PRAISE FOR MARK (

"A wildly original and magical twist on the Robin Hood narrative, Kendra Merritt's *By Winged Chair* is packed to the spokes with complex characters, wry humor, and flawless world building."

-Darby Karchut, best-selling author of DEL TORO MOON and FINN FINNEGAN

"With a wonderfully crafted blend of swords and sorcery and characters based on Robin Hood, Merritt tops this story off with the lead character readers need nowadays; a strong, independent, powerful female mage who also happens to be in a wheelchair. Readers will be constantly turning pages to see what happens next to this fun group of characters through the twists and turns they won't see coming."

-The Booklife Prize

"Kendra Merritt's prose is fresh, with one-line descriptions that crack like a whip, and she doesn't miss an opportunity to surprise the reader. From the first line to the last, I was enchanted with *By Winged Chair*."

-Todd Fahnestock, best-selling author of FAIRMIST and THE WISHING WORLD

ALSO BY KM MERRITT

Mishap's Heroes Series

Magic and Misrule

Death and Devotion

Trust and Treason

Illusions and Infamy

Sparks and Scales

Wastelands and War

Mark of the Least Novels

By Wingéd Chair

Skin Deep

Catching Cinders

Shroud for a Bride

A Matter of Blood

Mark of the Least Shorts

After the Darkness

When Quiet Comes to Call

Aria at the Opera

A Galadon Exile

Blood and Hope (in the *Fantastic Realms* anthology)

Faire-Weather Magic (in the *Wild* anthology)

Chasing Waves (in the *Girls of Might and Magic* anthology)

MISHAP'S HEROES

5

Sparks and Scales

KM MERRITT

BLUE FYRE PRESS

For Arielle, Miranda, Lacey, and Seth. Thanks for spinning fate with me.

ONE

VOLA COUNTED QUIETLY under her breath, listening for the sounds of movement from the others. There was the soft tread of a sandal on loam from Sorrel. A gasp and the heavy exhale of someone not used to the wilderness from Lillie. And nothing, not a sound or a breath or a whisper from Talon.

"Twenty-eight, twenty-nine, thirty."

Vola whistled the signal and surged upright in the underbrush. She charged forward with an orcish battle cry, and crashed her sword against her blackened shield, making as much noise as possible. Her charge flushed the family of warg out of hiding.

The big dog-like creatures startled and bolted out of the screening cover of the shrubs, across the empty dusty gully. Panicked grunts rang from the rocks. They tried to plunge back into the scrub on the other side, but a gray-clad halfling leaped from the underbrush, swinging a staff overhead, which crackled with lightning.

"Not today, beasties!" Sorrel cried.

The alpha warg skidded to a stop with a snarl, its rough gray fur standing on end. It spun to bolt through the opening the halfling had left to the north. Before it could escape with the other warg, a line of fire sprang between them and freedom.

Behind the flames, Vola could make out a plump woman, her eyes narrowed in concentration and hands outstretched. Lillie's outline wavered with heat, and her long blonde hair fluttered.

The lead warg spun, its lips pulled back, well and truly cornered. The female and the little wargs circled the alpha's legs, whining.

One opening remained to the south. But a new figure had appeared in the gap, cloak thrown back over her shoulders, her face obscured by a hood.

The ranger held her hands out in a calming gesture, making soothing noises through her teeth.

The warg's ears lay flat, then swiveled forward as if it couldn't decide between listening and charging.

Vola's fingers clenched on her hilt as a puff of warm air from Lillie's spell brushed her face. "Talon? Are we attacking or not?"

The hooded figure crouched, presenting a less intimidating presence. The warg eyed her warily.

"Give me a second."

Vola cast a glance at Sorrel and Lillie, but they both held their positions, keeping the warg from escaping.

A large black wolf brushed Vola's leg, and she laid her hand on his head, her fingers sinking into his thick fur.

"I know," she told Gruff. "It's not the plan. But I trust her."

Talon spoke quiet words the rest of them couldn't quite make out, and gradually the warg's lip lowered. The alpha lay down and listened with its head cocked.

Vola lowered her sword but kept her grip firm and ready.

Eventually, the alpha warg stood and shook himself. Talon raised her head.

"Drop the fire, Lillie," she said, voice a low growl.

The blonde wizard closed her fists and lowered her hands

without hesitation, and the wall of flames fell, leaving nothing but a line of blackened shrubbery.

Talon barked a word and the alpha warg led its family away to the north.

Lillie squeaked and stumbled out of their way, but the warg didn't pay her any attention, their mottled gray pelts helping them blend in and disappear until nothing remained of their passing.

Talon stood and brushed her hands off on her pants as Gruff raced to her and twined around her legs. "They'll stay out of the way of the villagers now," she said. "They don't like conflict any more than other animals, they're just way better at defending themselves when threatened. It makes for a bad reputation."

She pushed back her hood, revealing sandy-colored hair long enough to curl around her ears and the nape of her neck. She'd shaved that morning, and her jaw actually looked smooth for once. Maybe the cream Aunt Urag had given her was actually working.

Her eyes met Vola's and Vola read the question in them.

"It wasn't what I was expecting this morning when the village asked us to go warg hunting. But it worked," she said.

Talon's gaze shifted to the north, where the creatures had disappeared. "They didn't deserve to be hunted for one mistake. Revenge is a human thing. They wouldn't have understood it."

Lillie stepped across the line of scorched vegetation to the ranger. "Do you actually speak their language?" she said. "Or is it more of a spell that allows you to communicate with them?"

"More like a spell," Talon said as Sorrel trotted up to join them, slinging her staff back across her back. The little lightning bolts crackled and subsided. "I'm sorry you didn't get to hit anything," Talon told her.

The halfling monk shrugged. "It's fine. We got the job done. And if Rilla ever gets back with Anders's whereabouts, we'll have plenty of fighting to look forward to."

They turned to head back toward Vola's village to give them the good news that the warg threat had been taken care of.

"What do you think this Anders guy is doing with all the magic he's stealing?" Sorrel hopped over a patch of scrub, making her red-brown curls bounce.

Vola glanced at Lillie, their magic expert. "Any ideas?"

Lillie chewed her lip, watching her feet carefully. Her limp made this type of rocky forest that much harder to navigate. "I don't know," she said quietly. "But it can't be anything good."

"It's too bad none of the people working for him so far have known more than his name and the vague direction they were sending his super nefarious magical shenanigan supplies," Sorrel said. "Inga could have been so much more helpful in that case."

"If Vola hadn't pushed her out the window," Talon said. With her hood down, her smirk was clear.

"She'd just thrown my mother across the room." Vola's frown pulled at her thick eyebrows. "Any one of you could have been next. I was protecting you."

Lillie bit her lip on a laugh and gave Vola a dancing-eyed smile. "Our hero."

"I'm not saying she didn't need to go out the window," Sorrel said. "I'm just saying she could have been much more helpful before she died. She could have told us what this Anders character wants, how he intends to get it, where he normally holes up."

"What kind of defenses he has," Talon said.

"Exactly." Sorrel threw her arms over her head. "Hopefully Rilla is having more luck tracking him down."

Vola sniffed as they neared the village. Someone was barbecuing wargle ribs. Vola had a sneaking suspicion she knew who.

"I imagine the princess of the Dagger Throne will have far more resources than just us," Lillie said.

"And then we can stop killing time," Talon said.

Sorrel took a relieved breath. "Finally." Her eyes widened, and she held a hand out to Vola. "Not that it's not wonderful killing time with your family, Vola. Your mom has so many great stories about her and your dad from when they were mercenaries." She sighed. "I still can't believe I get to spar with Lydia Battlemane every morning."

"And your father is quite funny," Lillie added politely.

Vola's brow drew down. "Everything out of his mouth is a bad sex joke."

Lillie stopped dead in the middle of the dusty lane, her mouth dropping open. "Those were sex jokes?"

"I'm just saying," Sorrel said. "It's nice being here and all, but…"

Vola, Talon, and Sorrel drew up at the edge of the village and stared at the banner hanging across the road between two roof peaks. It glinted with fresh paint and glitter and read "THANK YOU MISHAP'S HEROES!"

"But Ella is really getting annoying," Sorrel finished, her shoulders sagging.

"We should not have told her our name," Talon growled under her breath.

Sorrel planted her hands on her hips. "Just because everyone calls us that doesn't mean it's actually our name. I never voted on it."

"If it was up to you, we'd be called 'super awesome bashing ladies,'" Lillie said.

"Do you think we can sneak back to my parents' house without any of them noticing?" Vola said.

"You wear plate armor," Talon said with a sniff. "You can't sneak anywhere."

"Too late anyway," Sorrel said in a stage whisper.

A slim figure with perfect hair, perfect skin, and perfect fingernails trotted out to greet them, carrying a cake.

"Vola, I'm so glad you've returned safely. Thank you so much for driving off the wargs. You've kept our village safe and we commend you for your sacrifice."

"I didn't even do anything this time, Ella," Vola said.

The girl just shook her head. "You're so modest. It's such an example for the rest of us." She thrust the cake into Vola's hands before she threw an arm around the paladin's shoulders and steered her through the center of town, where half the villagers had gathered to cheer as they passed.

Vola cringed. Sorrel and the others trailed after them, resigned. She could hear them whispering behind her.

"It's been like this the whole week."

"Well, we did save them all from Inga."

"Maybe Vola should have just left Ella there instead of carrying her out."

"Yeah, but a whole week of feasting?" Sorrel said. "Even I'm getting tired of booze and food."

There was a shocked gasp from Lillie and stunned silence from Talon. Even Vola shot a raised eyebrow over her shoulder at Sorrel.

"I didn't say I'd turn it down if offered," Sorrel said. "It's just, the novelty's worn off. Know what I mean?"

Ella slipped her arm through Vola's elbow and beamed up at her. Vola tried to smile through her tusks, but her heart wasn't in it.

This constant celebration certainly beat the ostracism of Vola's childhood. But enough was enough.

Why couldn't there be a place in between? A neutral spot where Vola could walk into a town, do her job, get paid, and move on. Like a normal person. Without the curled lips of her past or the hero worship of her present.

Near the center of the village, where the crowd was the thickest, Vola's parents' house stood. In the shadows, a figure leaned against the wall, surveying the party with amusement.

"Oh, thank Cleavah," Vola said under her breath. She pulled herself from Ella's clinging grasp with a half-baked excuse and hurried through the crowd. Sorrel, Talon, and Lillie were right on her heels having seen and recognized the dark green-clad figure as well.

The woman wore a leather jerkin and tight pants designed to blend in, and curly black hair rose in a frothy cloud around her head. No crown for this princess. She preferred to remain anonymous. And if anyone questioned her, a knife in the ribs worked just as well as royal privilege.

"It's about time, Rilla," Sorrel said.

"Did you learn anything new?" Lillie said. "Are we going to go after Anders now?"

Rilla's lip quirked, her eyes settling on the cake Vola still held. Then her gaze flicked to the party behind them. Ella had hopped to a bench to give a rousing speech about their brave heroes and how they'd defeated the warg pack and saved the village.

"Why? Ready to get out of here?" Rilla said, meeting Vola's eyes.

Vola heaved a relieved sigh. "Oh, my gods, yes. Give us a direction and we'll race you there."

Rilla gave them a theatrical pout. "But where else are you going to get this kind of treatment? Cake every day. Endless feasting and all the tail you could possibly want. Bet you have to beat the boys off with a stick."

Sorrel stuck her finger in Vola's cake and swiped up a huge glob of frosting. "It gets old after a while. Trust me." She stuck her finger in her mouth and grimaced.

Rilla raised an eyebrow at Sorrel, which she didn't notice.

"The cake gets old," Vola said. "She's talking about the feasting, not the boys."

Sorrel's brow furrowed in confusion. "What boys?"

Rilla hid a smile. "Never mind. It's time to pack up. If you can tear yourselves away, I've lined up a job on a caravan headed to dragon country."

"Dragon country?" Talon's voice went sharp and clipped.

"We're going after Anders."

Vola breathed a sigh of relief.

"You're coming, too?" Lillie said.

"Firewatch is out of Southglen's jurisdiction. You'll need my clout to get anywhere." Rilla shrugged. "Besides, I want to get this guy as much as you do. I can always portal back to the capital if I need to."

Talk about royal resources. Lillie could only teleport short distances, and she had to be sure of what was on the other side.

Sorrel clapped her hands. "Road trip!"

"A road trip toward danger," Talon reminded her. "Dragons are worse than anything we've faced so far."

"Yeah, but maybe Vola's mom will bake us cookies. They're so much better than Ella's cakes."

TWO

LYDIA DID MAKE COOKIES. There was also a lot less weeping and clinging than Vola expected there to be when they left the little cottage.

Lydia stood on the front doorstep with her hands on her hips, head cocked so her bushy mane of red hair fell over her bare shoulders.

"Well, to be honest, honey," she said. "We love you, and it was wonderful to fight beside you. But you and your friends don't need to be in our attic anymore." She cast a glance at Vola's father, who was examining a crack in his picket fence with a frown. Lydia licked her lips.

Talon grinned wide enough they could see her teeth even under her hood. "She means we're getting in the way of their fun times."

Vola cast her eyes toward the sky. "Yes, thank you, Talon. I got that."

"What do you mean getting in the way?" Sorrel said. "We're fun."

Talon snorted. "Never mind."

"You're taking your...creature, right?" Gorgo called.

Vola cast a grimace at the swamp monster. "Yes, Dad."

"Good. I think it's been eating the fence."

Rilla stood in the lane, rubbing the smile from her face as she waited for them.

Vola hurried her team and their employer out of her village and as far away from her parents as she could manage.

Visits home always seemed like a good idea. But between local baddies and parents who knew you too well, they always ended up awkward.

Vola's shoulders relaxed the further they traveled from her village.

The caravan Rilla had convinced to hire them was bigger than Vola had been expecting but still small enough to be ignored by most of the world. The owner seemed to know what he was doing, encouraging, coaxing, and cajoling the motley group to get on the road on time. Even with ten different merchants plus their wagons, livestock, and merchandise, keeping them all safe would be easier than a lot of the things Vola and the others had done to earn some coin in the past.

At least until they got to dragon lands.

They rolled along, leaving the familiar forests and plains of Southglen behind. They could have just huffed it across the countryside like normal, but they traveled with the princess of the Dagger Throne now, and she was nothing if not subtle. Not to mention paranoid.

So they walked alongside the caravan during the day and stood watch at night, pretending to be simple mercenaries, disguising their true purpose. Considering someone had already tried kidnapping the princesses of Southglen once that year, Vola wasn't complaining about the extra precautions.

So far it seemed to be working.

Vola strode around the perimeter of the campsite, hand on her hilt, eyes trained on the surrounding hills, even as she kept her ears open for anything unusual coming from within the campsite.

Nothing. Just the low crackle of the fire kept lit in the very center of the circle of wagons. She couldn't even hear Talon on the other side, walking the perimeter as well. The ranger moved like a shadow when she wanted to.

Vola stopped, letting the bulk of a nearby wagon consume the shape of her shadow, and stared into the darkness, letting her ears tell her where to watch.

Still nothing.

She was too used to conflict now. Expecting it around every corner and under every rock. A hazard of the job, but to be fair, it made her sharper than the average guard.

She moved on, stepping around the little hummocks of dry grass and poky shrubs. Nothing taller than a bush out here now. Apparently, the lands ahead of them were even dryer than anything they'd seen yet.

Vola couldn't really find it in herself to complain. This sure beat trekking through a swamp and nearly drowning inside a sinking tent.

Vola shuddered.

She paused at the fifth wagon in the circle, waiting for Talon. This was where they checked in with each other after every other pass.

Vola squinted and a lithe shadow detached itself from the wagon.

"Talon?"

"Who else did you expect?"

Talon stopped and stood facing the rest of the world, back to the fire and the caravan. She wore her hood less and less these days. Usually, she only hid her face when overwhelmed by large crowds or inundated by pestering strangers who looked at her and saw a man rather than a woman. It still happened occasionally even though she kept her face clean-shaven and wore a leather cuirass that cinched at the waist.

And Lillie had been doing something with Talon's hair—Vola had no idea what—pinning the ragged ends out of her face for a softer look. Soon it would be grown out enough to braid.

"Anything on your end?" Vola asked.

Talon remained motionless, staring off into the distance.

Vola straightened. "What is it?"

She didn't answer.

"Talon?" Vola whispered.

Talon jerked. "Hmm? What?"

"What do you see?"

Talon shook her head and took a step back. "Nothing. Sorry. What did you ask?"

Vola's brows drew down. "Are you all right?"

"Fine."

Vola crossed her arms and settled against the corner of the wagon. "Sure you are," she said. "Try again."

A couple of months ago, that would have shut Talon up for good. Tonight, she only hesitated for a bare second before opening her mouth.

"We're headed to dragon lands," she said.

Vola tilted her head. "Yeah. That's where Rilla says Anders is heading."

"It's also where dragons nest. Presumably."

Vola's breath blew out in the cool night air as she finally caught on. "Your original pack was killed by a dragon, weren't they?" she said quietly.

"Yes."

Talon had been raised by a wolf pack before she'd rejoined the human world. There were still some times when she looked at Vola and Vola could see the wolf in her eyes. Times when she was sure one wrong word or look would send Talon bolting.

But tonight, Talon turned to meet Vola's eyes, the firelight flickering across her face, and she seemed to really mean it when she said, "I'm fine, Vola. I promise."

"All right," Vola said. "I believe you."

"They're dead," Talon said. "They're gone. And nothing I do can change that. I've moved on. Like Gruff." She gestured to the long shape of the wolf lying beside the fire. He turned his head as if he could tell they were talking about him and his tongue lolled.

"I found a new pack," Talon said and flashed a rare smile at Vola. "But this trip is making me remember them."

Vola frowned.

"Not bad things," Talon said before she could respond. "I just...I want to be sure I remember them well."

"And how do you do that?"

"Honor the things they taught me," Talon said, turning back to the night. "Protect my new pack. Don't make the same mistakes twice."

"I thought maybe you were hoping for revenge."

Talon shook her head sharply. "What good would that do anyone? Besides, the dragon that did it is dead. It won't be hurting anyone ever again. I'm just worried about the ones we're headed toward."

Vola opened her mouth, but in the dark silence of the night, a twig snapped.

Talon's chin came up, and she sniffed the air. Behind them, Gruff rose to his feet, a growl starting in his throat.

Vola gave Talon a signal, pointing her to the right while Vola slipped left. Gruff passed between them, nothing more than a waft of breeze and a shadow against the darkness.

Vola unsheathed her sword as quietly as she could and settled her shield on her arm. She waited, tense and ready. She'd left the full plate armor in their tent, but sneaking wasn't her strong suit, so she stayed put until Talon gave her more to work with.

There. Four sharp whistles that could have been from a night bird but weren't. Then a long, swooping whistle — Talon letting her know what was going on. Gruff had found four enemies to their south.

Vola whistled back. She would close in on them from the left; Talon from the right.

She crouched low and scanned the horizon, waiting for movement. Finally she saw a shadow cross the stars between her and Talon.

She rose and charged the figure. A silent battering ram.

Orcs saw better in the dark, true, but the figure didn't become clear until she was nearly on top of him. He wore a motley selection of armor and carried a wicked-looking knife. Perfect for slitting sleeping throats. And no one friendly would be moving around in the dark without torches or a wizard's light.

Vola hit him before he even realized which direction she was coming from, and he went down without a cry.

There was a familiar sizzle behind her left ear, and she managed to turn a wince into a duck and roll as a flash of fire flew over her shoulder and struck the bare dirt where she'd been standing.

She came up, sword ready, but just as she found the spell caster a few feet away, an arrow sprouted from the woman's eye, and she went down.

"Two more," Talon growled, sliding up next to her.

"There." Vola pointed to two pale faces, fading back into the low scrub. "Tell Gruff to flush them out."

There was a growl, a short bark, and then a snarl. The remaining bandits yelped and leaped from the scant cover of the bushes.

Right into Vola and Talon. Talon tripped one and made sure he didn't get up again. Vola spun and slashed, taking her last opponent down with an anti-climactic sigh.

She stared at the bodies with a bemused frown.

"That was hardly worth the fight," Talon said.

"Tell Gruff to check the perimeter. Make sure there aren't any more of them lurking on the other side. These could be scouts for a larger party." Vola knelt to check the bodies as Gruff slipped away to sniff out any more intruders.

"Anything to identify them?" Talon asked.

"Broke bandits from the look of it," Vola said, emptying their wallets out onto her palm and finding only a few coins.

"Desperate bandits," Talon said. "If they decided four against a caravan was good odds."

"Middle of the night, just before watch change. Probably thought we'd be asleep on our feet."

Talon grinned, teeth flashing in the dark. "Too bad for them, Rilla doesn't hire fools."

Vola stood and dusted off her hands, almost feeling sorry for the enemy. They didn't have anything worth much on them, and their armor and weapons were shabby.

"When did we become the thing to be feared?" She rubbed her face. "Last I remember we were like these poor sods, knocking around Brisbene, trying to earn enough coin to get a bed for the night."

"You want to go back?" Talon said.

"Hel—er, heck no."

A wolf howled from the other side of the caravan, and Talon's head jerked up. "Gruff says it's clear."

Vola cocked her thumb at the campsite and led the way back to the wagons. "Let's make sure everything's still quiet."

A figure hovered in the opening between two wagons, silhouetted against the fire. Gregor, the caravan lead. He'd been the one to hire them, though Vola strongly suspected Rilla had insisted and then made him think it was his idea.

He craned his neck to look past them, squinting into the dark. "I heard something."

His son, Yevan, sidled up next to him, eyes trained on Vola.

She made sure to smile at him. The gangly youth was only twelve, but he reminded her strongly of Finn.

"Sorry to wake you," Vola said. "Just a couple of bandits. Nothing serious. We caught them before they even made their move."

Gregor's shoulders sagged, and he turned to let them back into the circle of firelight. He ran a hand through his shaggy blond hair, eyes darting between them and the darkness behind them.

"Thank the gods," he said. "You five are worth twice your fee, you know that, right?"

Vola gave him a look of mock horror. "Gregor, you're not supposed to tell us that. We might charge you double next time."

"He'd pay it," Yevan said, skipping to keep up with Vola.

"Gladly," Gregor said. "Your goddess must look after you personally." His eyes flicked to her shield with the spreading wings burnished into its blackened surface.

Most people didn't know what to think when they saw her shield. The surface blackened by holy fire was a mark of shame the world over. A symbol of a black paladin. A holy warrior stripped of their rank and position. But the shining symbol cutting through the black had wiped away part of the mark and made everyone she encountered look twice, wondering what it meant exactly. Vola was still trying to figure it out herself.

Gregor had decided after the first night when they'd fought off a family of manticores that she must have landed on the right side of whatever debate the gods had had over her shield.

"Who did you say you served again?" he said, eyes on the shining wings.

Talon glanced at Vola sharply as she hesitated for the

briefest of moments. Back in Inga's stronghold, her goddess had proved herself to be something more than a Lesser Virtue. Something more than a Greater Virtue too, maybe. But she hadn't deigned to explain to Vola just who—or what—she actually was.

"Cleavah," she said for simplicity's sake. That was the only name she knew her lady by, so that was the one she would continue to use.

"Goddess of Vengeful Housewives?" Gregor cocked his head so his big nose cast a shadow across his face.

"Yes," Vola said simply and quietly. She couldn't explain the differences even to herself, so getting into it would just give Gregor more questions.

Gregor shrugged. "I hope the lady of sharp implements continues to grace us with her favor," he said and gave her a little bow before herding Yevan back to their wagon.

Vola turned for their tent and Talon followed. A light still burned behind the canvas, casting the shadow of a woman with bushy hair hunched over a camp table.

Rilla stood pouring over her map under a swinging lantern. Sorrel and Lillie were already tumbling out of their bedrolls, rubbing their eyes and reaching for shoes.

"Figured it was about time for a shift change," Sorrel said with a yawn.

"Any trouble?" Lillie asked.

"Couple of bandits," Vola said. "From the south. We're pretty sure we got them all, but keep your eyes open. There's still a chance they were part of a larger group."

Lillie nodded as she tied her boots. "I can do a sweep to check for any signs of life sneaking up on us."

"Have you been up this whole time?" Talon asked Rilla.

The princess glanced up from the map, a frown line between her eyebrows. "Is it that late?"

Vola raised her eyebrows. "Yeah. What are you worrying about?"

"Not so much worrying as trying to imagine all the traps ahead of time," Rilla said, scowling at the lines on the paper. "It saves time later when you're trying to avoid them."

Vola joined the princess at the table. The pictures of mountains, the lines depicting rivers, and the boundaries between areas were all clear enough. But the names scrawled under each landmark swam in Vola's vision, and she blinked. Lillie claimed it was just part of her orc heritage, the main reason they passed down their history orally, but it didn't make it any easier to accept.

Rilla didn't seem to notice. She stabbed a dark finger at the line between an area covered with little pictures of scrub and the area surrounding the mountains.

"This is the border between Southglen and the dragon lands. Beyond that, my authority dwindles to that of a mere dignitary instead of a princess." She flashed a rueful grin at Vola. "That makes me snappy."

"Understandable," Sorrel said, standing on her tiptoes to see the map. Her brows drew down. "This table is not halfling friendly."

"If it was halfling friendly, the rest of us would be sitting on the floor," Talon said.

"What's wrong with that?"

"The dragon lands are not technically part of Southglen," Rilla said. "They're held jointly with the neighboring kingdoms as a sort of neutral zone. A place we all help to maintain where the dragons can roost or nest or whatever it is dragons do."

"Perch?" Sorrel said.

"Sure," Rilla said. "But what it means is that a bunch of humans and other sentient beings, dwarves, halflings, elves, even a few orcs, have made their home there where their former governments aren't technically allowed to touch them."

She stabbed the picture of a city tucked up against the mountains.

"An interesting situation," Lillie said over Talon's shoulder.

"A craptastic nuisance is what it is," Rilla said. "But Firewatch is well established now. They think of themselves as their own little kingdom out here. They've got their own council, their own culture and traditions cobbled together from scraps. And to be fair, they know how to navigate the dragon lands better than the rest of us. I feel like I'm walking into a bloody menagerie. But they live there. And manage to do it peacefully."

"It might not be that bad," Lillie said, chewing her lip while staring at the map. "The *draconis minimus*, the smaller dragons, are fairly ubiquitous. They're intelligent, they don't eat that much more than, say, another large predator like a bear. But they're small, docile, and easy to get along with as long as you respect them. It's the big ones, *draconis maximus*, that you have to worry about."

"Believe me, I'm worrying," Talon muttered.

"But they spend most of their time sleeping," Lillie continued. "They only wake every century or so to eat and…catch up on current events."

"You hesitated," Sorrel said. "Why did you hesitate?"

"Bad things tend to happen when the dragons wake." Lillie's gaze flicked to Talon. "A lot of Firewatch's resources go into making sure that doesn't happen early."

Talon didn't react.

Rilla glanced at Lillie, eyebrows raised. "That was very thorough."

"That's why we keep her around," Sorrel said. "That and the fireballs."

Lillie flushed. "My mother is supposed to be studying dragons." She glanced at the city on the map. "The last my father heard she was in Firewatch."

"If you remember any other tidbits, let me know," Rilla said.

Lillie nodded before slipping out of the tent to go stand watch, Sorrel trotting at her heels.

Rilla crossed her arms and tapped her lip. "My operatives tell me Anders is on his way to the city. If he's using the dragon lands to stage his...whatever it is he's planning, then he's most likely in Firewatch. Or will have a base within easy traveling distance." She straightened suddenly to tap her foot. "Do we still have to worry about the mind control Inga used? Will we have to worry about subverted city officials doing Anders's will?"

Vola raised her chin. "It's still a risk, but we know how to counter it now. Inga used relationships to pass Mulgash's influence from one victim to another. But you can use a relationship to spread the cure as well."

"Would we still need Cleavah to do it?" Talon asked quietly. "You used her power to heal us, didn't you?"

"Yes, but I don't think it's necessary in the long run. It just sped up the process." Vola frowned, remembering those frantic heartbeats staring into Lillie's hate-filled eyes, wondering if that was the last thing she'd ever see. "Considerably."

Rilla turned to plant her butt on the rickety table and pinned Vola with her gold gaze. "I thought you were cut off from her."

"I was," Vola said, spreading her hands. "The paladin council took my emblem."

Rilla froze. "Gods can't work through their followers without a physical connection," she said carefully.

"I think that's still true," Vola said. "For the rest of them. But I don't think it is for mine."

She could feel Cleavah—or the goddess she'd always known as Cleavah—as a burning weighted presence standing at her shoulder. But ever since Inga's stronghold collapsed, she'd had the feeling that all she had to do was turn her head and she'd brush against the goddess herself.

Had she always been that close, just…hidden? Or ignored?

"You can't ask her?" Rilla said.

Vola was dying to turn her head. To ask the question burning within her. Who are you? What's your name? Who am I serving?

But…

"If she's chosen to appear as a lesser goddess, she must have a good reason. I've learned to be careful with my questions. Because my goddess isn't afraid to answer them."

THREE

THEY TRAVELED with the caravan for two weeks, each day blurring into the next. The scenery shifted so gradually that it was three days before Vola realized they trudged through rolling dunes of fine-grain sand broken by rocky gullies instead of low dry scrub and grass. The sand got in their boots. It worked its way into the leather straps of Vola's armor. Lillie had to hold her books upside down and shake them to get sand out of the binding.

The only blessing was that it was dry. Like Talon had pointed out, it was far better than a swamp. Vola even glanced back now and then at the swamp monster trudging along behind the wagons, wondering if it had been such a good idea to bring the creature into a desert. Looking like a cross between a donkey and a crocodile, it was clearly made for the wet.

But the swamp monster glared at the scenery with the same bad temper it always showed. Vola couldn't see any difference in its temperament, and it still ate anything it could sink its teeth into, including the small rodents that ventured too close to the picket line when they camped at night.

On their fifteenth day with the caravan, Vola paused beside

the road and shaded her eyes. The wagons rumbled along the stones set deep enough into the ground with magic that the constant wind and bite of the sands would never move them. Dunes rose on either side so the road wound between them, a thin path of certainty in the desert that led to a smear of darkness on the horizon.

"The Firewall," Gregor said, stopping beside her to shade his own face. "The mountains themselves are too rugged to drive a caravan through. We have to make for the passes. But even those can be dangerous with dragons roosting in the heights."

"I thought they were sentient and docile," Vola said, resuming her march.

"Oh, aye. The ones who live in Firewatch aren't a problem. But the wild ones can be a nuisance if you get a clan of young ones all making trouble together. And the city officials always want you to hire a guide, to be sure you don't wake any of the big ones. They're the ones that level cities and start the apocalypse if they wake up early and grumpy."

The dark smudge on the horizon came into focus as they approached, revealing jagged peaks of flame-scoured rock towering over the desert below. The Firewall mountains.

The city of Firewatch sat nestled in the steep valley between two peaks, gold domes catching the light and deep crevices providing homes for the darker industries for a city of outcasts. Bridges connected the different layers, some built from rope and wood, sagging across the empty spaces between, some built from red stone, arching high and wide enough for the city's traffic.

Far above the buildings, a couple of towers perched on the jagged peaks, providing unbroken views across the entire desert.

"Those are the towers Firewatch is named for," Lillie said, staring into the distance. "Even peaceful dragons can be volatile. The residents have learned to live with them and guard against them at the same time."

Yevan, Gregor's lanky son, walked the ridge of a nearby dune, his arms out for balance. He'd been on this trade route often enough to know the importance of staying in sight. Vola spared a glance at him every few minutes just to make sure all her wards were accounted for.

Yevan stopped and raised his hand to shield his eyes, peering across the dunes away from the caravan.

"Dad," he called to Gregor. "There's something there."

"Be more specific," Gregor called back. "'Something's' not helpful. The last something was a dead raccoon. I'm not falling for that again." He muttered the last part under his breath.

Vola bit her lip on a chuckle.

"Dad!" The change in Yevan's tone raised the hair on the back of her neck, and she whipped her head around.

Black shadows crept along the ridge of sand at Yevan's feet, but the sky remained clear of any clouds or birds.

"Lillie…" Vola started. "What is that?"

"I don't know," Lillie said. "But it doesn't look natural."

Vola opened her mouth to call to Yevan, to tell him to get back to the caravan, but the boy skipped back a couple of steps from the creeping black, already on the same page.

The sand shifted under his boots, and he twisted. Yevan's scream pierced the hot air as he tumbled out of sight down the other side of the dune.

"Yevan!" Gregor shot forward, but Vola was already moving.

She grabbed Gregor's arm and hauled him back toward the wagons. "Stay here."

The merchants behind them were already starting to gasp and race for their wagons.

"But Yevan—"

"I'll get him," Vola said. "But it will be a lot harder if I have to rescue both of you."

Gregor gulped, but in a show of wisdom, he stayed put.

Vola signaled for Talon. "Get them all under the wagons," she told the ranger. "Shelter in place until I give the all-clear."

Talon nodded and began herding their charges toward safety.

Vola started for the dune. "Lillie, what am I heading into?" she called over her shoulder.

Lillie raised her hand and then pulled down from the sky, a streak of sparks following her fingers. The sparks flashed and formed the figure of a large raven. He swooped away from Lillie's hand and up into the air. She lifted her face toward him and closed her eyes.

"Rand says it's just black."

Not helpful. Vola clambered up the dune, her boots slipping in the sand. Behind her, Rilla and Sorrel caught up.

Sorrel scampered up the slope on hands and knees, reaching the top before Vola. She gasped and kicked her feet out to slide down the other side and out of sight.

Rilla drew even with Vola as she swore at the halfling's disappearance.

"That's what you get for wearing full plate," Rilla said.

"It always seems like a good idea in the morning. I don't have to stop and put it on before a fight."

Vola huffed to the ridgeline and straightened up to stare out across the desert.

Sorrel was helping Yevan back up the dune, slipping and sliding as they scrambled. But the boy seemed unharmed. Just shaken.

Vola's breath caught.

The desert stretched out, but instead of the golds and reds and warm browns that painted the landscape behind them, this was black. A dead sort of black that seemed to suck up the very sunlight and leave no warmth.

It didn't go on forever. There was a break just a few hundred yards away where the gold dunes started again. But here, this bit of the desert looked…dead.

"What in Ona's name is that?" Rilla said. And if a princess didn't know what was going on, Vola didn't feel so bad about letting her jaw drop.

"Yevan," Vola said. "Are you hurt?"

The boy shook his head as Sorrel stopped trying to drag him up the hill. Tendrils of black branched out from the dead circle, but they didn't move anymore, and Sorrel and Yevan were careful to stay away from the dark sand.

"Not hurt," he said. "Just scared. It was moving. Like it wanted to eat me. Then it just stopped."

Vola stepped forward, sliding down the sand dune.

"Vola," Lillie said, finally puffing to the top of the ridge. "Be careful."

"What else would I be?" Vola said. But she had to get closer.

Lillie's raven familiar swooped above her, keeping an eye out, and she trusted him to call if he saw anything creeping up on them.

She stepped over the sloping footprints where Yevan and Sorrel had passed and carefully approached the edge of the blackness.

She knelt and leaned forward.

Rilla joined her to stare at the blackened area.

"What is it?" Lillie called. But Vola had no answer.

Lillie huffed and slid down the hill. Yevan remained on the dune above them, but Sorrel came closer, watching their backs.

Vola gave Lillie a hand up at the bottom of the dunes.

"Is this common in dragon lands?" Rilla asked. "They breathe fire, after all."

Lillie held her hands out, hovering just on this side of the affected area. "It's not a burn," she said. "This isn't from fire. It's…it's almost like it's empty."

"Empty of what?" Sorrel said, planting her hands on her hips. "Color?"

"Life."

"How?" Rilla said, a frown creasing the skin between her eyebrows. "How is that possible?"

"I don't know." Lillie took an apple from the satchel at her side. She frowned at it, then tossed it into the direct center of the area.

It bounced and rolled to a stop. The shiny green surface gleamed against the black, unblemished by it.

Lillie held up her hands again. "Whatever happened here, it's done now. I think."

"That's not as reassuring as you think it is," Sorrel said. "I'd still like to know what happened."

Lillie frowned at her, then finally stuck her hand out, breaking the plane between the normal desert and the blackened zone.

Vola cried out, but Lillie just turned her hand over and over, watching it for any effect. Vola stood and yanked her back a step.

"You can't just jump into it to see what happens," she scolded.

"Well at some point hypothesis needs to move past observation." Lillie gave her a sidelong look, and Vola let go with a huff.

Lillie stepped forward as Vola held her breath. The black sand parted around her feet just like the normal stuff did, rolling away in a fine cascade of darkness. Vola expected it to glitter in the sun, but it was so black the light didn't even seem to touch it.

Lillie frowned and knelt to take a handful and let it run between her fingers. She squinted at her palm, then reached out to take a blackened twig from some low-lying scrub between her fingers. She pinched, and the twig cracked, but it didn't crumble.

"Definitely not a burn," she said. She took a rock from the area and drew her knife.

Rilla took a deep breath and then stepped across into the black. Still nothing happened. The princess strode to the exact center of what they could see and planted her hands on her hips to glare up at the sky.

Not to be outdone, Sorrel jumped feet first across the line, looked down to check herself, then jumped back.

Vola reached out a toe and nudged some of the blackened sand with her boot.

"Ouch." Lillie hissed in pain and shook her hand.

Vola jerked and stepped across into the blackened area. "What? What happened?"

"Oh, I was stupid. I was trying to score this rock. I thought maybe the black is just on the surface. But I slipped." The wizard dropped the rock and turned her hand to show Vola the slice across her palm.

"Not stupid, and lucky for you, you travel with a healer." Vola took Lillie's hand in hers and covered the gash. "Lady bless," she said, reaching for Cleavah.

And she came up empty.

Vola's breath froze in her chest. She reached again, but nothing met her except a sort of hollow emptiness.

"Vola?" Lillie asked, a crease forming between her brows as Vola just stood there, gaping at their hands.

"It's gone," she whispered, her voice catching.

"What's gone?" Lillie's fingers clenched on hers.

"Cleavah. Cleavah's power. It's gone. I can't feel it. This can't be happening again. She told me she would never be out of reach. She told me."

"Vola," Lillie said, her other hand reaching to grasp Vola's arm. "Don't panic. If she told you that, then she meant it."

Sorrel gazed around at the blackened area, then focused on Lillie.

"Cast a spell," she said.

"What?" Lillie's eyes still focused on Vola, who was trying to swallow down the panic climbing up her throat.

"Try casting a spell."

Lillie pulled away from Vola long enough to twitch her fingers and whisper under her breath. But nothing happened. Blood dripped down her hand in silence.

Lillie's eyes widened. "I can't cast," she said. Her breath hitched. "Oh my gods, Sorrel is right." She grabbed Vola's hand and hauled her off the black, back onto the normal sand. Vola stumbled over her feet.

"Now try it," Sorrel said.

Finally catching on to what the other two had already guessed at, Vola reached again for Cleavah's power. A well of burning energy rose at her call.

"Lady bless," she said, placing her hand over the gash in Lillie's palm.

White light flashed between them, and when Lillie drew her hand back, her skin gleamed unmarked in the sun. A mirrored cut stung Vola's palm.

"That's better," Lillie murmured. She snapped her fingers and a little ball of fire appeared on her palm, crackling happily.

Vola blew out her breath, relief pounding through her so hard it gave her a headache.

"It's the spot," Sorrel said, frowning at the black sand beneath her sandals. "It's not just dead…"

"It's devoid of magic," Lillie said, stepping away from Vola.

"But how did it affect us?" Vola said. "I'm pretty sure I'm not magic."

"Spells have to come from somewhere. Some of us study a long time to learn how to use them, but the power comes from somewhere." She gestured around her, her hands fluttering through the air. "Wizards learn how to harness the world's magic for their spells. Inside that circle, there is no magic to harness."

"What about me?" Vola said.

Lillie chewed her lip. "Paladins get their power from the gods, yes? Well, the gods are connected to the world in a very funda-mental way. They were the ones who created it. They're the ones who guide it. Without that connection…"

"They're powerless," Vola finished. "And that means so was I."

Vola's shoulders sagged. Sorrel and Lillie exchanged anxious ideas and Rilla interjected sharp questions, but Vola pushed all the sound away and focused inward toward that presence that always hovered just over her shoulder.

"Lady?" she whispered.

"I am here, Vola," the voice said. But it came without the normal rush of acceptance and love. This felt…worried with an edge of the same panic Vola had just felt. "I do not know what this is. And that…is not good."

That was the understatement of the century. Whoever or whatever Cleavah really was, if she didn't know what was going on here, it could only mean trouble of a spectacular sort.

"Someone or something stole the magic out of this section of desert," Rilla said, bringing Vola back to the present. "Enough that spell casters and healers can't even reach their own magic or their gods."

"I didn't even know that was possible," Lillie said quietly, wringing her hands.

"Well, we didn't know stealing magic out of dead people or out of the Thrones was possible either," Sorrel said, face unusu-ally sober. "And Anders was managing that. With help."

Another figure came up over the ridge to stand beside Yevan.

"Talon," Vola called and gave her the signal that it was safe to come down.

Talon slid down the slope, sending a cascade of sand before her.

"Sorry," Vola said. "We weren't sure what was going on so we didn't give the all-clear yet…What's wrong?"

Talon's burned, peeling nose and cheeks had gone white, and she stared at the dead spot.

"Are you all right?" Sorrel asked.

"I've seen this," Talon said, voice cracking on the last word.

"Where?" Rilla moved closer.

"When…my pack died. There were spots like this. The dragon left them."

Lillie shook her head. "It's not a burn—"

"I know it's not a burn," Talon snapped. "Believe me, I know the difference. This is empty. The land no longer speaks to me, as if it's dead."

Lillie pressed her lips together and stared at her boots.

"The dragon used these spots to kill my pack," Talon said. "They were all over the forest where we lived and the pack was gone."

They all looked up, searching the skies for the shape of spreading wings. There was nothing but Rand turning and turning above them.

But off in the distance, little draconic shapes wheeled over the city.

"One of the great ones has woken up," Talon said.

"Wouldn't we have seen one of the big ones if it had been here?" Sorrel said. She raised her hands when Talon rounded on her. "I'm just making sure. It's pretty hard to hide anything in this wasteland. Let alone a big honking scaly thing."

"There are many spells that can be cast at a distance," Lillie said quietly. "And…well, there are dragons nearby. We know they sleep in the Firewall mountains."

"Could a dragon really do this?" Rilla asked. She glanced at Lillie.

Lillie put a hand on her hip. "Why does everyone always look at me when they ask things like that?"

"Probably because you usually have the answer," Sorrel said.

Lillie rolled her eyes. "My mother is the one who studies *draconis maximus*. Not me. I suggest you seek her out."

Rilla straightened her shoulders and strode back toward the dune, where Yevan waited, his eyes wide and worried.

"Let's get moving. We need to get to the city."

"Wait, are you really going to find Lillie's mother?" Sorrel asked as she passed.

Lillie gulped.

"No, I'm going to warn Firewatch that a dragon has woken." Rilla turned on her heel to meet Vola's eyes.

Vola raised her chin. "What do you need from us, princess?" she said, quiet and steady.

"Get the caravan to the city. Finish the job. Then get yourselves fitted for an extended expedition into the mountains. A great dragon waking before its time is a threat to Southglen as well as Firewatch. These things start apocalypses when they're angry. So follow this lead until you get to the end and smash the threat into as many pieces as you can manage."

"Yes, ma'am," Vola said as Sorrel gave her jaunty salute.

"Smashing things is our favorite," the halfling said.

"I'll meet you at our inn as soon as I have anything substantial. Maybe this isn't the first of these spots. Maybe the city already knows about this threat."

"Maybe they have leads we can follow as well," Lillie added.

"Go," Rilla said.

Sorrel scrambled up the dune toward Yevan.

Rilla paused far enough away from the dead spot and yanked her hand through the air, tearing open a portal edged with green and black light. Rilla cast one look back over her shoulder before disappearing into the portal with a whoosh. It snapped closed behind her.

Vola turned to herd the rest of her party up the slope, but

Talon stood at the edge of the blackened area, staring at the dark sand.

Vola's gut twisted. This was exactly what the ranger had been worried about. And they'd walked right into it. Now, her new pack was in the exact same danger as her old one.

Vola reached to touch her shoulder, but Talon turned to trudge after Sorrel and Yevan, too absorbed in her thoughts to notice.

Vola dropped her hand.

Lillie limped forward to stand at Vola's shoulder, and they watched Talon walk away together.

"Is she going to be all right?" Lillie asked.

Vola didn't answer. Talon insisted she wasn't still affected by her grief and turmoil. But this had to change things. This had to bring back more bad memories. It had to feel like history repeating itself.

"You know that this follows Anders's pattern," Lillie said quietly. "Right?"

Vola's lips tightened. "Are you saying you don't believe her?"

"Of course, I believe her," Lillie said. "But...what if they're connected?"

"Are you saying Anders could be controlling the dragons?"

"I'm not sure what I'm saying yet. I just don't want to be the only one thinking of the possibility."

Vola blew out her breath and pushed her sweaty hair back from her forehead. "Then we're going after the man who was responsible for the death of Talon's pack. I don't think that changes anything. Do you?"

"It makes me angrier."

"Ah." Vola turned to head back toward the dune. "Remind me to point you in the right direction and stay out of your way, then."

Lillie flashed her a smile before they started climbing. Creaks from the wagons and the sounds of whips and curses came floating to them over the ridgeline. Sorrel had obviously gotten Yevan back to the caravan and gotten them underway again. A joke and a smile from Sorrel could move mountains. Which was why Vola counted on her as her second.

"I forgot how disconcerting it is to see Rilla worried," Lillie said, puffing to the top of the dune.

"I'm not sure we've ever seen her really thrown before," Vola said. "Even when she was cut off from her Throne, it made her more angry than anything."

"Forgive me if I'd like to keep her from getting angry again. She tends to stab things," Lillie said.

"I mean, so do we. If we're honest."

FOUR

THEY DIDN'T ENCOUNTER any more trouble on the way into Firewatch. Nor did they see any more dead spots along the road.

The paved path led all the way through the rocky foothills, up into the narrow, jagged valley of Firewatch. There was no gate and no wall. Without a national government to answer to, there was no reason to keep people out. This was a city made for refugees, a city built to escape into. And with the surrounding peaks inhabited by dragons, no one had ever been brave enough to try invading. The little ones breathed fire and flew, dive-bombing their enemies, but the big ones could level armies in a single stoop.

The caravan made its way along crowded narrow streets to park outside a bazaar tucked up under a rocky overhang. There was more shade here with the buildings blocking a lot of the sun but the air hung heavy between the walls, cut off from the breezes across the open desert.

Vola and the others said goodbye to the merchants there. Gregor pressed a hefty bonus into Vola's palm before they left, telling them they had a job with him any time they wanted. Vola still wasn't sure if he'd guessed that Rilla was a princess, and she wasn't about to point it out.

Rand, Lillie's familiar, had left them near the entrance to the city, flapping off to find Rilla. An hour after they arrived, he returned with a message.

"Change of plans. I'm ass-deep in negotiations up here. They didn't even want to let me into the city, bastards. Get up to the council rooms prepared to argue."

At the bottom of the page was an address.

Vola and the others glanced up at the city looming above them. It was a mishmash of pieces salvaged and looted from wagons, land barges, and carriages. Stone from distant lands, pilfered and transported across the desert. Elegant golden domes sat next to rickety towers where dragons had tried to add to the eclectic mix and ended up with something more cluttered than Vola's parents' attic.

"How are we going to find it in all of that?" Sorrel said.

"Was there a map somewhere that we missed?" Talon said.

Vola glanced around, looking for signposts, but all she saw were hundreds of people going about their lives. Carrying produce, hurrying to and from the bazaar booths, gossiping in corners.

Every now and then, a large, horse-sized dragon flew overhead, but no one seemed to pay any more attention to them than you would to say a horse.

Throughout the bazaar flitted little dragons about the size of Rand. The familiar eyed them suspiciously. The swamp beast tried to snatch one out of the air to snack on. The little green dragon trilled and stuck out its tongue before darting away through the crowd.

Vola frowned at it. "I didn't realize there were tiny ones, too."

"I don't remember reading about them along with their larger cousins," Lillie said, holding her hand up to entice one closer. It hummed as it hovered, then dodged away. "Maybe they were bred more as pets."

Vola watched carefully as a nearby group of women lured one of the little dragons in with a piece of meat. When they let it go again, it hovered before them as they followed, going slow enough so that they could keep up.

"Or as local guides," Talon said.

"Rand," Vola said. "Could you catch one and bring it here?"

The raven ruffled his feathers, then launched himself into the air. Gruff watched, and Vola could almost imagine an envious gleam in his eye. The familiar had been a gift to Lillie just a few weeks ago, but he'd already made himself invaluable, as much a member of the party as Gruff was or the swamp beast.

The swamp beast eyed Rand, but its look was much more speculative and hungrier.

Okay, not like the swamp beast.

The familiar circled above, then dove on one of the little dragons. They collided with a squawk. His momentum carried them to the ground at their feet.

Vola swooped in and grabbed the little dragon as Rand extricated himself. And she held up a strip of dried meat from her pack.

"Can you take us to the council rooms?" she said, then read off the address.

The little bronze-colored creature cocked its head and eyed them with a slitted golden pupil. Then it snatched the meat and its wings whirred. Vola let go, and the creature sprang into the air and zipped away over the crowd.

"What if it leads us off a cliff?" Sorrel said, but Vola was already moving. She pushed through the bazaar shoppers, keeping the swamp beast on a tight leash behind her. They'd learned well enough that it did *not* pay to lose track of the swamp monster in an unfamiliar city. That's how it ended up living in sewers, terrorizing the populace from beneath their feet.

The little dragon led them up through the patchwork city, through narrow alleys made from recycled wood, and up big thoroughfares of solid stone. They crossed the valley on a small but serviceable bridge and ended up on the other mountainside.

Their guide stopped outside one of the big white-washed towers with a gold dome. It trilled, then zipped away, its wings whirring too fast to see.

Sorrel squinted at the sign out front and then up at the disappearing dragon. "What do you know; it worked."

Vola tied the swamp beast to a railing she assumed was a hitching post and glared it into submission. "Don't eat anyone," she said as the others filed through the ornate door.

The swamp beast narrowed its eyes and snorted, spitting a wad of yellow mucus onto Vola's breastplate. It sizzled.

She just sighed and scrubbed it off with a spare polishing cloth she kept in her back pocket. It paid to be prepared when traveling with a walking snot factory.

Inside the tower, the others had paused to wait for her. Or to admire their surroundings, one of the two. Vola wouldn't be insulted if it was the latter.

The round reception hall could have fit their entire caravan, and it was paved in a mosaic of colored stone and glass gathered from all over the world. She recognized a bit of blue stone from the quarries near her home and something green she was sure she'd seen on the tor in the swamp near Water's Edge.

Two staircases rose before them, hugging the walls so they curved around and met in the middle of the opposite wall, where a door hung slightly ajar.

A voice floated from that second story opening.

"What do you mean, am I sure? Of course, I'm damn sure. I came all this way up here to argue about it with you. Do you think I'm enjoying myself…Well, screw that. I don't have to cater to your bloody insecurities."

Vola exchanged a glance with Lillie as Rilla stormed through the door above them and stomped down the steps.

Lillie cleared her throat delicately. "Trouble?"

"This level of stupidity is astounding. We have a real problem heading this way, and all the council can do is worry that a princess of Southglen is trying to steal their authority."

Sorrel tilted her head. "Are you trying to steal it?"

"Trust me, it's not worth stealing," Rilla growled. "They can do whatever the hell they want on top of this cute little city they've built. I don't care. What I care about is that there's a dragon out there with the power to suck magic out of the earth itself. But I'm so wrapped up in the local bureaucracy they haven't even acknowledged the threat creeping up on them."

She paced to the foot of the left staircase, then spun on her heel and paced to the foot of the right, her boots clicking against the colored stones.

"I thought it was their job to keep the dragons from waking up," Vola said with a glance at Lillie. "Isn't that what they're so worried about?"

"Yeah," Rilla said. "But they've been doing it for so long that they think they know everything there is to know about sleeping dragons. There's no proof, they said. Nothing to show that a dragon has woken. And by insinuating that one has, I insulted them and their sacred duty."

Vola winced. She could imagine Rilla insulting a lot of people in the course of her job. The princess could be subtle when she wished, but clearly, she did not wish right now.

"Proof?" Talon's voice grated even more than it usually did. "They want proof."

Rilla stopped pacing and faced the ranger. "I'm sorry," she

said quietly. "A dead wolf pack however many years ago and miles away won't convince them."

Talon stiffened. "Unfortunately, a dead pack is all I have to offer. What the hell else can I say or do to make them believe me?"

"I believe you," a voice said. A dwarf stepped through the door above them and closed it softly behind him. Squat and round, he would only come up to Vola's belly button in his bare feet. His shoulder-length dark hair was caught in a tail at the nape of his neck and he jingled in a fortune of custom chainmail and leather as he descended the stairs.

"I heard your arguments," he said as he came even with them. "And I believe you."

Rilla's eyes narrowed on the dwarf. "I don't remember you in there."

"I'm not a councilor. I was watching from the gallery. Fedor Gerrickson," he said, thrusting his hand out to Rilla. "Captain of the city militia and professional dragon hunter."

Rilla shook it, keeping her hesitance at an acceptable level.

The dwarf turned to Talon and jerked his chin up to meet her eyes. "You've got a personal stake in this."

"I've seen it before," Talon said. "A dragon killed my family."

"And did you kill it right back?" Fedor asked, eyes boring into her.

The corner of Talon's mouth twitched. "I did. With help."

Fedor waved a hand. "Then you're practically a professional, too."

"I wouldn't have guessed there'd be much call for dragon hunters," Lillie said, clasping her hands in front of her. "Considering the *draconis maximus* are supposed to remain sleeping."

"Yeah, but they don't always, do they?" Fedor said sharply. He gestured to Talon. "Accidents happen and the big beasts have to be put down for the sake of the world. And I have no problem occupying myself in between. After taking one of the big ones down, things like the little horse-sized ones and bears and minotaurs are easy."

"True," Vola said. But she kept her eye on Talon. She didn't look like she'd met a kindred spirit. Mostly, she looked worried.

Fedor took a step closer to Talon. "I know what it's like," he said. "To have everything you love wiped out by something that barely sees you as an ant. That's why I'm here. One day, I'll convince the council that we need to burn out the problem at its source. We need to strike the beasts where they lay and kill them before they rise."

Talon took in a sharp breath while Lillie blinked.

"All of them?" the wizard said.

"'Course. It's the only way to be safe," Fedor said.

Talon's mouth drew tight. "Attacking them for no reason would just wake them up earlier and put more people at risk."

"Not if we do it right. It's called nipping the problem in the bud."

"It's called murder," Sorrel said, cocking her head.

"Do you murder a bear or a boar that's gone savage?" Fedor said. "Or do you slaughter it? *You* understand." He met Talon's eyes.

Talon grimaced. Then she opened her mouth but hesitated.

"Killing them before they threaten everything is the only way to keep everyone safe," Fedor said. "They're much more dangerous once they're awake."

"Which is why we have to deal with this one before it does any more damage," Rilla said, making Talon jump.

The ranger backed up a step, her brow coming down. "She's right. There's one awake right now. We can't deal with a sleeping threat until we deal with the threat that's already here."

Fedor shrugged. "Fine with me. I enjoy killing them either way. Revenge is sweetest when it's shared. Am I right?"

He bumped his shoulder into Talon's elbow making her stagger.

Talon, who didn't like physical contact at the best of times, lifted her lip. Gruff rose from his spot by the door and slunk between them, neatly putting himself in Fedor's way.

Fedor frowned down at the wolf.

"What do you suggest?" Vola said, drawing his attention away from the ranger and her companion. "Since you're the professional."

"Find proof," he said. "Something that will convince the council that you know what you're talking about."

"An expert opinion might sway them." Lillie tapped her lip, eyes distant. "This is where the experts on dragons gather, anyway. They must respect them and their results."

Fedor made a face. "I was thinking find the dragon and show the council the danger. Personally. But yeah sure. Experts. That works, too. There's a monk at the All-Pantheon temple who might be able to help. A Master Bao. He was asking me about where the dragons roost. Maybe he's got something up his sleeve."

"Master Bao?" Sorrel cried. "My Master Bao?"

"I didn't know you had a Master Bao," Talon said.

Fedor squinted at the halfling. "He was dressed a lot like you. Claimed he was from one of Maxim's monasteries."

"That's him, then," Sorrel said.

Vola tilted her head. "Why would one of your masters be all the way out here, looking for dragons?"

"Obviously, that will be the first thing I ask when we talk to him."

"Obviously," Vola said.

"What are you going to be doing?" Talon asked Fedor.

"I have my eye on several dragon lairs around Firewatch," he said. "And associates posted up and down the mountain range. I'm going to check to see if any of them are suddenly empty."

A solid plan. "Good luck," Vola said.

Fedor gave them a jaunty salute and headed for the door, his mail jingling with every step.

"An interesting character," Lillie said, as he disappeared out the door.

Rilla crossed her arms. "He might have been disparaging of it, but I liked your idea of experts. Did you have anyone in mind?"

Lillie flushed. "Sort of. I mean, my mother. She's supposed to be around here somewhere, studying dragons."

"Perfect place to start then."

"Are you sure that's a good idea?" Vola asked.

"Why not?" Lillie asked, shoulders going back. "She's...she's family. And she knows what she's talking about, presumably. And...well, it might be nice to meet her."

Vola's brow drew down, reading a lot more into the pauses than what Lillie was saying. The woman had left the Ephyra family after Lillie was born, having completed her side of the marriage contract. Vola didn't see the worth in a woman who saw a family and children as a contract, but also, she'd gotten to grow up with her own mother. She could see how it would be different for someone who hadn't.

"Do it, then," Rilla said. "You're better able to ask questions than I am, right now." She pinned Lillie with her glance. "And I trust you not to let anything personal get in the way."

Lillie raised her chin. "Of course, Your Highness."

"I'm gonna swear at the wall some more. It'll be good practice for when they let me back in the council chambers."

"You're going back in?" Vola asked.

"I have to get them to admit there's even a problem. Meanwhile, you're going to have to be my eyes and ears and hands."

"Will they let us do our job?" Talon asked. "If they don't like you, why would they like us?"

"I don't think anyone here knows you work for Southglen. Unless the caravan spreads it around."

"I'm not sure Gregor ever guessed you were a princess," Lillie said.

"Probably hasn't met any," Vola said.

"Especially not ones that swear so much," Talon muttered.

FIVE

WHEN RILLA HAD HIRED them back in Brisbene, she'd promised them room and board, as well as their salary, and she hadn't disappointed them yet. The hotel in Firewatch wasn't as fancy as the one in Glenhaven, but it was clean and there was actually room service.

Although Rilla's parting words as she left the next morning were, "Have fun, but stay away from the eggs."

"I think I should have listened to her," Sorrel groaned as she and Vola made their way through the winding paths of the city toward the All-Pantheon temple. It stood beside a House of the Broken, a healing center dedicated to the Greater Virtue of Righteousness.

"I don't know why you didn't. The rest of us did," Vola said.

"It was clearly a challenge." Sorrel rubbed her stomach. "You can't just let a challenge like that go."

"It was clearly a warning." Vola squinted up at the facade which comprised three different architecture styles, each story representing a different culture and technique. It was probably supposed to mean something like unity and togetherness, but mostly it came out looking like a badly done puzzle. "So, you seemed pretty excited about this Master Bao."

"He was my fighting master."

"And he treated you okay?" Vola asked, knowing the answer might not be yes. The rest of the monks hadn't been particularly good to Sorrel.

Sorrel grinned, her gaze going distant with memory. "He refused to train me at first. Said I was too small."

"That doesn't sound very nice."

Sorrel grinned. "Well, I was four. But I climbed to the roof where I could see them in the yard and mimicked everything he did until he finally agreed. I was his favorite after that."

They stepped up through the wide archway of mismatched plaster. There wasn't even a door. Just an open portal into the dark interior.

They'd decided that morning to split up. Sorrel had obviously wanted to track down Master Bao while Lillie had to find her mother's address at the city's registry before she had a hope of talking to her.

Talon and Vola had exchanged a wordless look and they split as well, Vola to watch Sorrel's back and Talon to watch Lillie's.

Vola might have had an ulterior motive for following Sorrel to the temple. She could talk to Cleavah anywhere, true, but some conversations just felt better in a place of worship.

The space inside was cool and dim. Only a few worshipers stood beneath the arranged statues to pray. The Greater Virtues all stood lined up under the steep roof while little altars to the Lesser Virtues and Obstacles lay at their feet.

"I'm going to find an acolyte," Sorrel said. The staff across her back sizzled and lightning crackled over its surface, lighting up the statue of Maxim for a moment. "Maybe one of them will know...huh."

"Huh, what?"

"Well, I was going to say maybe one of them will know where Master Bao is, but he's right there."

An ancient human with skin as dark and dry as the desert outside ambled around the statue of Ona, Greater Virtue of Honor. He wore a gray wrap-around tunic just like Sorrel's, and his stark white beard had been pulled together into a long braid.

"Master Bao," Sorrel said, her voice carrying up the walls. She raced to the old man.

As she drew even with him, he stuck one foot between her legs and twisted her over his hip to send her flying across the floor.

Vola cried out and rushed forward, drawing her sword, but Sorrel hit the ground rolling and bounced upright with a grin.

"Just checking your reflexes." Master Bao's voice scraped like leather across the stone, but his lively eyes glinted.

"They're as good as you made them," Sorrel said, stepping back to them. This time Master Bao didn't throw her.

He tsked. "That is not the compliment you mean it to be. They should be better by now. You should have made them better yourself."

Sorrel rolled her eyes. "Master Bao, I thought you'd be back at the monastery, making sure Hazel didn't make any mistakes in her first year as abbess."

"Hazel is doing fine. You were wise to pick her." His eyes flicked to the staff across Sorrel's back, and Vola had a feeling he knew it was the real thing while Hazel had gone home with a replica. "She can do without me. Indefinitely."

Sorrel's brow drew down. "What does that mean? What are you doing in Firewatch?"

His mouth twisted in a self-deprecating grin. "I'm retiring, Sorrel."

Sorrel's eyes went wide, and she sucked in a breath. "No."

Vola's gaze flicked between the two of them. Retiring didn't sound that bad, but from Sorrel's expression, she must be missing something.

"Congratulations?" Vola said.

Sorrel shook her head. "You can't," she cried. "Master Bao, you're not done."

"I am, little one. I have taught many. I have lived years beyond my normal life, thanks to Maxim. I have seen much of this world. And now I'm ready to meditate with my god."

"That actually sounds rather peaceful," Vola told Sorrel.

"You don't get it. When a monk retires, they don't just not work or fight anymore. What it means is they go off into the wilderness to 'meditate.' Forever. No food, no water."

"Until we return to the earth we were born from," Master Bao said.

Sorrel jerked her chin up. "Until they die of starvation and exposure, you mean."

"It is my choice, Sorrel." A bit of steel came into Master Bao's voice.

"Well, it's a stupid one. Some dragon hunter up the hill said you were looking for dragons. I thought you were going to fight one or something."

"I am done fighting. Maxim was once considered the brother of dragons along with the other Virtues. I wanted to spend my final days meditating in a place closer to him."

Vola winced. Personally, she didn't think it would matter all that much where Master Bao chose to do his dying. Maxim hadn't proved he cared.

But it was still Master Bao's choice.

"I'm not letting you do this," Sorrel said.

Vola put her hand on the halfling's shoulder. "Sorrel."

Sorrel shrugged it off. "No. He still has so much left to do in the world."

"Like what?" Master Bao said, more gently than Vola would have.

Sorrel's mouth worked, but she couldn't seem to come up with anything.

Master Bao stepped around them, heading for the door.

"Like helping us with this dragon," Sorrel said, going after him. "A big one is out there, causing trouble."

"And you are the best ones to take care of it." He paused and met her eyes. "I made sure of it."

Master Bao walked out the door empty-handed. He didn't take any supplies or a weapon. He didn't need to.

A range of expressions flickered across Sorrel's face, making her eyebrows twitch and lower and her mouth pinch.

She took a deep shuddering breath and cast a glance up at Vola. "This isn't over. I'm not done arguing. Wait here." And she followed Master Bao out of the temple.

Vola took a step and then shook her head. She wasn't going to be any use in the conversation. She could see both sides, but she didn't have a reason to argue for Sorrel. The halfling argued well enough on her own. And Master Bao was fully capable of making his own decisions. And defending them.

And the thing Sorrel might be too upset to think of yet was that it took a while for someone to die of starvation and exposure. Especially someone who'd spent a lifetime making their body into a weapon the way Master Bao had. They still had time to change his mind.

Vola moved closer to the statues, gazing up at the still marble faces of the gods. As usual in an all-pantheon temple, the Greater Virtues had their statues arrayed around the far wall, towering over the little alcoves where the Lesser Virtues had their altars. There were fifteen. Fifteen Greater Virtues who carried the righteous traits of the world. Gods like Ona, who carried a scale and represented honor. Bierhel, who posed with her arms up in dance, representing joy and honesty. And Maxim, who stood fist to his heart, representing strength and loyalty. His stony face didn't seem to care that Master Bao was heading off to "commune" with a distant god who never answered.

At the end of the line stood the Broken, a scarred woman missing an arm and most of her left leg. Flames climbed behind her like fiery wings.

Vola stood in front of the Greater Virtues, surveying the alcoves at their feet. Somewhere down there, among hundreds of others, there would be an altar to Cleavah. Lesser Virtue of Vengeful Housewives. Mother of sharp implements. A mystery who was more than what she seemed.

The air moved as if someone stepped up to stand behind Vola's shoulder, and she breathed in deep. The scent of warm bread, fresh-cut grass, and the salt breeze from the sea washed over her even here in the desert.

"My lady," Vola said without turning around.

"My knight," Cleavah said in a voice that sounded like bells in the wind.

Vola's fingers twitched, and she just kept herself from touching the shield on her back in response, pride swelling through her. Standing here in the temple with the statues of the Greater Virtues in front of her, it was so tempting to try to match the voice with a face. She knew what Cleavah looked like. As the goddess of vengeful housewives, her altar lay beneath the Greater Virtues' feet. But she belonged up there, standing shoulder to shoulder with Maxim, Bierhel, Ona, and the Broken. Didn't she?

"Do you know all of them?" Vola asked instead of the question she really wanted to ask. She raised her other hand to gesture to the statues. "The Greater Virtues?"

Cleavah hesitated before answering. "Very well," she finally said. "Bierhel might be my favorite. She always knows a good joke. Maxim...well, he's a good man, but a bit dour."

Vola took a deep breath and turned. Cleavah stood in the dim temple, her golden skin glowing slightly, her long curling hair moving as if in an unseen breeze. Just as she'd always looked. She didn't look like she had the power to reach through all the rules and regulations to touch Vola.

"My lady, what happened in the desert? In that dead spot? You told me you could never be taken away from me as long as I reached out for you."

Cleavah's mouth drew tight and her eyes pinched. "I was not taken from you, Vola. But there is something in the desert that is able to steal power out of the world. And a god's power is directly tied to the world. Without that connection…" She spread her hands. "We are left in the dark. When you stepped into the dead space, nothing connected me to you anymore. Nothing connected me to that part of the world."

Vola gulped. "That's possible?"

"It shouldn't be," Cleavah said, her voice growing firm. "It never has been before. But this…this could be something new. It *is* new. And the world has been toppled by new things before."

"What about something that's very, very old but doing a new thing?"

Cleavah tipped her head in question.

"Could it be one of the dragons? They start apocalypses apparently."

Cleavah's lips thinned. "Perhaps. The dragons were there when the gods made the world. They are like siblings. And all siblings squabble."

"So they could be powerful enough."

"All together, yes. But something would have to wake them first."

"One might already be awake."

"I did not know that." Cleavah tapped her lips. "Siblings don't always talk to each other." Her eyes strayed to the statues of the Greater Virtues.

Vola opened her mouth to ask. She was going to do it. Three little words. Who are you?

The shush of sandals grabbed her attention. Sorrel strode across the quiet temple. Her staff sizzled as she passed Maxim's statue again. A bruise was forming under one eye and her clothes shed sand. "Well, he threw me across the street and disappeared, so I guess the argument's over. Hiya, Cleavah."

"Hello, Sorrel." Cleavah waited a beat longer, giving Vola time to ask.

She didn't.

She just watched as Cleavah turned and stepped into the shadows of the temple, heading for the door. Vola's eyes tracked her movement, but by the time she reached the sunlight outside, she was gone.

"Don't worry about Master Bao," Vola said as they exited the temple. There was no sign of Cleavah or the ancient monk outside on the street. "We have a little time. We can still track him down."

Sorrel trudged down the steps, her head down as if thinking.

A raven cawed, and Vola lifted her chin to find Rand perched on the railing opposite them. He flapped up over the crowd in the street and landed on Vola's shoulder.

She lifted her hand, and the raven dropped a note into her palm.

"Did Lillie and Talon find her mom?" Sorrel asked, not looking up.

"She works at the field museum, apparently," Vola said, squinting at the small page. Lillie always made sure to write her letters big and blocky so Vola could read them without them crawling all over the page. "They're headed there now."

Sorrel rolled her shoulders and cracked her neck. "Enough moping, then. Let's go meet them. Hopefully, Lillie's mom will have a better idea where to look for the dragon."

They followed Rand as he swooped over the heads of the crowd and led them nearly to the top of one of the peaks.

The museum itself was built overlooking the city from a rocky crag. Wide windows glinted in the sunlight and reflected the other side of the city climbing up the mountain opposite them.

Lillie and Talon stood on the steps leading up the last few hundred feet. Lillie's mouth hung open.

"It looks like a ship, doesn't it? Like the cabin of a ship. How did they get it up here?"

Vola squinted at the museum, which did resemble the back end of a ship sticking out over the empty space at the edge of the rock. The building beyond was quite a bit larger but obviously made up of pieces of other vessels and structures.

"Magic," she said.

Lillie spluttered and limped up the steps to the front door. "Of course, it was magic. I meant more specifically. We're miles from any bodies of water. The amount of power and energy it would take to transport this across the desert..."

Lillie continued babbling to herself as they pushed through the doors and stepped into the cool quiet of the museum.

Vola's eyes widened as they adjusted to the dim light inside. Strung across the wide hall was the lithe, shiny skeleton of a dragon. One of the *draconis minimus,* otherwise it would never have fit inside. But it was still larger than any of the other dragons Vola had seen flitting around the city so far. Along the walls stretched murals of dragons in their natural habitats.

The museum seemed dedicated to draconic natural history, but a few other species made appearances here and there. A manticore's stinger sat on a pedestal before a painting depicting the angry beast. And on their left, a tooth from an earth giant rested against the wall, nearly as tall as Vola.

"Huh," Sorrel said, hands on hips as she gazed around. "Maybe we can sell them the swamp beast. It would feel right at home here, I think."

"I agree," Talon said. "I can see it fitting right there." She held up her hands to frame a bare patch of wall across from them. "Stuffed, preferably."

"They'd have to kill it first," Vola muttered. "Which is more than we've managed."

Sorrel cocked her head as several well-dressed patrons passed, ogling the displays. "Who do you suppose is in charge?" she said. "None of these look like they work here."

"Are you looking for someone in particular?" a voice said, accompanied by a slithery, serpentine noise. Like scales on stone.

Vola turned to catch the speaker and found herself face to face with one of the small dragons. This one was red and gold with its wings folded tightly to its back so it didn't knock anything over. It sat on its haunches, waiting.

Vola's eyes narrowed. She hadn't seen that many dragons this close yet, but this one seemed sort of familiar. Its coloring would gleam as bright as flames under a clear sky.

"Hurren," Lillie said, quicker than Vola to place the dragon.

"Mishap's Heroes," the dragon said, the crest above her eyes raised in what looked like surprise. "Well, hi."

"Oh, now I remember," Sorrel said. "You were bouncing for Fang in Brisbene last we saw you."

"And you kicked my tail," Hurren said with a light laugh that didn't seem at all resentful. The dragon purred deep in her throat. "That was fun."

"What are you doing here?" Lillie said.

"Working," she said. "I retired from pit fighting a couple of months ago. There's only so many adventurers you can bop on the head before you get tired of it and go home."

"So, you got a job at the museum?" Lillie said, perking up. "I had no idea you were so interested in history."

The dragon shrugged, her gold scales glittering. "I mostly carry things. And answer the really stupid questions tourists have about dragons. Like 'are you sure you don't want to eat me?' and 'where's the toilet?'"

"Speaking of toilets..." Sorrel grimaced and rubbed her stomach.

"Out of order for the day, unfortunately," Hurren said.

Sorrel sagged. "Figures."

"Rilla told us not to eat the eggs," Talon muttered.

"You don't mind working beside...er, a blatant display of draconic mortality?" Lillie's eyes flicked to the skeleton hanging in the center of the room.

Hurren followed her gaze. "What? Brocker? No, he was a dick. He deserved to be strung up for display. About the only thing nice about him was his bones." The dragon batted her eyes at Lillie. "Unlike you."

Lillie flushed.

"Still casting that net pretty wide, huh?" Vola said.

"Hey, dragons like pretty things," Hurren purred. Her gaze flicked from Lillie to Vola. "And I have a broad definition of pretty."

"Yeah, yeah, keep it in your pants," Sorrel said, rolling her eyes. "We know we're beautiful. But we're not interested in being collected. We have our own questions."

Hurren sighed and settled back on her haunches. "Let me know if you ever change your minds. What would you like to know?"

"We're looking for an elf named Shereille. She works here." Her words were a statement, but her voice rose at the end, betraying her nerves.

"Oh, Shereille." Hurren rolled her eyes. "Yeah, sure. Everyone here at the museum knows Shereille. She's one of our lead researchers."

Lillie's eyes fluttered, and she looked simultaneously terrified and exalted. "Oh. Oh, is she here?" Her gaze flicked around the hall. But all Vola could see were the tourists gathered around the manticore stinger, reading the plaque.

Hurren shook her head, and Lillie's shoulders slumped.

"She's out with her team. Isn't due back for a couple of weeks." Hurren cocked her red and gold head. "I can give you a map, if you'd like. She wouldn't be that hard to find since she studies Listrell—the dragon closest to the city."

Vola glanced at Lillie for an answer.

Lillie pressed her lips together and nodded. "Yes, please. We need to talk to her. Unless…Hurren, if one of the *draconis maximus* had woken, would you be aware?"

Hurren snorted. "Gods, yes."

"You have a connection?" Talon asked. "Because you're all dragons?"

"Nothing as complicated as that. Everyone would know. The world would know. The big guys are noisy, and if one woke up early, it would be angry. Believe me. Everyone would know."

Talon took a deep breath through her nose.

Vola gave her a look. "It's not proof either way. We still need to find an expert."

Lillie squared her shoulders. "Yes. I think we'll need that map, Hurren."

SIX

HURREN WASN'T WRONG. Shereille's campsite might have been well up into the mountains that flanked Firewatch, but there was a broad path leading through the rocky crags and jagged bluffs. The morning sun beat down on Vola's head, making her regret the choice to wear the full armor of her calling.

"Well, it is a desert," Sorrel said, pausing at a bend in the path to shield her eyes and survey the view. She wasn't even panting in her loose linen tunic and trousers. Although she was shifting from foot to foot and holding her stomach.

Talon had pulled her hood low over her face to protect her fair skin. The end of her nose was already peeling from their long trek across the sands the last few days.

At least they'd left the swamp monster stabled back in the city, with Gruff standing guard to make sure it didn't eat anything important.

Lillie's red face glistened, and she stopped to swipe at her forehead with a damp handkerchief. "This is…really quite…oh, I can't even come up with words for how hot it is. Are you all right?"

Vola stopped and rested her hands on her knees to concentrate on breathing. "I think I could double as an oven, right now. There's enough sweat under this breastplate to drown a horse."

Raven swooped over them, cawing.

Lillie shaded her face. "It's just around the bend, he says. There's a camp and people and shade."

"Woohoo." Sorrel scampered up the trail after him. "I hope they have a bathroom."

Talon picked up her pace, too.

Vola started to follow but noticed Lillie hesitate. She turned, ready to offer a hand. The wizard didn't draw attention to her limp very often, but it had to be bothering her going up these hills and avoiding the rocks and gravel.

But Lillie stared up the path, teeth chewing her bottom lip.

"You can make it," Vola told her quietly.

"That's not what I'm afraid of," Lillie said. She met Vola's eyes. "I...I haven't actually met my mother, Vola. She left when I was barely a week old. Is it really childish to say I hope she likes me?"

Vola snorted. "Not at all. You want to make her proud."

Lillie rolled her eyes. "That doesn't make me sound like any more of an adult."

"No. You're right. It makes you sound like a child. But you are her child. No matter how grown-up you are, you will always be her child."

Lillie's lips pulled into a slow, sweet smile. "Yes. Yes, of course. Thank you, Vola. You always manage to put things into perspective. She is my mother and always will be and that counts for a lot." Lillie gathered herself and climbed the path past Vola.

Vola frowned. Wanting to impress a parent made absolute sense. But she hoped Lillie didn't think that impressing her would magically make Shereille into a better mother than she had been.

Vola brought up the rear in case Lillie slipped in the gravel that lined the path. The jagged spires of rock gave way to a little hidden valley between the peaks. Here the sloping mountains flattened out a bit, leaving a broad smooth area large enough for several tents that looked semi-permanent and about a dozen sturdy tables. Crates and baskets of supplies sat in neat stacks between the tents.

There were at least twenty humans and elves dressed in dusty shirts and trousers striding purposely around the campsite. A few leaned over the tables, notes spread before them. A couple manned the cookpot over a central fire-pit, while others checked the supplies, taking notes.

They looked a little surprised to see them appear from the path, but no one seemed ready to kick them out, either.

Sorrel clasped her hands over her heart. "Look. Latrines."

"You're leaving now?" Talon asked as Sorrel started for the line of little tents big enough to hold one person standing up. "What if Lillie needs your moral support?"

Vola was pretty sure Talon was just messing with Sorrel, but the halfling glanced between the latrines and Lillie.

"Oh, all right. I suppose it's not an emergency. Yet." She stopped the first person to pass within shouting distance. "Where can we find Shereille?"

The woman tucked her hair behind her ear and jerked her head toward the large tent at the back of the campsite. It backed up against the nearest peak, and a steady glow shone from the open flap.

Definitely not hard to find. Probably because Lillie's mother wasn't really hiding. She was just living a life free of any kind of familial obligation.

Sorrel trotted forward without hesitation. Lillie stumbled after her.

The tent at the far end of the camp had been erected atop a wood platform, as if the researchers expected to be in one place for a while. Through the flap, Vola glimpsed several full book-shelves, a neatly made cot, and a desk dominating the center.

A tall, slim figure with blonde hair tied up in a no-nonsense bun leaned over the desk.

"Aster, I'm going to need another wizard light in a few hours. Would you be so good as to have one ready when this one gives up?" a lyrical voice said.

Vola glanced at Lillie, but she seemed frozen, her foot just hovering over the step up to the platform.

Well, introductions weren't going to happen any time soon. At least not without help.

Vola cleared her throat and stepped up, her boots clanking against the boards. "Shereille Moonhallowed?"

The woman straightened and turned. "Oh, you're not Aster. I'm so sorry. What can I do for you?" She tilted her head, revealing sharply pointed ears, and smoothed her hands down her front as if she wore a court gown and not a pair of dusty overalls and a stained apron.

"Er," Vola said and glanced at Lillie, waiting for the wizard to take over. Nothing. "I'm Volagra Lightless. Paladin. We're here investigating some disturbances with the dragons. We came to find you because…well, you're the expert. But also, um, Lillie? You want to help me out here?"

Lillie shook her head, like breaking free of a reverie, and took the step up into the tent. "Yes," she said softly. "Um, hello. It's lovely to meet you finally. I'm—my name is Lilliara Ephyra."

The woman blinked. "Ephyra. As in Lord Ephyra. Of Glenhaven?"

"Yes."

Sorrel rolled her eyes and bounced forward. "Yes, Ephyra. Miss Shereille, meet your daughter. Daughter…" She gestured to Lillie. "Meet your mom."

Well, Sorrel hadn't made it any *more* awkward.

Shereille's eyes flickered over Lillie's form, her face, her hair, and eyes. Vola couldn't help comparing as well. Lillie had gotten her stature and a lot of her features from her father. But her hair and eyes, those came directly from the woman standing before them.

"Oh," Shereille said on an escaped breath. "Lilliara." Finally, she beamed. "Welcome. I'm glad to have finally met you."

But she didn't immediately step forward and sweep Lillie into a hug. Vola couldn't tell if Lillie was glad or not.

"You've grown," Shereille said. "You were so tiny when I left."

"That is what babies do," Lillie said with a twitchy little smile.

"I suppose so." Shereille tilted her head. "Elves take much longer to mature. That must be the human part of you. I guess I remember that from your brothers. They were a bit older. I got to know them so I might even recognize them now."

Lille bit her lip hard enough to turn it white, and Vola could tell she wanted to ask why she didn't stay to get to know her daughter, too. But she didn't.

"What do you do with yourself now?" Shereille said as if searching for something to talk about.

"I'm a wizard," Lillie said. "I went to the university in Glenhaven."

Shereille brightened. "Oh. A researcher?"

"Er, no. I took a more practical route." Lillie glanced at Vola and the others. "I help solve problems."

Vola nodded. "Not a bad way to put it."

"Oh, well that's useful, too, I suppose," Shereille said. "I remember your father being very studious. He surely instilled a curiosity and love of learning early. I would never have signed the contract otherwise."

"Are contracts like that common among elves?" Sorrel said, leaning on her staff. Her eyes kept flickering to the latrines.

"Common enough," Shereille said. "Marriage among our own

kind is similar to the other races, but we live so much longer than humans, it's hardly practical to find a life mate so young. Especially not one of another species." She paused with a small smile. "Still, Ephyra was nice enough. And we had lots in common so we had plenty to talk about while under contract. It passed the time pleasantly."

"That's...good?" Sorrel said.

"Oh, yes. It's rather dull when your partner can only provide excitement in bed."

Lillie let out a little squeak. "That's all right. That's not something we have to talk about."

Vola bit down a smile. "No, I get it." She turned to Shereille. "It is much nicer when you can rely on someone's wit as well as their...prowess."

"Yes," Shereille said brightly. "Ephyra wasn't as robust as some, but what he lacked in stamina he made up for in enthusiasm."

"Stop talking," Lillie hissed at Vola.

Vola leaned toward Sorrel. "You're right. This is much more fun when it's someone else's parents."

"Glad I don't have any," Sorrel said with a grin.

"Me too," Talon added.

"What about your research?" Lillie asked in a rush. "I'm so interested in what you're doing out here. Please, tell me about it."

Shereille turned her brilliant smile on her daughter and Lillie staggered a little. It must have been disconcerting to be on the other side of that brilliance for once. "Oh, I'm so glad you're interested. We're out here studying the great dragon, Listrell, while she sleeps. She is one of the most powerful of the greater dragons."

"You're not worried about waking her up?" Talon said.

Shereille laughed. "There is very little that could wake a greater dragon. They're tied to the land, and the land sustains them in slumber. They are its guardians even while it shelters them." Her eyes narrowed. "But why are you here? You mentioned something about a disturbance with one of them."

Because meeting her daughter wasn't enough. Vola fought not to huff. "We think one has woken," she said instead. "There are dead spots out in the desert. Places where magic was sucked out of the ground. And the last time anyone saw anything like it, a dragon was involved."

Shereille's frown creased her forehead. "Impossible."

"Excuse you, but we've seen it," Sorrel said.

"I'm not sure what you've seen, but it's impossible for it to have been a dragon."

Talon crossed her arms. "The last one killed an entire village and the local wildlife near my home. There were half a dozen spots just like it and a rampaging dragon on the loose. Don't tell me they're not related."

Lillie wrung her hands, her eyes darting between Shereille and Talon.

"I'm sorry," Shereille said, tilting her head. "But *draconis maximus* are tied to the land. The way the *draconis minimus* are tied to water. They govern it. They would never do anything to harm it. And believe me, if one of the greater dragons had woken up and gone rogue, we would know."

Vola read outrage in the stiffness of Talon's shoulders but also a creeping doubt.

"I have it on good authority that it's possible," Vola said, inching closer to Talon.

"What authority?" Shereille said.

"A goddess. One of the Virtues."

Shereille smiled indulgently. "Well, a goddess isn't really the expert on these things, is she? I am."

Vola's eyebrows went up.

Lillie stepped forward. "Perhaps you would like to examine

the dead spot with us. It would be helpful to have a trained eye to see anything we might have missed. And we were looking for an expert for a reason." She gave Vola a look.

"That would be helpful," Vola said, her voice barely above a growl.

"I'm afraid I can't spare anyone from my team." Shereille turned back to her table, shuffling her notes. "Unless you'd like to take a closer look at Listrell. She occupies my time nowadays."

"You're not even curious?" Vola said, glancing at Lillie. Lillie was curious about everything.

"Not really," Shereille answered flatly. "I don't believe it's connected to my work. But let me know if you want a glimpse of Listrell. She's quite fascinating even in this dormant state."

Lillie glanced at Vola. "We could take a look, couldn't we? We might see something that's related to the dead spots."

Vola didn't miss the note of pleading that crept into Lillie's voice. She sighed. Of course Lillie wanted to steal every moment with her mother that she could. She couldn't blame her. And she couldn't be the heartless git that stood in her way.

"Sure," Vola said quietly. "It wouldn't hurt. And maybe Talon will spot something familiar."

Talon hesitated and then nodded.

Lillie turned back to her mother. "We'd love to take a look."

"Wonderful," Shereille said, turning back to her desk. "I'll have Aster show you up to the lookout point. I'm sure you'll love it, and she can answer any questions you have while you're up there."

Vola was close enough to hear the little sip of air as Lillie's chest caved. But the wizard just smiled a strained smile and turned away from her mother who had already gone back to work, dismissing her as easily as she'd done as an infant.

SEVEN

THEY TRUDGED up the hill after Aster, a plump young woman with short curling brown hair and a perpetually cheerful expression. She scrambled up the narrow trail ahead of them, clearly familiar with the terrain. Dry shrubs grew between cracks in the rock. There was a lot more shade here and little depressions and crevices where water could gather so the plant life wasn't instantly vaporized by the desert sun.

"It's not far up here," Aster said, without having the decency to sound winded. "We have a perfect overlook where we can observe Listrell as she sleeps. There's still so much we don't know about the great dragons since they haven't been awake in centuries."

"You almost sound sad about that," Talon said.

"Well, obviously no one wants them to wake up. It would be a disaster. But...can you imagine if one did? Think of everything we could learn."

Lillie hung behind, her attention on the ground in front of her. Vola had expected her to ask a billion questions and take notes. But she didn't even look up.

Rand swooped down to light on her shoulder. He fluffed his feathers and bobbed his head the way he did when he had a gift for the wizard. She held out her hand and he dropped a blue stone into her palm.

"Thank you, Rand," Lillie said, polite even in her distraction.

Vola climbed up next to her. "I'm sorry meeting your mom was awkward."

Lillie's eyes flicked to her and then back to the rocky trail. "I don't know what I was expecting. I'm awkward about everything. I can't help overthinking every word and gesture and so it all comes out stiff. I just wish I could have had all the right things to say. Just once, when it counted."

Vola frowned at Lillie's back as she climbed past.

As she hurried to follow, she stepped headfirst into a draft of air smelling like fire-warmed rock and year-old carrion.

"Whoof, what is that?" Sorrel asked as Vola caught up to the group.

"Listrell," Aster said. "There's a shaft up ahead that vents fresh air into her sleeping chamber."

"And hundred-year-old morning breath out."

"You're one to talk," Talon muttered, climbing the path directly behind Sorrel. "Rilla said not to eat the eggs."

Aster bounced a little as she walked. "We can actually look straight down the shaft and see Listrell's flank move with her breathing. Mistress Moonhallowed often posts someone there to make the daily observations."

"How long have you worked with my m—with Shereille?" Lillie said.

"Almost two years now."

"Is she...a good boss?"

"Oh yes. I mean, she's demanding, sure, but you have to be in this field. She's extremely choosy about who she devotes time to, so it's an honor just to get to work with her."

"I'm sure," Lillie murmured miserably.

If it had been Vola, she would have been glaring a hole in the girl's back, blaming her for stealing Shereille's time. But Lillie's focus seemed to be diving further and further inward, looking for the fault in herself, probably. What had she done wrong? What did she do to drive her mother away?

Vola placed her hand on Lillie's shoulder and leaned to whisper in her ear. "Stop that."

Lillie glanced at her, eyes wide. "Stop wh —"

"I give up!" Sorrel threw her hands in the air, making Lillie jump. She hopped over one of the rocks at the edge of the path and disappeared.

"Where are you going?" Vola asked.

"Where do you think?"

"Why didn't you go back at the camp?"

"I second-guessed myself, okay? You've never done that before? But the non-emergency has now become an emergency. Just keep going. I'll catch up if it really is as close as Shereille said."

Talon stifled a snort behind her hand.

Aster had paused in the middle of the trail. "Is everything all right?"

"Fine," Vola said and tried to start up the path again.

But Talon had frozen, smile falling from her face.

"What is it?" Vola said.

Aster waited above them, blinking at their hesitance.

Talon turned her head, her nose in the air like she smelled something worse than the dragon.

"Talon?" Vola said quietly.

Talon's gaze dropped to the ground and she knelt to place her fingers against the dirt. "It's happening again," she said. "The magic, it's leaving. It's being pulled out of the land."

"Another dead spot is forming?" Lillie said. "Here?"

Vola didn't doubt Talon knew what she was talking about. The ranger's magic came from the land so she could probably feel it even before Lillie. Not to mention she had a personal connection to the problem.

Vola drew her sword and settled her shield on her arm. "Where is it going?" she said. "Where is it being drawn to?"

Talon stood and pointed up the trail. Aster stepped to the side, gazing at them with wide eyes.

Vola led the way, charging up the narrow path and dodging around the sharp boulders that jutted into their way.

"Sorrel, we need you," Lillie called as she and Talon followed.

"Kinda in the middle of something here!"

The trail twisted one last time, hiding the overlook, and Vola barreled around the corner to see the path even out and stretch all the way to a cliff with a sharp drop off on two sides and a steep slope up the other.

A short figure in long brown robes knelt in the center of the overlook. She glanced up as they came around the corner and Vola registered big eyes, wide ears, and round cheeks reddened by the sun. A gnome, dressed in a robe that hung from her waist in long, tattered strips. She held a gnarled staff with a clump of black feathers tied to the top.

Vola skidded to a stop.

She couldn't feel the magic sucking out of the world like Talon, but the colors of the rock beneath her feet writhed and twisted, like snakes or worms wriggling across the stone and sand. It made Vola's stomach roil, and she lurched back a step.

The stone around the gnome's feet grew black, absorbing the light until nothing remained but the darkness. And the black spread out, sending tendrils across the overlook as if stealing all the color from the world.

Vola instinctively crowded the others back with the feeling in the pit of her stomach that it would be very bad to be standing where the gnome was working.

"What...what is happening?" Aster said from behind Vola. She'd managed to keep up.

"It's her," Talon said. "It's not a dragon, it's her."

Vola leveled her sword at the gnome. "Stop that. Stop doing... whatever it is you're doing?" The words felt stupid, but what else could she do?

The gnome grinned at her, showing off a set of wide, perfect teeth. "Well, hello to you, too."

"I said stop it."

The gnome rolled her eyes. "Uh, no. Then the spell will be all ruined, duh."

"You're hurting the land," Talon said, squeezing in beside Vola. There wasn't a lot of room where the trail opened onto the overlook. "You're taking the magic right out of it."

"Well, yeah. That's the point." The gnome sighed like they were being really slow. "I can't use its power if it's locked away in the land."

"It's not yours to use," Talon cried at the same time Lillie said, "Use it for what?"

"Well, it's not yours either," the gnome said, planting her free fist on her hip while keeping her staff planted firmly against the rock. "Why shouldn't I claim some to power my spells? No one's going to miss it." She flung out her hand. "We're in the middle of a desert, in case you missed it."

"Stop it right now," Vola said. "You're stealing power from the world."

"And that's...bad," the gnome said. Her gaze flicked to Vola's shield. "Why would a black paladin care? Aren't you like the expert on bad?"

Vola growled.

Then the gnome's eyes widened. "Oh. Oh, I recognize you

now. An orc, an elf, and a…" She waved a hand at Talon. "Whatever you are. You're Mishap's Heroes. You've been wandering all over Southglen doing good. Where's the halfling?"

"Indisposed," Talon growled.

The gnome cocked her head. "Huh."

"What?" Vola yelled.

The gnome shrugged. "Nothing. Nothing at all."

"Obviously you were going to say something," Lillie said, a frown creasing her forehead.

"It's just…you're shorter than I was expecting."

"Speak for yourself," Talon growled.

"Yeah, but I'm a gnome. What's your excuse?" The gnome raised an eyebrow at Talon. "I guess the fact that you're here means you're going to try to stop me."

The blackness spread through the rock under their feet. They were running out of places to stand.

The gnome grinned. "Kind of hard, when you can't get close."

There was a whisper behind Vola's shoulder, and she didn't flinch as a fireball flew past her head to explode at the gnome's feet.

The gnome waved her hand in front of her face and coughed, a little singed but no worse than the sunburn peeling the end of Talon's nose. "Oh, good try. You must be Lilliara Ephyra."

"You have the advantage of me," Lillie grated through her teeth.

The gnome bowed from the waist. "Nargilla Pipwattle, the Unbeaten."

"Nice title," Talon said. "You come up with that yourself?"

"Yes. I'm rather proud of it."

"Enough," Vola said. "Talon, put an arrow through her ear. Maybe that will get her to stop."

"Gladly," Talon said and swung her bow up.

Pipwattle twisted, dodging the arrow meant for her head.

"Too slow," she cried. "Aaaand done!" She lifted her staff from the ground, leaving only a large spread of black where the rich reds and browns of the rock had been.

Vola uttered a war cry and charged the cocky figure, shield down, sword ready for a swing.

The gnome raised her staff as if to block the blow.

Before they struck, there was a violent rumble beneath their feet, and Vola stumbled past Pipwattle into the steep cliff beyond.

Vola spun to see if this was some trick. But Pipwattle stared at the blackened ground, a crease along her forehead. "Huh," she said.

"Oh, my gods," Aster said, eyes wide enough to reflect the overlook and the sky beyond.

"What was that?" Lillie hissed.

There was another deep rumble and a noise that started like a shiver at the base of Vola's spine and rose until it became a roar that echoed off the sharp cliffs around them.

"Oh, my gods, the dragon," Aster said. "It's Listrell."

Nargilla Pipwattle stepped to the edge of the overlook and glanced down. "Phew. I guess they don't have the equivalent of beauty sleep for a dragon, do they?"

Vola gaped at her, but the vibration under her boots was more immediately concerning. The rumble became constant and a waft of smoke curled from the vent beside the overlook, snaking and weaving into the sky.

"The land," Aster whimpered. "Dragons are tied to the land. And you just took all the magic out of this spot."

"Pff, she should learn to share then, shouldn't she?" Pipwattle said.

The peak beside them shivered, like a sleeping bear rising

from its hibernation, and between one second and the next, it erupted in a shower of earth and rock that blotted out the desert sun.

A shape so big Vola could barely register its size climbed from the jagged broken mountain, spewing a mouthful of fire into the sky. It unfurled wings of brilliant turquoise as bits of dirt and gravel pattered around them.

The dragon, Listrell, turned her head and opened her jaws to let out a roar that made Vola's sword ring in her hand. She dropped it to clap her hands over her ears.

The dragon's long neck snaked forward and her eyes fixed on the overlook. Slitted gold pupils pinned Vola to the rock against her back.

"Well, that was unexpected," Pipwattle said, gazing up at the giant silhouette against the sun. "But I'll take it."

"What the hell are you guys doing up he—Whoa, that's a dragon." Sorrel skidded to a stop at the top of the path, her mouth wide and her hands frozen on the ties of her pants.

"Nice of the halfling to join us finally," the gnome said. "Just in time to say good bye and good luck."

She spun to give Vola a jaunty salute and then stepped backward off the cliff edge.

Vola lunged forward, landing on her knees at the edge. Pipwattle floated downward as if held by a gentle breeze, her gnarled staff in her hand, and the strips of her robe fluttering around her. She alighted at the base of the cliff among jagged rocks and kept her balance like the distant cousin of a mountain goat. She flashed a grin up at Vola and then vanished among the rocks.

"Shit," Vola said. A little lightning bolt struck the ground beside her hand.

"Not to distract you or anything," Sorrel said. "But we have a much bigger problem heading this way."

Vola glanced up to see Listrell raise her wings, muscles bunched beneath her. She launched herself into the air, wingbeats like thunder that set their bones to shaking.

Listrell turned at the top of her arc and dove. Straight for the overlook.

Vola scrambled backward, snatching at her fallen sword, and she had a split second to wonder what good the blade would do against a dragon.

Then Listrell's bulk blocked out the light, casting a shadow over the blackened surface of the overlook.

Vola stared up at her, turquoise scales shining all along her back, wings slanted overhead, and Vola's gibbering brain said, "well, at least it's shade."

Then she kicked herself into action and raised her shield.

Listrell opened her huge jaw, and Vola found herself staring down the dark, empty stretch of teeth to the flames gathering at the back of her throat.

Fire shot out, but just before it reached Vola, there was a crack of air and Lillie manifested in front of her. The flames parted around them, flickering like they hit an invisible wall.

"Thanks," Vola gasped. "But isn't that usually my job?"

"You'll have plenty of opportunities. I don't know how many times I can do this."

The fire didn't let up.

Sorrel, tiny compared to the beast in front of them, leaped on the dragon's snout. She was no bigger than the dragon's eye, but she slammed Maxim's staff into the dragon's snout, letting a ripple of lightning crackle across the scales.

The fire stopped abruptly as the dragon's breath hitched. Vola didn't squander the opportunity. As Sorrel leaped free of the snout and snapping teeth, Vola lunged around Lillie and swung her blade at the nostrils just within range. She connected with a clang, and her blade slid off the scales. But she swung again and again—it had to at least be making a dent because the dragon grunted and shook her head.

Arrows sprouted from the beast's hide, and Vola glanced back to find Talon sniping from behind a rock on the trail.

Sorrel scampered past and leaped again, using the arrows as handholds to climb up the dragon's slick hide. Her feet were sure as she raced down the length of the snout, and the dragon went cross-eyed trying to keep track of her. Sorrel snapped out and bashed her staff into the beast's forehead, right between her eyes.

Listrell roared, and Vola lunged forward to plunge her sword hilt deep in the dragon's gums.

A precisely timed arc of lightning shot from Lillie's hands into the open maw, and Listrell gurgled in pain.

She jerked back, yanking Vola's sword out of her hand. Vola stumbled a couple of steps as the dragon reared back and Sorrel landed beside her, rolling into the cliff.

With another ear splitting shriek, Listrell pushed off from the overlook, beating her wings and sending a wave of air to press them back. She gained height and spun above them, roaring the entire time.

Then she wheeled and headed toward the city, spouting gouts of flame at the ground as she passed.

"Oh no," Lillie said. "She's going for Firewatch."

"And she took my sword with her," Vola grumbled.

"Well, you did stick it in her mouth," Lillie said. "Sorrel, are you all right?"

"Peachy," Sorrel said. She lay upside down, her feet up the side of the cliff, her arms flat against the ground as she stared up at the sky. Her staff lay in the dirt beside her. "Luckily monks are made out of rubber. You know, fighting dragons sounds so romantic in the stories, but it's a lot of bad breath and just whacking away at something until it falls over."

"Except she hasn't fallen over yet. She's headed for the city," Vola said.

Talon peered behind another rock, finding Aster, who cowered there with her arms over her head. "Get to the camp," she said. "Tell the researchers to evacuate. Get under cover. The camp is too open if the dragon decides to come back and take her revenge on anyone nearby."

"Revenge?" Aster said, sitting up. "Why would she want revenge? We didn't have anything to do with waking her up."

Talon frowned at the sky. "This is exactly what happened to my pack."

Vola straightened and winced when her back popped.

"Is it?" Lillie said quietly.

Talon spun around. "Yes. It's not exactly what I thought it was. It mustn't have just been a dragon that time, either. But I think the dead spots woke it up, and it was angry. It attacked everything in sight. That's the important part. I don't care who's to blame, but if we don't do something about Listrell, many will die."

Aster gasped and followed her gaze. "What about the city?"

"We'll get to the city. You get the researchers to safety."

EIGHT

THEY RACED back down the narrow track, following Talon, who didn't bother to pause at the researcher's camp. Lillie hesitated when Aster split off and rushed for Shereille's tent, but she kept going down the trail before Vola could even open her mouth.

Vola wanted to stop and take stock for just a second, to wrap her head around the fact that they'd just fought a *dragon* and they were heading toward *another* fight with a dragon. But she decided they couldn't spare the time when Listrell made a swooping pass over them, making the air hum, and then she winged away toward the city, flames spouting from her jaw.

Clearly, the threat was ahead of them. And it wasn't like they could find Pipwattle to exact justice.

Besides, Talon had seen this before. And Vola trusted Talon. If the ranger said to hustle, she'd hustle.

It had taken them two hours to walk from the city to the researcher's camp, but they made it back in half an hour.

Nothing kept them from running straight into the city. It wasn't like the dragon had laid siege to it. She was still airborne, doing her best to burn the whole thing to the ground.

Vola hadn't thought Firewatch could get any hotter, but with flames licking up the eclectic collections of wood structures, she was half convinced she was going to melt inside her tin can armor. Civilians ran by, knocking into them in a panic, some running into buildings that still stood. Others tried to escape the burning city with what few belonging they could save. Ash began to gather on the street softening their footfalls.

Vola's nose burned from the acrid smoke as she whipped around, mind racing. What the hell could they do against a dragon? How could they defend an entire city?

She squinted, spotting a familiar figure on one of the stone bridges spanning the gap between the two halves of the city. She gestured to the rest to follow and sprinted up the sloping road to the bridge.

"Now do you believe me?" Rilla waved her hands over her head as she confronted a man in a flowing blue robe with a cream-colored tunic underneath.

"Dragon," the man gibbered towards the sky. "It's a dragon. What is it doing awake?"

Rilla took him by the shoulders and shook. "Your city is literally called Firewatch! You live in the middle of dragon lands. How can you not be prepared for a dragon attack?"

"We haven't had one in hundreds of years!" the man yelled back. "Our strength lies in the ability to reason with and live peacefully with the creatures. The little ones live here as well. They don't want to burn it down."

"Well, you've got a big one trying to do just that! What are you doing about it?"

The man gestured as a civilian ran past with a bucket, water sloshing across the stones at their feet. "Look, the brigades are already forming. They'll pull water from the cisterns inside the mountain."

"Great, so you can save the buildings. Hopefully, there will still be people to live in them! What are you doing about the dragon?"

The man hesitated, his mouth wide.

Rilla growled deep in her throat and turned to Vola and the others as they drew even with her. "This is fucking ridiculous. They built the city to withstand dragons centuries ago, but now when they actually need it, they've forgotten everything they learned." Rilla gestured to the nearest building, which smoldered uncontrolled. "They let people build with wood on top of the stone. And now they act surprised when it's all burning."

"The dragons have left us alone for years," the official said behind her. "Why would one attack now?" His eye caught on Rilla, and he leveled his finger in her face. "You came here talking of a dragon attack. What did you do to wake the creature?"

"It wasn't us," Vola said. "The dead spots out in the desert that she warned you about. We found the one who's doing it. She woke the dragon up by draining the land."

The official clutched his dark hair with both hands. "We must drive it away from the city. Long enough to regroup and put the fires out. Only then can we solve the problem of who woke the thing."

"You four." Rilla pointed to Vola and the others. "You're on dragon duty. Get that thing to leave us alone. Join whatever defense these people have cobbled together."

"Captain Fedor Gerrickson will be on the Heights," the official said, pointing to the jagged peaks. "He's in charge of the city militia."

"The dragon hunter?" Talon said.

"Well, we don't let him go around waking up dragons, so what else is he good for?"

There was a squeal and a shape the size of a horse with nasty teeth and worse breath slithered by, the light of the fire reflecting from its scales. Gruff ran after it with an angry bark.

"Oh no," Lillie said.

"It must have escaped the inn in the confusion," Sorrel said.

Rilla rolled her eyes. "I'll catch your swamp monster. You get to the Heights."

Vola gave Rilla a snappy salute and led the way through the conflagration. She didn't have a map and didn't think it would be helpful with most of the city burning, anyway. But she figured all they had to do was keep moving up, and they'd eventually reach the Heights.

Sparks swirled through the air along the lower levels, stinging Vola's skin as they settled, but the higher they got, the more smoke stung her eyes and caught in her chest.

Vola squinted and led them up the last tower. From there, a wooden bridge spanned the gap to the bare peak, where figures swarmed in the smoke.

She gestured the others across, bringing up the rear, but the wood smoldered under her boots and crumbled behind her heels.

"Go, go, go," she called. "This is a one-way trip."

Lillie took one look over her shoulder and then grabbed Talon and popped out of existence, the two of them reappearing on the peak. Sorrel stopped suddenly and threw herself onto the wood slats.

Vola sprinted past her. "What are you d—"

The rope railing snapped with a violent twang. Vola threw herself toward the end of the bridge but landed halfway over the edge with a painful gasp. She kicked and scrambled her way to solid ground.

"Sorrel!" Lillie called.

Vola leaped to her feet and peered over the edge, expecting the worst, but Sorrel had wrapped her arm through the railing and ridden the bridge down. Their side was still attached so that the loose bridge dangled over the empty space above the city. Sorrel just grinned and climbed up it like a ladder.

"That was fun," she said. "What's next?"

Vola heaved a sigh and coughed on smoke. "Would you not do that?" she choked out.

Sorrel patted her on the back, but there was an ominous flapping noise coming from all around them and Vola didn't dare sit there recovering for any longer.

She straightened and glanced around. A few guardsmen in soot-stained uniforms shot from the peak and a couple more manned an ancient ballista.

"Fedor?" Vola called, squinting through the smoke. "Are you up here?"

The dwarf's head popped up from the other side of the ballista, topped with a smudged helmet. A grin wreathed his face as soon as he saw them.

"Proof!" he cried. "That's some damn fine proof!"

"We're here to help," Vola said.

"Great." He bent his head to aim the ballista. "We'll take anything you can give us. Grab a bow and start shooting. Unless you have anything else that can bring down a dragon."

A gust of wind drove the smoke away from the peak in swathes of swirling darkness, revealing Listrell. The great dragon dove for their tiny defense.

The guardsmen yelled. Fedor fired the ballista, shooting off a great crossbow bolt that struck Listrell's side and bounced off.

"Shit." Fedor lunged out of the way as the dragon landed on the ballista.

The ancient wood crunched beneath her talons. She swung her head around, teeth snapping, and a guardsman leaped from the peak with a scream, not waiting to be dragon food.

Vola reached for her sword and remembered it was still stuck somewhere in the dragon's maw. If she hadn't swallowed it already. All she had left was a pair of matching hand axes.

Before she could draw, Sorrel had charged the dragon, staff

crackling with lightning, and got in two solid blows which cracked like thunder.

Listrell grunted. Her muscles bunched, and she sprang into the air again.

Talon was already taking aim beside Vola, and Lillie had her hands raised calling forth lightning or fire. Sorrel couldn't follow the dragon into the air, but she did carry a god's weapon with many uses. The staff morphed in her hand until she held a bow nearly as tall as she was. Vola had never seen her use one, but she'd grown up in a martially-minded monastery and the staff answered to her almost as if she was Maxim herself. So Vola didn't doubt she could use it.

Which left Vola standing there useless unless Listrell chose to land again.

The guardsmen all scrambled to their feet and Fedor called orders for them to form a rank and send a volley of arrows at their enemy. Vola had to give them points for bravery.

She rubbed the smoke and soot from her eyes and followed Listrell's movements. The dragon circled just out of range of the guardsmen's shortbows. The only thing hitting her were Lillie's spells and whatever Talon and Sorrel could fling at her with their longbows.

They had to get closer. Bring the fight to the dragon rather than waiting for her to come to them.

Vola's eyes narrowed. She had a crazy idea, but since the normal ideas weren't going to be enough right now...

She grasped Lillie's shoulder. "Can you get me onto her back?"

Lillie gaped at her, soot streaking her round face. "Get you —? You mean teleport you there? Are you insane?"

"Not since the last time I checked. Look, we have to drive her off, not bring her in closer. Get me up there, and I think I can do it."

There was a roar, and they ducked as Listrell swept past, raking the peak with her claws and taking several guardsmen with her.

"Now, Lillie. Before she kills anyone else."

Lillie's lips thinned like she was going to argue. Then she blew out her breath. "Shit."

"I always know it's a fun idea when Lillie swears," Sorrel said with a grin.

Vola slung her shield across her back—at least it hadn't gone down the dragon's gullet—and drew her axes.

Lillie took her arm and muttered a few words.

Vola's ears popped, and the world went white for a second.

Then slick turquoise scales heaved under her feet and air rushed past her like a storm across the deck of a ship, only way worse. She staggered and grabbed Lillie before either of them could fall from the dragon's back.

"Go," she yelled in Lillie's ear. "Back to the others. You'll be safer there than here."

"Be careful," Lillie said, then flashed out from under Vola's hand.

Vola crouched low, trying to keep her balance as Listrell banked. The dragon's back tilted and Vola lunged to grab hold of one of the spikes marching along her spine.

As the beast leveled out, Vola stood and tripped forward, using the change in momentum to fight the rush of air.

Vola squinted into the wind and caught sight of the peak ahead of them, growing closer by the second. The dragon was going in for another pass.

Vola quit trying to get to Listrell's head and swung her right ax at the spot where her wing met her body.

The dragon screamed and veered to the left, and Vola grabbed a scaly spine. It was a long way down if she lost her grip or her footing.

She swung again, trying not to think about what would happen if she made the dragon fall from the sky rather than flee the fight.

Listrell roared and shuddered, trying to shake her free, but Vola clung to the spike for dear life.

There was a pop, and Lillie appeared beside her with Sorrel.

"I told you to stay on the peak with the others," Vola yelled.

"My fault," Sorrel said. "I was jealous you got to bash her up close."

Lillie just rolled her eyes before teleporting away again.

"All right," Sorrel said. "Let's see if we can annoy her into leaving."

Beside them, an arrow streaked through Listrell's wing, leaving a gap big enough to ride a horse through.

"That'll help," Vola said. She made for the beast's head again, this time with Sorrel in tow.

Vola leaped the last few steps and planted an ax blade between Listrell's eyes. Sorrel followed it up with a blow to the eyebrow ridge. The Warhammer had changed back into a staff for her.

Listrell roared, and Vola kept up the onslaught.

"It's not worth staying," she yelled, wondering if the creature could hear her. "We're just going to keep bothering you."

Sorrel aimed a kick at her eye. "We're very annoying like that."

Listrell jerked, and Vola lost her footing. She flung her arms around the dragon's neck, just fast enough to avoid a long plummet.

Sorrel tumbled down the dragon's back, and Vola gasped. But the halfling caught hold of one of the spine ridges, halting her fall. She adjusted herself, then raised her fist and brought it down with a crack right on Listrell's spine.

The dragon screamed and wheeled again, only this time

instead of circling the city, she straightened her course and made for the mountains.

"It's working," Vola called to Sorrel.

"Great, now how do we get off? I can't imagine she's gonna like having stowaways when she gets wherever she's going."

Vola scanned the ground as the city sped beneath them. Then she spotted one of the fire watch towers ahead of them.

It was perfect, but they weren't going to get close enough. Sorrel might be able to make it, but there was no way Vola could jump that far.

Vola squinted, searching for another option. High on the cliff above them, a figure appeared and drew a longbow.

"Talon," Vola whispered.

An arrow whistled through the air, close enough to the dragon's eye to make her grunt and swerve. Now they headed directly for the fire watch tower.

"Thanks, Talon," Vola said under her breath, then she called to Sorrel. "Get ready to jump."

"I mean, I'm always up for jumping but are you sure —"

"Now!"

Vola flung herself from the dragon's back, trusting Sorrel to follow her.

She overshot and had to grab the tower railing as she went by. Her momentum swung her around, and she crashed into the side of the tower, smashing through a plywood wall.

At least that gave her plenty of hand and footholds. She hung there, gasping for a moment, half in and half out of the hole she'd made in the tower.

"Hey, it worked." Sorrel stood above her, leaning nonchalantly on what was left of the tower's railing. The rest lay below them in pieces.

Stupid monk had probably landed on her feet.

"You always sound so surprised when you say that," Vola said. "Don't you believe any of my plans will work?"

Sorrel scratched the back of her neck. "Well, I mean there's believing and then there's *believing*. I will follow you anywhere, but I usually pray for luck before I do."

A distant roar made her glance up to see Listrell hesitate in the air. She hung there for a moment, and her head swung around, glinting eyes finding Vola and Sorrel on their tower.

One last arrow streaked close enough to make Listrell flinch, and the dragon banked away, aiming for the nearby cliff.

"No!" Vola called.

Talon flung up her arm to ward off the dragon, but the creature's claws raked the stone, catching in her cloak. Listrell pushed off from the rock, and Talon dangled from her grip.

The dragon winged away into the mountains, carrying the ranger with her.

Vola cried out and nearly lost her grip on the tower. She fought down her instinct to leap after the enemy who'd snatched her friend. What could she do? She was stuck at the top of a broken tower, and all she could do was watch them disappear.

Gray clouds roiled overhead and a rumble of thunder rolled far closer than any normal storm. In seconds, torrential rain blanketed the city, pouring over the fires still smoldering below.

Above them, on the highest peak, Vola could just make out Lillie with her hands raised, directing the storm to the most damaged parts of the city.

Vola let her head fall back, and the rain washed over her face. Numbness spread from the water's touch, matching the cold inside her.

NINE

IT TOOK CONSIDERABLY MORE effort to climb down from the tower than it had to jump from the dragon's back. And Vola was having a hard time making her hands and feet work through the haze of red that threatened to swamp her vision.

The monk, of course, had no trouble. She scampered around the tower like an insect, finding hand and footholds that were obvious enough that even Vola could see them. And she kept up a steady stream of words, keeping Vola anchored here and now instead of flying away with Talon and the dragon.

"A little to the left. Keep going, you're doing great. Only thirty more feet."

"Sorrel…"

"We'll get down. Don't worry."

"That's not…"

Sorrel met her eyes where she clung less than halfway up the tower. "We'll get her back. Don't worry about that either."

The halfling glanced between Vola's trembling arms and the ground. "Maybe I should go find some mattresses…"

That made Vola laugh, and she found the strength to slip and slide the rest of the way until she planted her feet firmly back on the ground again.

"Hey, with Lillie's rain you can hardly tell what's water and what's sweat," Sorrel said, head cocked as she stared up at Vola's face. "I guess you don't like heights."

"Let's never speak of this again," Vola said. "Come on. We have to find Rilla and Lillie."

They found the princess about halfway up the city with the same official, directing bucket brigades to the parts that still burned. Big wafts of black smoke billowed into the air, obscuring the sunset and making twilight fall a lot earlier than usual.

Lillie limped up from the opposite direction with Fedor. Vola didn't feel particularly steady, but instinct made her catch Lillie as the wizard sagged.

"Good job," Rilla said, pausing long enough to give their soot-streaked forms a once over. "We've saved at least half the city. I think. But damn, there's a lot to do here." She ran a hand over her forehead, leaving a streak of sweat and grime. "We need to get after the one that woke the dragon—"

"We need to go after Listrell," Vola growled. The numbness had spread through her chest and made it hard to breathe, let alone speak the words she needed to say.

Rilla's brows drew down, and she opened her mouth to argue.

"She took Talon," Sorrel said.

Lillie gasped, her body going stiff against Vola's, and Rilla froze.

"The dragon?" she said.

Vola drew in a painful breath. "Talon covered our escape from the dragon's back, but Listrell snatched her just as she left."

"Gods, I'm sorry," Rilla said, jaw slack. In better circumstances Vola would have been proud. They rarely managed to shock the princess.

Fedor pounded his fist into his palm. "Then we go after the

creature. Pin it down in its lair and make sure it never harms another soul."

"You're not going anywhere," the city official said. His blue robes were considerably shorter and ended in a ragged, burnt line, but to his credit, he was still on his feet. "We hired you to protect the city. How can you do that if you're gallivanting around the mountains?"

"Gallivanting?" Fedor said. "Listen here, you. I'm a dragon hunter—"

"Which should make you uniquely suited to protect us from dragons."

"Which I can't do if you don't let me go after any."

"Freelance on your own time, Gerrickson. You'd need a permit to hunt one of the greater beasts anyway and the council isn't granting you one. They, however, are another case entirely." The official cocked his thumb at Vola and Sorrel and Lillie.

Fedor glared at them, his eyes glinting from underneath his sweat-streaked hair.

Vola shook off his look. She didn't care about Fedor one way or another. He could be an asset or a hindrance. Right now, she just wanted her teammate back.

She made sure Lillie was steady on her feet before she straightened up. "We're going after Listrell. Now. I'm not leaving Talon—"

Rilla held up her hands. "I'm not trying to stop you, but you just fell off a dragon—"

"Jumped. And we're fine."

"Vola," Sorrel said quietly. "She's right. We're exhausted and half-crisped."

"So is Talon," Vola snapped.

"And we won't be able to do anything to help her if we die on the way there." Sorrel's words were steady and pragmatic and impossible to ignore.

A yip made her start and a long black shape wove through the crowds of refugees and the crates and boxes stacked along the edges of the walkway.

Gruff twined around Vola's legs. The big wolf liked to be touched about as much as Talon did, but now he cuddled against her, seeking comfort. She knelt and buried her hands in his fur. He turned his head to lean his skull against her chest.

Vola gazed up at her battered team. Ash settled on Lillie's pale cheeks, the rain making more of a mess instead of washing it away. Sorrel's tunic hung limp and stained from her thin shoulders.

Rilla didn't look nearly so battered, but she stared back at Vola all the same. She could order them to wait. She could order them to do whatever she wanted. But she didn't. She waited.

"All right," Vola said quietly. "All right. We'll go after her in the morning. We're not prepared for a desert expedition, anyway." And logic said that ridiculous speed wouldn't help them, anyway. If the dragon wanted to eat Talon, there was no chance they'd get there in time to save her. Listrell could move faster than any of them and was probably already settling into her lair. Whatever she planned to do with Talon was already done or started.

All they could do was catch up in order to find out what it was.

"We'll find her in the morning," Vola said, mostly to herself and Gruff. "I promise."

They slept in their hotel, which smelled like damp, burned wood, an unpleasant combination that kept Vola awake for most of the night. Gruff slept curled up against her back. Rilla had tracked down the swamp monster and tethered it back in its stall so the thing couldn't wander off again. Vola strongly suspected the fires were the only thing that had kept it in the city in the first place.

In the morning, they collected their monster and dragged it

along with them, visiting the shops and crafters that were still open after yesterday's attack.

Everything in Vola urged her to go racing out of the city, but she was as responsible for Lillie and Sorrel and now Gruff as she was for Talon. While their brief trek to Shereille's research camp had not required much in the way of equipment, a rescue mission did.

The selection was pretty poor. Two out of every three shops were closed along the main pathway down through the city.

Vola paused outside one with a shopfront narrower than a desert snake. It didn't have any writing on the sign, just a pickaxe nailed over top of a coil of rope.

"Camping supplies?" Vola mused out loud.

"I suppose pickaxes and rope are too niche of a market to support an entire shop," Lillie said.

Vola tied the swamp monster up on the railing and pushed inside.

A couple of oil lanterns lit the dim interior. More tools and wares were nailed to the walls.

"To be fair, it is a much easier way to display your goods than say glass cases," Lillie muttered.

"If you buy something, do you have to pull it off the wall yourself?" Sorrel said.

"Ooh," Lillie said, touching the brim of a wide straw hat which hung from a peg.

"Not really your normal style," Sorrel said.

"Who cares if it keeps the sun off my face?"

The shopkeeper stepped through a door in the back wall. "What did you need?" she asked. She was as broad as a horse and almost as tall, and she scowled at Vola.

"We're headed into the mountains for a prolonged mission," Vola said, trying a smile.

The shopkeeper frowned at her tusks.

"Can you tell us what gear we might need?"

The shopkeeper squinted one eye. "I wasn't talking to you," she said. "I'll speak with the humans, thank you."

Vola kept her eyebrow from twitching, but it was a near thing.

Sorrel snorted. "That'll be hard. None of us is completely human." She looked Lillie up and down. "I suppose you're closest."

The shopkeeper spit, apparently not caring that it was her floor she'd have to clean later. "Fine. I'll talk to anyone who's not that one."

"Excuse me?" Lillie said, voice gone calm and quiet. "Vola is our leader. She's the one who speaks for us. It doesn't matter that she's a half-orc, and it shouldn't matter to you."

"Don't care if she's green," the shopkeeper said. "I care that her shield is black." She gestured to the shield slung on Vola's back. "I don't deal with black paladins. Can't trust them."

Red flickered at the edges of Vola's vision. But instead of thrusting it down, she welcomed the surge of anger, letting it rise and holding it at a simmer just below the surface.

"Now what did you need, ma'am?" The shopkeeper focused on Lillie.

Lillie crossed her arms, her mouth set in a thin line.

"Let's not set anything on fire now that we've saved it," Vola muttered to her.

"What about you?" the shopkeeper asked Sorrel.

Sorrel exchanged a look with Lillie. "I'll be outside. You can talk to our leader or you can lose our business." Sorrel trotted outside.

Lillie smiled her coldest, politest smile and followed her.

Vola turned her gaze back to the shopkeeper and huffed a mirthless little laugh. One of her teammates was missing, and this woman was a fool if she thought she could delay Vola for another second.

"Can't help but notice you drove off the only two witnesses." She put her hand down on the counter and leaned. "You know the best part about being a black paladin? No one cares when you break the rules."

The woman's face went white and she glanced at her wares. Vola could see her calculating how much her pride was worth.

A half an hour later, Vola left with armfuls of gear to load onto the swamp beast.

Lillie leaned against an intact portion of the railing, well outside biting distance from the swamp monster. Sorrel squatted next to her, watching as Rand dove over the swamp beast's head, taunting the creature.

"You're going to get your tail feathers snatched," Vola told him.

"He's much too fast for that," Lillie said with a proud smirk.

"So how much did you have to threaten her?" Sorrel asked, examining her nails.

"I didn't threaten," Vola said. "I just leaned. And pointed out the flaws in her logic. That's always more fun, anyway." Vola tossed Lillie the straw hat she'd been eying. "Try that on."

Lillie beamed at her and placed it on her head while Vola dumped the rest of her load onto the swamp beast's back. It had been a while since they'd had enough gear to use the swamp beast for its original purpose, and she grinned at it while it hissed.

Sorrel stood to help and glanced up at the peaks surrounding the city. The one just north was a completely different shape than it had been the day before. The top had exploded out under the force of Listrell's exit, and now the whole peak looked like some giant had taken a bite out of the top with a set of uneven teeth.

"Talon is the priority," Sorrel said quietly. "But Master Bao was supposed to be up there somewhere, too."

Lillie took the hat off and bit her lip before stowing it behind the swamp monster's harness. "I'm sure he's fine," she said.

Vola tried not to wince. He'd been suicidal. None of his self-preservation instincts would have been working properly.

"We'll keep an eye out for him," Vola said anyway. Though she couldn't promise more than that. If Master Bao had been anywhere on that mountain when Listrell had burst through, there wouldn't be a lot left for them to find.

"Do we even know where to start looking for them?" Sorrel asked, turning back to check the swamp beast's straps. "I doubt Listrell has gone back to the same lair where we can find her easily. Dragons are supposed to be smart, right?"

"They are incredibly intelligent," a lyrical voice said. "And no, she would not have returned to her sleeping lair. But I know where to find her now."

They all turned. A tall, blonde elf dressed in sensible trousers and a linen shirt sat on a pile of luggage at the next corner.

"Moth—I mean, Shereille?" Lillie squeaked.

Shereille beamed. "Hello again."

"What are you...what are you doing here?" Vola asked, casting a look at Lillie.

Shereille blinked. "I was looking for you. You're quite famous around town now, you know."

Lillie made a noise in the back of her throat, but before she or Vola could respond, Sorrel said, "You know where the dragon might be?"

"Of course. I am the foremost expert on Listrell."

"You weren't that interested in helping us yesterday," Vola said.

"You were spouting nonsense about how Listrell had caused your dead spots. It couldn't possibly be true and had nothing to do with my research since Listrell was sound asleep." She gestured vaguely to the sky, which was still a little hazy from all the smoke. "Of course, that's all changed now. Fascinating times we live in, don't we?"

"Right. Fascinating." Vola's eyes narrowed.

"Why—" Lillie stopped to clear her throat. "Why were you looking for us?"

Shereille stood, brushing down her trousers. "You are going after the dragon, are you not?"

"Yes," Vola said. "She took one of our teammates."

"I would like you to escort me to her hideout, as well."

"Um..." Sorrel said.

"You are adventurers," she said, her green-blue eyes flicking between them. "You accept money to...solve problems, I believe is how you put it. Well, I wish to study the dragon up close. Now that she's awoken, we will be able to gather so much more information than before. It's a truly unique, once-in-a-lifetime opportunity. And I'm not going to miss it."

"You're hiring us to take you into a dragon's lair?" Sorrel tilted her head. "Don't damsels usually want people to rescue them from dragons?"

Shereille raised her chin and looked down her nose. "I assure you I am perfectly capable of taking care of myself, if that's your concern. You will be paid for your time, and this is a wonderful opportunity for many things." Her gaze landed on Lillie.

Lillie flushed a deep red and cast a beseeching look at Vola and Sorrel.

Vola's eyes narrowed a fraction. Well, maybe Shereille was actually trying to make an effort now. Maybe this was her way of spending more time with a daughter she hardly knew. Motherhood probably didn't come naturally to everyone; some people had to work on it. And she couldn't fault Shereille if she was doing her best and trying to get better.

She cast a glance at Sorrel to assess her reaction. The halfling gave a little nod.

"You're aware that we might be killing the very thing you're trying to study, right? Listrell took Talon, and if we have to kill her, we will."

Shereille surveyed them, a calculating look on her face. "Slaying a *draconis maximus* would provide me with enough research to publish for the rest of my life. If you think you're capable. Just do me a favor and don't mess up the cadaver when you do so. I'd like to do a dissection and lopped off limbs are very frustrating."

"That's...very reasonable," Vola said, trying to find the catch. Oh right, the catch was they'd be trying to kill a dragon. Which they were already heading off to do, so what difference did it make?

"All right then," Vola said.

Lillie squeaked again and covered her mouth with her hand.

Vola raised her eyebrows but went back to Shereille. "We'll draw up the contract. We can't take a wagon up into the mountains, so most of your things will have to stay behind. And we're on a rescue mission so we're moving quickly."

Shereille gave them a serene smile and reached to pluck one case from the pile of luggage. "Don't worry. I am capable of traveling light when it's important. The rest of my equipment I'll have shipped back to my residence."

She came to stand beside Lillie. "Well," she said. "Won't this be pleasant?"

Lillie beamed at Vola, bouncing up and down on the balls of her feet.

Vola just shook her head. *Pleasant is one way to put it,* she thought. *But I probably would have chosen awkward.*

TEN

VOLA WOULD GIVE SHEREILLE THIS. She was right about knowing how to travel light. They tossed her case onto the swamp beast's back with the rest of their equipment, and it didn't seem to bother the creature any more than usual.

Though the swamp beast did its best to bother Shereille.

As they passed out of the city and turned into the desert sun, the swamp monster reached out its long neck and took a snap at the researcher.

Lillie cried out and smacked the beast on the nose. "Millford, don't you dare."

She crowded the beast back and spun to check on her mother. "Are you all right? Did it get you?"

Shereille rubbed her back end surreptitiously. "That creature bit me."

Sorrel leaned over and squinted at the elf's butt. "You're not missing the back of your trousers so you're doing better than most people it eats."

Shereille's eyes widened. "It eats people."

"No," Lillie said sharply, glaring at Sorrel. "It does not eat people."

"Not regularly," Sorrel mumbled.

Lillie transferred her glare to the monk. "We don't let it."

"Because that makes it better," Vola said, but she wasn't sure Lillie heard her.

Shereille eyed the swamp monster, who ambled along through the sand, leaving wide webbed footprints. Slobber dribbled from its chin and hissed when it struck the sand. It stared balefully over the crest of a dune and then squealed and lunged forward. When it straightened up, an armadillo's tail hung from its mouth. It swallowed with obvious relish.

Shereille's eye twitched. "And you keep this thing as a...pet?"

"Not on purpose," Sorrel said cheerily. She whistled as she scrambled up the next dune, then stopped to stare up at the rocky foothills, her hand shading her eyes.

"It's more of a beast of burden," Lillie said.

Shereille did not look convinced.

"It grows on you," Lillie tried to say, and then choked on the words. "Actually, it doesn't. We feel sort of responsible for it. And if we are taking care of it, then at least the rest of the world isn't subjected to it."

Shereille's lips thinned, but then she shrugged and continued walking. "I suppose that is honorable in a way."

The elf didn't notice, but Lillie beamed behind her back.

"I have colleagues who would be fascinated by such a creature," Shereille said. "I, however..." she cast a glance back at the swamp monster, who was drooling again. "I think I would prefer dissection."

"If you can think of a way to kill it, you can have it," Sorrel said.

Shereille did not react, and Vola wondered if she just hadn't heard or if she was pretending not to.

Vola joined Sorrel at the top of the dune and shaded her eyes. "Where is Listrell holed up now?" she asked Shereille.

Shereille pointed along the ridgeline of the mountains. "She will have found herself a new lair, since the old one is no more than a crater. We should follow the mountains."

"And then I imagine we follow the scorch marks," Vola said. She could already see a streak of blackened rock spreading into the next valley.

Valleys in the Firewall range were a bit different than anything Vola had seen before. They weren't the verdant green she was used to in Southglen. Instead, they were uneven trenches zig-zagging through jagged rocky cliffs.

As they climbed into the foothills, Vola kept a sharp eye on the trail, peering around the sudden corners to check for lurking threats, while Sorrel followed with her staff in her hand and her eyes on what sky they could see between the cliffs.

Rand swooped between the rock formations and dropped to Lillie's shoulder. She smiled at him, and he reached out his beak to drop a shiny bit of quartz in her palm.

"Oh, thank you," Lillie told him. "What a lovely gift."

Rand ruffled his feathers in pleasure and croaked, then ran his beak through her bright hair and took off again. Vola trusted him to alert them of anything that might be sneaking up on them from the hidden trail up ahead.

"Your familiar?" Shereille said, eying Lillie.

"Yes." Lillie tracked his flight with her gaze.

"Hmm," Shereille said. "Ravens aren't very majestic creatures, are they? Not like owls. Or dragons."

Lillie's jaw hardened. "He was a gift from a friend. And he's much cleverer than the owls I've met."

"More loyal, too," Sorrel said. "And I've never seen him run into a tree. Not even once."

Lillie turned her frown on her mother, eyes expectant, as if waiting for a response. Any kind of response.

Vola suspected Lillie of reacting indignantly on purpose. She'd seen the wizard hold her tongue against the worst of insults, so maybe Lillie was trying to get a reaction out of her mother.

It didn't work, though. Shereille blinked as if puzzled, then just shrugged. "All right," she said and trudged after Vola.

Lillie's shoulders sagged the barest bit. Vola only noticed because she was watching for it.

Lillie limped unevenly after Shereille. "Do you have a familiar?"

"I am a researcher, my dear. Not a practical wizard. I don't have the same insecurities that require constant companionship."

Vola and Sorrel winced.

"Do you think Lillie would flame her own mom?" Sorrel whispered.

Vola cleared her throat. "Shereille, maybe you should be up here with me."

Shereille tilted her head. "I don't know a lot about combat, but I imagine the front position is the most dangerous."

"Yes, but it's also the closest to me so I can protect you." Because Vola wouldn't be at all surprised if Lillie snapped and ended up killing her. "Besides, you're the one who knows where Listrell most likely went to ground. I'm hoping you can spot her before she spots us."

"I suppose that is true." Shereille gamely trotted to catch up with Vola. Like Aster, she didn't even have the decency to look winded. Researching dragons must involve a lot of climbing and hiking.

The ground under Vola's boots vibrated, making the soles of her feet tingle. "What the —"

"Is the dragon coming back?" Sorrel said, searching the skies.

"Rand says no," Lillie said. "He doesn't see anything unusual from above."

"Well, then, where is it coming from?" Vola glanced down.

Just in time for a round mouth to erupt from the rock at her feet.

"Geez!" She stumbled back, dragging Shereille out of the way.

The mouth gaped, showing off rows of needle-thin teeth as a long tubular body stretched from the rock face.

"What the hell is that?" Vola said. She looked at Lillie.

But it was Shereille who answered. "Rock wyrm. Cousin to the more common sand wyrm."

The thing reared back and up, looming over them where they stood on the narrow trail. It looked a lot like the garden worms Vola's Aunt Urag pulled out of her vegetable patch, except this one was big enough to eat an orc. Purple veins pulsed under its pale hide, and its long thin body ended in a circular mouth designed to latch onto something and suck.

A low moan made its way from the rock wyrm's throat, and Vola had a second's warning before it lashed forward.

Vola dove and rolled, coming up with one of her hand axes drawn. Sorrel shot past her, staff a blur in her hands.

Vola took the opportunity Sorrel gave her to shove Shereille down behind a rock outcropping.

"Stay there," she said.

"I could help—"

"No. Our job is to get you to the dragon safely. To get us all to the dragon. The best thing you can do is stay out of the way."

There was another shiver in the rock below, and Vola danced to the side as a rock wyrm's head gnashed its teeth at her feet. She brought her ax down, but the wyrm ducked back into the rock and the blade rang against stone.

"Heads up," she called. "There's more than one."

The swamp monster chewed silently on what was left of the

armadillo while Lillie ducked out from behind a rock and shot a stream of fire at the wyrm still waving above them. It's thick, translucent hide reflected the flames so they bounced right off.

The ground under Vola's feet erupted, and she stumbled back a step, but not fast enough. The second rock wyrm's mouth collided with her torso, and its teeth scraped across her armor with a chilling squeal.

She went down under its undulating body with a yell.

"Vola!" Lillie's voice rang against the rocky cliffs, and a blast of fire made Vola's skin shiver. It charred the rock around them, but the rock wyrm just moaned, and its head shot forward again, oblivious to the heat as it tried to attach itself to Vola's breastplate.

"Ha, hah, yah!" A column of air struck the wyrm in the side and lifted it clear off Vola. Sorrel followed it, fist outstretched.

Lillie flashed out of existence and reappeared on an outcropping above them.

Vola flipped to her feet and charged the first wyrm since Sorrel was busy with the second now. She dodged as it lunged and slashed the long body. Instead of biting into the creature's hide, the ax crunched and slid aside. Almost like she'd struck...

"Rock," Lillie called. "They've taken in the essence of their home and used it as armor."

Sorrel spun in a flurry of fists and feet and then fell back, panting. "Essence of what now?"

"How do we fight stone?" Vola called. She still had her ax but held it at her side since it wouldn't do any good.

"Stand back," Lillie said. Then she raised her hands.

Vola knew that gesture well enough. She grabbed the back of Sorrel's tunic and dove for Shereille's shelter.

With a crack that sounded like the air itself split, lightning streaked from the sky and struck the first rock wyrm just as it reared back to strike. It froze there, bits of lightning crackling over its hide. A second branch arced between it and the second wyrm, limning its outline with blue-white light.

The moans of the rock wyrms rose to screams and after a long moment, they toppled to the ground like giant fleshy trees.

"Bleh," Sorrel said, clambering out from their hiding place. "Rock wyrms win the prize for the most disgusting thing we've fought so far."

"You think these beat the giant flesh golem thing in Myron's lab?" Vola said.

"Or what about the time we crawled through the sewer to fight the traitors in Glenhaven?" Lillie pointed out.

"Those were just human traitors." Sorrel climbed to the top of one of the dead wyrms and turned with her hands on her hips. "How are they disgusting?"

"Well, we were covered in, er—" she glanced at her mother, "—poop at the time."

Sorrel gave a shrug. "Then I think we would be the disgusting thing in that scenario."

Lillie flashed back down to the ground and limped to the rock that hid Shereille. "Mother? I mean, Shereille. Are you all right?"

Shereille climbed to her feet and stared dispassionately at the dead wyrms. "How did you know to use lightning?"

Lillie bit her lip. "I do a lot of research before we enter an area. On its inhabitants—both sentient and non—in order to better understand what we might be up against."

"She was reading almost the entire way here," Talon said.

"But then she's always reading, so it's hard to tell when we should pay attention sometimes," Sorrel said.

"Hmm," Shereille said. "Impressive."

Lillie blushed a brilliant scarlet. Shereille didn't look at all shaken from the attack. She just kept climbing up the path. Lillie scampered after her, her lips twitching in a careful smile.

ELEVEN

"WE'RE LOOKING for a long corridor through the mountains," Shereille said as Lillie sent Rand to circle overhead. "I imagine it will be quite obvious from the air and it should lead us to Shereille's new lair."

"Doesn't that seem a little easy?" Sorrel said. "Like a great big arrow saying 'look at my hideout.'"

"Many texts mention some sort of guardian." Shereille tilted her head. "I imagine the challenges will become clear as we get closer to Listrell."

"Great," Vola muttered.

Lillie's eyes went blank as she watched what Rand was seeing. "I don't see a corridor, yet. But there's another scorch mark to the north," she said. "It looks like they extend straight that way."

"Any sign of Talon?" Vola asked quietly.

Lillie shook her head gravely.

Vola wasn't even sure what they were looking for. What signs would Talon have been able to leave? If she was able to leave any...

She shook her head. They just had to find the dragon. If they found the dragon, they'd find Talon. They had to. There were no other options.

"Any more signs of rock wyrms?" Sorrel asked.

Lillie blinked, her attention returning to them. "No, but we wouldn't be able to see them from above, either. They travel directly through the rock and only emerge where they feel vibrations from their prey." She tilted her head as Vola and Sorrel started climbing again. "I wonder if you could set up some sort of machine to thump the ground and draw them away from high traffic areas."

"That's exactly what we do when we camp near known sand and rock wyrm territories," Shereille said. "Well done."

"Oh," Lillie said on a little puff of surprised air.

"It's a mechanism that looks mostly like a hammer. And it thumps the ground to draw the wyrms."

"In a regular cadence? Or are the wyrms smart enough to recognize the difference between a footstep and something tapping?"

"They do recognize the difference." Shereille's eyes lit up as she spoke. "It was actually an intriguing problem for a while. How to imitate the random noises and vibrations caused by a camp."

Lillie tapped her lip. "I'll bet you could do something with gears. Set up an interlocking system with different numbers of teeth in different sizes to create a randomized output."

"Exactly." Shereille threw her hands in the air, and she and Lillie beamed at each other.

Vola cleared her throat. "I'm glad you're having fun, but are we still going the right way?"

Lillie jerked and glanced up at Rand, who circled lazily above. "Rand says yes." She frowned and squinted. "Wait..." She turned slowly in a circle. "I think I see the corridor Shereille was talking about. That way." She pointed toward a cliff in the distance.

It was too steep to climb easily, so Vola had been angling them parallel to it.

Lillie closed her eyes as Rand dove out of sight behind the rock face. "It's like a valley cut through the cliff. It doesn't look natural." She opened her eyes again and caught Vola's glance. "It follows the scorch marks."

"Any sign of the guardians Shereille mentioned?"

Lillie's brow creased. "No. It's...empty."

Vola huffed up one side of a fall of rocks and slid down the other, leading them closer to the cliff. The path had given up some ways back, and now they had to scramble over the stone and scree.

Vola came up against the cliff face and squinted toward the top. There was no way she was getting up without help. The ridgeline flattened out about three times her height.

"Could you teleport us in?" she said.

"Not blindly." Lillie slid down the rocks behind her and winced. She stood, rubbing her rear end. "And it would take so many trips I'd be useless for anything else if we encountered trouble in there."

Vola surveyed the cliff, then met Sorrel's eyes as she hopped down next to her. "Can you get up there?"

Sorrel didn't answer, just made a noise like "pfft" and started digging in the swamp beast's bags. The swamp monster bared its teeth, and Vola lunged forward to keep it from snapping at the monk.

Sorrel turned with a coil of light rope and a stack of metal stakes.

"Pylons," Sorrel said. "Remember the set we almost sank in the swamp? I wondered if we'd ever need them."

"You mean pitons," Lillie said as Sorrel draped the rope over her shoulder. "Did that nasty shopkeeper sell you these?"

"At a discount, even," Vola said with a vicious grin.

"I'll take the rope up and secure it along the way," Sorrel said. "That way you guys can follow."

"We'll have to rig something special for the swamp beast," Lillie added.

Sorrel snorted. "Good luck with that." She took a running jump at the rock face and stuck to the wall six feet up.

"Will she be able to get up that?" Shereille asked, eyes wide as Sorrel scrambled higher.

"Easily," Lillie said. "I've seen her climb sheer walls. She broke us out of prison once."

Vola cleared her throat violently and shook her head before Lillie could tell that particular story.

Sorrel reached the top of the cliff and stood at the ridge line, hands on her hips. She whistled as she gazed over the far edge. "Would you look at that?"

"We can't yet," Vola said. "Stop gawking and do your thing."

Sorrel tied the end off and tossed the rest down the cliff. Then she climbed down a lot slower, stopping every few feet to hammer a piton into the wall and secure the rope to it.

"All right, let's move," Vola said, stepping to the wall.

Shereille glanced dubiously at the rope trail leading up the cliff, but she gamely took hold and started climbing. Sorrel reached the bottom and hesitated a moment before climbing back up to show Shereille the best hand and footholds.

Lillie froze at the base of the cliff.

"I'll give you a boost," Vola said quietly, guessing at Lillie's discomfort.

"It's really not that hard," Lillie said. "I'd just rather no one watched."

"Well, Shereille is pretty distracted. Come on."

Lillie reached for the rope and placed her foot as high as her leg would go. Quickly enough to stall Lillie's protests, Vola put her shoulder under the wizard and heaved.

With a startled "oof," Lillie rose halfway up the cliff and clung to the rope.

"There," Vola said. "Half the work is done."

"Yes, thank you," Lillie snapped. "But maybe with a little less gusto next time."

"At least I can toss you," Vola grumbled, then turned to the swamp monster, who leveled a glare at her. As if daring her to do the same with it.

Gruff had disappeared, maybe to make his own way up and avoid the humiliation of being tossed. But of course, they couldn't count on the swamp beast to solve the problem for them.

"Wait," Sorrel called from above. "I have an idea." She scampered down and hung on the cliff face at about Vola's height, safely off to one side so she didn't get in the way of the climbers. Then she waggled her butt in the air.

Vola gaped. "What are you —"

"Come and get me, you smelly thing," Sorrel called.

"There is no way that will work."

Sorrel bent over to peer through her legs and stuck her tongue out at the beast.

The swamp monster squealed and launched itself at her.

So fast Vola barely registered the movement, Sorrel scaled the cliff again.

And the swamp monster followed, swift and sure as a mountain goat. At the top, it lunged for Sorrel.

The monk ducked out of the way, and the swamp beast sailed past her and out of sight. There was an indignant bellow from the other side.

"Problem solved." Sorrel brushed her hands off and straddled the ridgeline, swinging her feet.

Vola just shook her head and climbed up after them.

At the top, she had to echo Sorrel's whistle. A long corridor had been carved through the mountains with steep walls and a smooth floor leading north and a little east for as far as Vola could see. Once they were in, it would be a lot harder to get out. Sorrel would be able to manage it, no problem, but the rest of them would be stuck.

Gruff walked carefully down the ridgeline to sit next to Vola, having found his own way to the top.

"This seems like the perfect place for an ambush," she said. "A custom-made funnel, channeling us right to whatever's waiting."

"Listrell, hopefully," Shereille said, lowering herself to the ground alongside Sorrel. "This is the thoroughfare leading us to her lair. That is where you wanted to go, isn't it?" Shereille raised an eyebrow.

Vola surveyed the corridor as Lillie slipped the last couple of feet to the ground and landed with an "oof" next to Sorrel and Shereille.

There was nothing in the corridor now. At least not within sight. And any "guardians" trying to get in to ambush them would have the same difficulties scaling the walls.

Unless, of course, they could fly.

Vola lowered herself uneasily to the ground after the others.

"I'll send Rand ahead," Lillie said. "Do you suppose Gruff can scout without being spotted?"

Vola glanced up at the wolf, who sat dejectedly on the ridge-line. "Gruff," she said, trying to imitate Talon. Then she gave him the hand signal the ranger had always used.

The wolf whined once, then shot away along the top of the wall. His course took him parallel to their path.

They followed the corridor to the north, Rand flying high to check ahead.

Five minutes later, they came across a scorch mark, a streak of black soot that stretched from one side of the corridor to the other.

Shereille knelt and ran a finger through the black. She rubbed her fingertips together. "Is this what you were talking about? Dead spots?"

Vola shook her head. "No. This is just burned. Not dead. The land is still alive."

"The spots that we've found have no magic," Lillie said. "Talon could feel it drained out of the land itself. I couldn't cast spells, and Vola couldn't reach her goddess."

"That is…troubling," Shereille said.

Vola wanted to say it was a damn sight more than troubling, but this was the first time Shereille had acknowledged an interest in something outside her area of research, and it didn't seem prudent to mock her.

They marched on, leaving the scorch mark behind. The sun blazed directly overhead, glaring along the trench they followed so there was no shade.

Sorrel didn't seem to mind at all. Vola felt hot but was pretty sure that was a product of wearing a metal chest plate that could double as an oven if needed.

Shereille pulled a floppy hat from her back pocket that unfolded until the enormous brim shaded her head and shoulders.

Lillie glanced at her, then bounced from foot to foot before she pulled the straw hat Vola had bought her out from the swamp beast's packs.

Shereille raised an impressed eyebrow, and she and Lillie spent the next hour comparing notes on big hats. Vola was glad Lillie had finally found some common ground with her mother, but they really couldn't have picked a more boring subject.

Ahead, shapes came into view, and Vola slowed. Rand swooped over them in the signal for all-clear, but it sure looked like large figures lined the corridor in front of them.

Vola gave the signal to wait, and the others fell silent as she crept forward. On the ridge above, Gruff mirrored her progress.

Vola reached the first figure and huffed a laugh.

"Statues," she called to the others. "They're statues."

"Yes, but of what?" Sorrel said as they trotted forward.

Vola tilted her head to examine the carved stone. They stood almost two heads taller than Vola herself and had been chiseled from the same red-brown rock that surrounded them. The figure was humanoid in that it had two arms and two legs, but a draconic head stared down at them and a scaly tail jutted out behind the figure.

"They're beautiful," Lillie said, creeping closer to the one opposite. She reached out, but her hand stopped before she actually touched the armor carved across the statue's chest. "So lifelike."

"These must be the guardians the texts talked about," Shereille said, voice hushed and reverent. "We must be getting close to Listrell's lair."

"What do you mean?" Lillie asked.

"These statues. I could write so many papers on these alone. Perhaps they were placed by the ancient peoples who worshiped dragons."

"Wasn't Listrell sleeping somewhere else?" Sorrel asked. "In that mountain she destroyed yesterday. Why would these be here and not there?"

"Dragons don't sleep in the same lairs where they spend their time awake."

"Really?" Sorrel said, squinting up at one of the statues. "Why? I mean, besides the fact that she destroyed hers when she woke up."

"Would you want to spend another minute in the bed where you'd just spent a hundred years?" Lillie said.

Sorrel shrugged. "Fair point."

"We spent most of our time near her sleeping lair, so I've never actually seen them before." Shereille stepped right up next to one. "I should have sent an expedition out here to study these before she woke. I always figured we had time. And I hoped she wouldn't wake up quite so angry so I'd have a chance to talk to her."

"But you're sure you still want to study her now that she's trying to burn everything to the ground?" Vola said.

"Oh, of course. Even just five minutes of observation would make a huge difference in our understanding."

Lillie shifted her feet. "I'm not sure you'll have a chance to talk to her. We need to make sure she doesn't go on any more rampages."

Shereille gave her a little smile. "All knowledge is good knowledge. I am very much looking forward to seeing how she fights. I will attempt to take copious notes before you do what needs to be done. I wish I could take the time to sketch these statues as well, but I suppose you want to move on."

"No need to worry," Lillie said, holding up her notebook. "Already done."

Shereille's lips parted on a smile. "You work fast."

"I suppose I've had a lot of practice."

"Good, that means we can go," Vola said.

"Yeah, these things look like they're ready to come alive and jump us," Sorrel said.

A growl rumbled from the surround rock. "You ruined the surprise," the low, rough voice came from the statue in front of Vola.

"Heaagh!" Vola jumped back as the draconic statue moved, stretching its limbs.

It cracked its neck and then fixed Vola with a beady glare. All the statues around them creaked to life, blinking in the sun and shaking out their arms as if they'd been asleep awhile.

Sorrel stared around them with her hands on her hips. Shereille looked absolutely delighted.

"They aren't statues," Lillie whispered. "They're alive."

"We're all watching," Vola snapped. "You don't have to narrate everything."

"How do you do that?" Sorrel tilted her head back to ask the nearest guardian. "Stay so still?"

His lips pulled back from his teeth in a grin. "We enter a fugue state." He seemed to be the only one interested in conversing. The others checked their weapons and armor. All along the corridor as far as Vola could see, hundreds of draconic statues came alive, ready for a fight.

"It slows our breathing and our heart rate so we may remain stationary for centuries if necessary."

"Can you teach me that?" Lillie asked.

"I cannot," the guardian replied. Color returned to his scales as they spoke, streaking the reddish-brown under his armor with subtle flashes of green and blue. "Dragon blood is required. And I believe we will be busy with other things." He rolled his shoulders and settled his massive warhammer in his hands. "We cannot allow you to disturb Listrell."

"Disturb?" Sorrel said. "She's set fire to an entire city and we're disturbing her?"

"We will not let you pass."

The other guardians moved to stand at his shoulders. Each one had a subtle pattern of colors moving along their skin. And each one carried their weapon like they'd had centuries to perfect their skill.

"I don't suppose reasoned argument is going to change your mind," Vola said.

The lead guardian's lip twitched, revealing a long row of very sharp teeth. "No. But it was nice of you to try long enough for my warriors to breathe life back into their limbs."

"You're welcome," Vola said sourly, unsheathing her axes.

"This is not personal," the guardian said. "Only duty."

"Keep telling yourself that, buddy," Sorrel said. She spun her staff so it whirred through the air. "If it makes you feel better."

The guardian lunged for Vola.

She twisted out of the way, trapping the guardian's forward arm under hers. Then she brought her knee up into his gut.

The breath that whooshed from his lungs was dry and hot as the desert wind.

The ridge of scales above his eye that looked like an eyebrow rose. "All right, this will not be as easy as I thought," he wheezed.

"Damn right it won't," Vola said. Then she yanked him around so Cleavah's lightning struck him squarely in the back.

Vola pushed away in time to avoid getting singed.

"I always knew that would come in handy someday," Sorrel said and threw herself at the clump of stunned guardians. She scrambled up one, using its own armor as her footholds, bashed it over the head with her staff, and then launched herself at another.

Lillie stepped aside, muttering over her hands before she shot lightning into the nearest guardian. The arc of energy zipped from one figure to the next, to the next, curving to avoid Vola and Sorrel.

A howl echoed from the walls of the corridor, and Gruff dropped on a guardian. His teeth screeched across scales as he tore at the figure's throat. But the guardian did not fall.

None of them fell. Even the one in front of Vola had regained his wind and pressed forward.

Vola huffed and called out, "Gruff, guard Shereille. Guard!"

The wolf lunged away from the guardian, teeth bared, and then raced to herd the elven researcher against the wall. He circled in front of her, keeping the other guardians at bay while Shereille watched with shining eyes.

As an experiment, Vola slashed the nearest guardian's arm.

Her ax blade drew little blood from the scaly skin and the creature didn't seem fazed at all.

The guardians were as living as Vola and the others, but they were nearly as hard as the statues they resembled. Sorrel was having a little more luck with blunt force and Lillie had her lightning, but through the sweat stinging her eyes, Vola could see the inevitable.

The corridor was narrow enough that the guardians couldn't get around their sides to flank them, but the figures stretched ahead of them, nearly endless. Hundreds still waited for their turn to attack the intruders.

Blood beat in Vola's ears. There were too many and they took too long to cut down. She and the others would fight well, yes. Maybe even for hours. But inevitably they'd fall exhausted amid the hordes of guardians. Unless they could pull an ace out of their sleeve.

Cleavah had said the dragons were like siblings. They were there when the Greater Virtues created the world. Did that include the servants of dragons?

Only one way to find out, and they didn't have a lot of options if they wanted to press forward to find Talon. Vola wasn't a Greater Virtue. But she knew someone who was. Maybe.

The lead guardian brought his warhammer down, and Vola caught it on her crossed axes. Her muscles strained to keep the wicked point from falling any further.

"Lady," she croaked.

"I am here." A breath of wind touched her cheek.

"Will they obey you?"

After only the briefest hesitation, the blades of Vola's axes burst into flames.

"Let's find out," Cleavah said.

The guardian flinched away from the flames, and his

warhammer slipped against Vola's weapons. She heaved and threw him off. He stumbled back a step and fell to one knee.

He raised his head as if it pained him.

"What—? How are you—?" His slitted green eyes widened. "You are a Greater Virtue."

Vola snorted. "No. But I have one on my side."

The flames flickered in the eyes of the guardians, and one by one they fell to their knees around their leader.

"What will you do now?" he asked.

Vola took a deep breath, her shoulders relaxing a bit. But she didn't dare loosen her grip on her axes.

"It seems to me like this would be the perfect time to get rid of them," Shereille said. "Make sure they don't get back up again or hinder us from our purpose."

Vola winced. She didn't like the idea of leaving an enemy at her back, but she also wasn't in the habit of slaying a thinking creature who knelt before her in submission.

But Talon still waited for rescue.

"Let us through," Vola said.

"I cannot." The guardian dropped his eyes.

"Not even at the command of a greater god?" That was stretching it a little. But Cleavah had just confirmed her place in the pantheon, even if Vola still didn't know her real name.

"No," the guardian said with a growl. "I am bound so that none may pass me while I still live."

"We don't want to kill you," Sorrel said.

"We don't?" Shereille tilted her head.

"No," Lillie said. "They don't fight us while Vola controls them."

"She's right," Vola said. "We don't want to kill you."

"But will you kill Listrell?" the guardian asked.

Vola's lips thinned. "I can't guarantee anything past this point."

The guardian bowed his head. "That is...better than I thought. If I cannot fight you and I cannot let you pass, then I have only one option."

He stood smoothly and signaled the other guardians. In a wave of movement, they all rose from their knees, and together they retreated down the corridor. The lead guardian's eyes remained on Vola until they disappeared from sight.

TWELVE

"ALL RIGHT, I admire your elegant solution to a hopeless fight," Lillie whispered after the guardians had disappeared. "But what are we going to do when we get to the lair? We're just delaying the inevitable. They know we're coming, and they won't let us kill their dragon."

Vola ground her teeth, thinking the same things. "We might have better terrain for an assault when we get there."

"Better terrain?" Sorrel said. "In a dragon's lair, inside a mountain, which she probably picked specifically to be defensible."

"I don't know. I'm just following our normal procedure."

"You mean, making it up as we go?"

Vola made a face. "It sounds so much worse when you say it out loud."

Lillie patted her arm. "Perhaps it will all work out. We're good at improvising. It's why Rilla calls us Mishap's Heroes. Even if Sorrel refuses to acknowledge the name."

Sorrel plugged her ears and skipped ahead. "Not listening," she sang.

Vola shook her head.

"Will you be able to do what you did before?" Lillie said, gesturing to Vola's axes. "With Listrell instead?"

Vola glanced at her weapons. The flames sputtered and flickered out, but Vola could still see the sheen of orange and yellow along the blades.

"No," Cleavah said in her ear, but from the way Lillie and Sorrel straightened, they heard her, too.

Shereille had pulled out her notebook and was scribbling furiously, bright head bent over the page. For that moment, she looked just like Lillie.

"My authority extends to draconic servants," Cleavah said. "But I doubt one of the great dragons will bow to my authority. Even if we called them sisters and brothers once."

"Well, I guess that answers that question," Sorrel said to the air. "You really are a greater god."

"We knew that." Lillie addressed the spot over Vola's shoulder. "The remaining question is which one."

The air remained silent and expectant, and Vola got the distinct impression Cleavah was waiting for her to add something.

"Cleavah is good enough for me," she said.

Sorrel rolled her eyes and turned to start down the corridor. "One day you'll have to as —" She fell in the sand with a grunt.

"What was that?" Vola said.

Sorrel kicked her feet. "I tripped over something."

"You? Tripped?" Lillie said, kneeling to brush the sand away, revealing the cold ashes of a long-dead fire. A couple logs created lumps in the sand.

"It happens sometimes," Sorrel said. "And that's not what caught me. It was this." She snagged the strap of a satchel and pulled it from the sand.

"Wait." Vola lunged forward and caught the bag, so it stopped swinging. She swiped sand from the flap.

A complicated knot was burned into the outside, matching the ones that crawled the length of Sorrel's staff. The symbol for Maxim's followers.

"This was Master Bao's," Vola said. "He was carrying it when we saw him in the all-pantheon temple."

Sorrel yanked the satchel from Vola and tore open the flap to rummage inside.

"Did you literally trip over a clue?" Vola said. "I can't decide if that's good luck or bad."

"Maybe your goddess isn't the only one getting involved here," Lillie said. "I'd believe it was a coincidence if it was me. But Sorrel hardly ever trips over anything. Perhaps Maxim wanted her to find it."

Vola made a face. It would be a first if Maxim decided to pay attention to anything down here.

Sorrel pulled a battered journal from the satchel and flipped through the pages.

"What's in it?" Vola asked. "How does it end? Anything helpful about what might have happened to him?"

"Unfortunately, no. No convenient cause of death."

"When I die, I'll be sure to leave you a written record of the event," Lillie said.

"I really can't tell if you're being facetious or not," Vola said.

Lillie grinned at her.

"There is this, though," Sorrel said, her mouth drawing down at the corners. It was the most unamused face Sorrel had ever managed. She held up the last page of the journal.

Vola squinted to make the words stop swimming and read aloud.

"I've made my choice, Sorrel. Stop following me."

Lillie rubbed her lips, hiding a smile.

"Well, at least now we know it wasn't a coincidence," Vola said.

Sorrel stuffed the journal back in the satchel and stalked toward the swamp beast. "No, he meant for me to find it. This was his last camping spot. He had to have seen Listrell erupt from here, but he's still going through with his plan to up and die in the mountains somewhere."

She snatched the swamp monster's lead rope and avoided its bite to tie the satchel to the rest of their supplies.

"Then we still have time to find him," Vola said. "After we find Talon."

Shereille slipped her pen back in her pocket and snapped her notebook shut. "Of course, Listrell flew this way last night. She could have snatched your master the same way she snatched your teammate."

Vola glared at Shereille as Sorrel went green. "That was so helpful, thanks."

"There's no blood," Lillie pointed out. "Or claw marks. If Master Bao encountered Listrell, he has the same chance of survival as Talon, I imagine."

"Unless the guardians got him." Sorrel brushed the sand from her pants.

Vola shook her head. "They didn't come alive until we started talking about what we would do when we reached Listrell. I think we must have activated their defenses somehow. If he was just camping here, they might not have bothered him."

"Which means Listrell is our best chance of finding both of them right now," Lillie said.

Sorrel nodded and turned to continue down the corridor. This time she carried her staff in her hand, ready.

The sun had started falling toward the horizon, dipping behind the ragged peaks by the time the corridor ended abruptly in a rock wall. A stone doorway large enough to admit a dragon opened into the cliff, the deep black maw stretching into the mountain itself.

"Needs a welcome mat," Sorrel said, tapping her teeth.

"I'm not sure Listrell is really open to visitors," Lillie said.

"How are we doing this?" Sorrel said. "The guardians will be ready for us." She pointed to the sand in front of the door, which was pitted and marked with hundreds of footprints.

"Maybe she has a back door," Vola said and glanced at Shereille. "Any ideas?"

"Her last lair was riddled with openings," Shereille said, examining the facade. "Air holes like the one we made our observations through. *Draconis maximus* might be tied to the land but they still need fresh air."

"Holes big enough to sneak into?"

Shereille pursed her lips. "Usually. An air hole for a dragon is a sizable tunnel for anyone else."

"So we find one of those instead of knocking on the front door. I think this has a better chance of working if Listrell is at least surprised by *how* we come in. Our goal is to save Talon. Not kill a dragon. If we can sneak in to do it, all the better."

"You won't fight her?" Shereille said.

Vola cast her a disgruntled glance. "Not if we don't have to. Not if it endangers our teammate. If we can find and free Talon without risking anyone's life or limbs, then we will."

"I do like my limbs," Sorrel said.

Between Sorrel, who could climb, and Rand's swooping passes, they found a nearby tunnel much more subdued than the big entrance by the corridor. A healthy breeze of hot, dry air threaded steadily into the entrance.

"Hey, it's not stinky," Sorrel said, poking her head into the entrance.

"Well, it hasn't had a dragon sleeping in it for the last century." Vola dragged her back from the entrance. "We're supposed to be sneaking, remember?"

"I'm naturally sneaky," Sorrel said. "People don't see me because I'm so short."

"They can still hear you." Vola rolled her eyes. "Sorrel goes in first. Lillie and I after them. Shereille, you'll stay here with the swamp monster."

"What?" Shereille said with a dubious glance at the swamp creature. "I'm not staying here. I'm supposed to be studying Listrell."

"You can come see her up close as soon as we've...er... subdued the situation."

Shereille opened her mouth again.

"We're not arguing about this," Vola said, putting on her paladin face. "You hired us to get you to your subject safely. So let us do our job." Plus, Vola didn't want to worry about protecting her while they were trying to find Talon.

Shereille scowled, but she snapped her mouth shut and didn't argue again.

Vola signaled Sorrel forward while Shereille sullenly grabbed the swamp beast's halter.

Lillie bit her lip. "Just don't get too close to its head," she told her mother. "It really doesn't care what it eats."

Vola dragged her into the tunnel after Talon and Sorrel.

"You didn't have to be so harsh with her," Lillie whispered fiercely. "She just wants to see her life's work fulfilled."

"And I'd prefer she stay alive while she's doing it, wouldn't you?"

Lillie shut up.

The tunnel was narrow and close, but Vola could stand most of the way upright, which was better than a lot of places they'd stormed. She tried to walk carefully without a lot of clanking and made sure she didn't scrape against the rough walls. Gruff stayed pressed against her side.

Air still streamed past them, as if something on the far side sucked it through a straw. They hadn't lit any torches, and Lillie kept her spells dark and silent, so Vola trailed one hand on the wall and trusted Sorrel to lead them through the dark.

Gradually, Vola realized a faint glow grew ahead of them, mostly blocked by Lillie's head. The tunnel continued to lighten until Vola could make out Sorrel silhouetted against the lighter cavern opening.

The halfling turned and held her finger to her lips but didn't signal them to wait, so Vola and Lillie crept up behind her.

An enormous cavern opened beyond the mouth of the tunnel carved into the very center of the mountain. Massive amounts of stone had been chiseled away, leaving great columns stretching to support the arch of the ceiling so far above it was lost in darkness.

The rock face sloped away from their feet down to the cavern floor where rank upon rank of draconic guardians had gathered. They knelt in a wide circle, weapons ready and facing out, as still as the statues they'd originally mistaken them for. Behind them they could finally see what made the cavern glow.

Listrell paced back and forth from one end of the cavern to the other, her turquoise scales pulsing with her anger. She was the light source for the entire cave.

As impressive as the sight was, it wasn't what Vola had been looking for.

"Where's Talon?" Lillie whispered.

Vola didn't see any sign of the ranger. And it wasn't like there were a lot of hiding spots, at least ones that weren't directly under the dragon.

"Maybe she escaped," Sorrel said, eying the other openings around the cavern

It was a nice hope, but Vola couldn't seem to fit it around the knot of pain and worry in her gut.

"Look," Lillie said, her voice flat. She pointed, and Vola and Sorrel followed her focus to the dark cloth caught in Listrell's claws.

It was just black fabric. It shouldn't have made Vola's insides twist with pain. But she'd seen that cloak every day for months now, and her gut recognized it even before her mind had caught up.

Her sharp inhale echoed in the tunnel behind them. "Talon."

The ranger herself was gone. All that remained was that tattered bit of clothing slashed almost beyond recognition.

"She can't be —" Sorrel choked, cutting off the rest of what she was about to say.

Lillie held her hands over her mouth.

Vola's fingers clenched on the edge of the ledge, and she forced herself to breathe as little flickers of red licked at the edges of her vision.

"We can't..." Lillie cleared her throat. "We can't assume. Look. The guardians haven't noticed us yet. We can still leave. We'll follow Listrell's flight path back to the city. She might have dropped her somewhere in the mountains —"

A squeal of rage rang from the walls behind them, making Vola jump.

Lillie and Sorrel flattened themselves against the wall, and Vola ducked as a shape came charging down the tunnel.

"Oh, fu —" Vola lunged for the swamp beast's halter as it sped past, but she missed, and the creature shot off the edge. Straight into the sea of guardians below.

Listrell didn't even wait for the guardians to defend her.

She lurched forward, head snaking out on her long neck. The dragon's jaw snapped shut on the swamp beast, who disappeared with a cut-off snort.

Vola froze at the edge of the tunnel and stared.

"Uh, so that just happened," Sorrel said.

Boots pounded up behind them, and Vola turned to catch Shereille skidding to a stop, her eyes wide. "I'm so sorry. I couldn't catch it."

"Guys," Sorrel said.

Hot air blasted past them, and Vola glanced up to find Listrell looming over them, her nostrils glowing as she took a deep breath. Her eyes focused on them in the tunnel mouth.

This...this thing had killed Talon. Eaten her as easily as it had eaten the swamp creature. Vola welcomed the red that smeared her vision, welcomed the rage that swelled through her, and lent strength to her limbs. She opened her mouth and roared at the dragon.

"Well, this is happening," Sorrel said. "Lillie, cover us from the right. Vola, I assume you want to go down the middle with me."

"Yes," she growled.

"Great, don't get crisped."

"I'll just...stay here and take notes, then?" Shereille said behind them.

Lillie popped out of existence and reappeared on a shelf halfway up the wall to the right.

Vola crouched, holding her shield over her head. Sorrel leaped onto its flat surface, and Vola heaved, flipping her into the air.

The moment Sorrel was airborne, Vola ducked and dove out of the way as a stream of fire struck the wall behind them and sparks flew. Shereille didn't even flinch. She just pulled out her notebook and started taking down her observations.

Sorrel landed on Listrell's snout as Vola hit the slope and turned her dive into a roll. She found her feet at the bottom and raced between the guardians, who shifted and stood. Gruff hit the ground seconds behind her and dove into the fray with his teeth bared.

Sorrel spun atop the dragon's muzzle and brought her staff down between Listrell's eyes. "Ha!"

Listrell shook her head violently, but Sorrel clung to the ridge over her eyes, flapping around like a shirt on a washing line.

Gruff snarled and snapped, then suddenly he froze, sniffing the air. He threw his head back and howled long and high. Without any other warning, he shot off toward one of the other air holes in the opposite side of the cavern.

"Gruff!" Vola called. Talon would never forgive her if the wolf got himself lost or killed.

But before she could follow, Listrell swung her head and snapped at Vola. Vola threw up her shield and deflected the dragon's snout, glistening teeth closing inches from her face.

A boom echoed above them, and a wash of heat heralded Lillie's first fireball of the day.

Listrell raised her head, and Vola darted into the space she'd left and swung her hand ax at the dragon's claw, right where the talon met the skin.

Listrell shrieked and pushed herself up to stand on two legs, wings spread. Vola's eyes widened as she realized how big the cavern really was if she could do that without clipping her wings on either side.

A voice full of roaring wind spoke in her ear. "Behind you."

Vola spun in time to catch the lead guardian's warhammer against her shield. But in the moment she was distracted, the dragon fell back onto all fours and whipped around.

Vola yelped and brought her shield up. But instead of snapping at her again, the dragon's tail whistled through the air and caught her from behind.

Vola flew through the air and struck the wall with a clang. She crumpled to the floor, one long ache. The cavern spun around her, and she blinked, trying to focus through the pain. Vague shapes started converging, and she tried to remember why that was a bad thing.

"Vola!" she heard as if from a great distance.

Claws descended and pinned her to the ground. She still held her ax, but she couldn't even lift it, not with the dragon's strength holding her down.

She blinked at the guardians who leveled their weapons at her as she tried to call back the red rage that lent her strength. But she just felt empty, her chest caving inward under the crushing weight of her armor and the dragon's claw.

"Why do you invade my home?" a voice boomed above her, and Vola focused her watering eyes on the dragon.

"You...killed my...friend," she wheezed.

"It's possible. I kill anything that threatens me and mine."

Vola bared her teeth, but that was all she managed. She tried to struggle, but her wrists just flopped uselessly against the ground. Even at full strength she'd have been pinned, and hitting the wall had knocked her silly before that.

The dragon arched her neck and sucked in a huge breath, the air whistling past Vola. Little flames flickered at the corners of Listrell's mouth.

Vola refused to close her eyes, even though she knew what was coming.

A figure, blurred through Vola's pain, leaped onto the dragon's claw. Vola gasped as their weight landed. The figure planted two long daggers in the foot that pinned Vola.

Listrell shrieked and yanked her claws back, shaking the figure loose.

Vola raised her head and blinked the fog from her eyes.

The figure stood between Vola and the dragon and all the

guardians surrounding them. A figure wearing a dark cuirass with sandy-colored hair growing out of a short cut. Gruff growled beside her.

Vola heaved in a painful breath. "Talon," she wheezed.

THIRTEEN

TALON STOOD THERE, features outlined in blood and soot and her clothes torn. But her eyes were bright and fierce. She looked like she'd fallen off a cliff. Or got in a fight with a dragon.

Listrell drew back her lips, baring teeth as silver as Talon's blades.

Vola rolled, ignoring the grating pain in her chest, and pushed up onto her elbows. She needed to rise, to defend and protect. This was about to go so badly. Talon had said she didn't want revenge on all dragons, but this one had attacked her new pack. What was going through her head?

Black crept across Vola's vision and she collapsed on the ground again.

Listrell lunged.

Talon spun aside, dodging the teeth, and slashed her twin blades across the dragon's face.

Most of Vola's blows had just slid off the impervious scales, but Talon must have hit something sensitive. Listrell yanked back with a hiss and raised her front claws to hold her face.

A collective gasp went through the guardians, and they pulled their weapons back as if to charge.

Talon spoke, her voice as harsh as usual, but her words were guttural and unfamiliar. They rang against the cavern walls, echoing back to them a hundred times. It wasn't a language Vola recognized, but Listrell certainly did.

The dragon snorted and jerked her head up. The guardians fell back a step, shaking their heads in confusion. The lead guardian they'd talked to in the corridor tilted his head back and stared up at Listrell as if asking for orders.

A skidding sound distracted Vola, and suddenly Sorrel's sandals appeared in her view. "Talon!"

Lillie's boots joined them a few inches from Vola's nose. "We thought you were dead." Her voice quavered, as if she still didn't quite believe the truth.

Vola tried once more to lever herself to her feet, using the wall for balance. Lillie rushed to help her, sliding her shoulder under Vola's arm. They wobbled for a precarious moment before Vola gained her feet.

Talon remained between them and the dragon.

Listrell waited, eying them with a swirling green eye.

"Talon," Vola grated. Her voice didn't sound right, either from the damage in her chest or the way her heart squeezed, Vola wasn't sure.

Sorrel stepped up beside the ranger, leveling her staff at the guardians and the dragon beyond. "Shall we finish this?" she said with a feral grin.

"No," Talon said.

"What?" Lillie said as Sorrel's mouth dropped open.

"No."

"I heard that part," Lillie said. "Perhaps I should clarify the question. Why not?"

"She killed you," Sorrel said. "Er, well, I mean, I guess she didn't actually kill you. But we sure thought she did. And she carried you away. And she ate the swamp beast and set fire to the city."

Talon remained poised, knives in her hands, eyes trained on Listrell. But she didn't make a move to attack.

"We're not going to kill her because she didn't kill me," Talon said. Her voice grated like normal, but she spoke with grudging respect. "And because she's not killing us now." She gestured to the dragon, who waited beyond her wall of guardians, watching them warily.

"What did you say to her?" Vola asked.

"I said I knew she was Pipwattle's victim."

"That is surprisingly reasonable," Listrell rumbled. "I don't meet a lot of reasonable adventurers. And definitely not any that speak my language." She lowered her head to gaze at them steadily. "Truce?"

"Truce," Talon said.

"Great," Vola wheezed. "I never really set out to slay dragons, anyway."

Sorrel shrugged and let her staff fall from its guard position. "Yeah, it's no fun to kill things that aren't trying to kill me back."

Since the guardians had all lowered their weapons and the dragon sat back on her haunches, staring at them with her head tilted, Vola finally felt safe enough to drop one of her axes and take care of the rib stabbing her lungs.

She laid her hand over her chest and whispered, "Lady bless."

Power flowed out of her center and then in through her hand, resetting bone and knitting it. The pain eased.

"You have the power of one of the greater gods," Listrell said.

"It's more like she lets me borrow it." Vola finally took a deep breath and straightened away from Lillie's support. She faced Talon.

"I thought you'd been killed," she said. "We came out here to rescue you and when we couldn't find you, we thought you'd been eaten."

"Ha," Sorrel said. "Then you saved us instead."

Talon's lips twisted in a little smirk. Blood had dried in a streak down the side of her face. "I appreciate the thought, at least."

Vola wanted to throw her arms around the ranger to make sure she was real and unhurt. But Talon wasn't a hugger. She held herself apart, even from them, and probably wouldn't appreciate almost seven feet of paladin blubbering on her shoulder.

"No offense, but why aren't you dead?" Sorrel said.

"She dropped me," Talon said. "As she flew over some of the closer peaks, she let me go. It took me this long to catch up with you."

Which explained why Talon looked like she'd rolled off a cliff.

"Are you all right?" Vola asked quietly.

Talon rolled her shoulder and winced. "A little banged up. Nothing a couple of full nights of rest won't help."

Vola glared at Listrell.

"She could have circled back and eaten me, Vola," Talon said to her personally. "She didn't."

"That doesn't make her good," Sorrel said, glaring at the dragon. "That's like the lowest standard of living, not eating people. And she set fire to the city."

"An emotional reaction, I assure you," Listrell said. She covered her mouth with a claw and let out a loud gassy burp. Then cleared her throat. "Excuse me. You've never woken up on the wrong side of the cave?"

"Of course, except when I wake up angry, I don't level whole cities." Sorrel planted her hands on her hips.

"I don't usually," Listrell said, avoiding their eyes sheepishly. "But I don't respond well to pain. It's a personal flaw that I'm working on." She burped again and looked surprised. "I'm sorry, something I ate isn't agreeing with me."

"What do you mean, pain?" Lillie asked.

"The land I am tied to, I am its caretaker. But also, it is my source of power. And someone drained all the magic out of a piece of it. It woke me up early, and it feels like a hole burned right through my hide." She scratched the side of her belly.

They exchanged a look.

"The dead spots," Lillie said.

"They hurt her," Talon said. "It's like someone stabbing you awake."

"You understand," Listrell said, leveling her gaze on Talon. "I like this one. I was thinking about eating you. That's why I grabbed you. But the moment I flew away from the city, you stopped fighting me."

"Because there wasn't a reason anymore. We were just trying to protect the people there."

"The way I was just trying to protect my people and the land we are connected to." She jerked her snout at the guardians.

"We have a common enemy then," Talon said.

"The one who's draining magic out of the land," Vola said.

"The gnome," Listrell added.

"How did you know that part?" Sorrel asked.

Listrell shrugged her massive shoulders. "I have resources."

Then she made a gagging noise, covered her mouth, and hunkered down to heave something big and wet onto the floor of the cavern.

The swamp monster rolled to its feet and shook the goo from its scaly hide.

The party ducked with various cries of disgust and outrage.

"I'm so sorry," Listrell said. "Usually I'm a very neat eater. But bleh, my mouth tastes like three-day-old fish."

FOURTEEN

"I'M NOT surprised it didn't agree with you," Vola said as Sorrel took advantage of the opportunity and snagged the swamp monster's halter. "It's never agreed with anyone that we can tell."

"But you still let me eat it." The guardians around Listrell shifted out of their combative stances and moved away toward the edges of the cavern, leaving only the lead guardian they'd talked to in the corridor.

"Should we hang a sign around its neck that says 'may cause stomach upset?'" Sorrel asked.

"If we're on the same side, then we can't go around talking about who ate whose swamp monster and who attacked who on a cliff outside Firewatch," Talon said, crossing her arms.

"I already apologized for that. Oh, you mean before I flamed the city." Listrell shuffled her feet. "Fair point. Wait, then are you the ones..." She dug around in her mouth with a claw and winced as she pulled Vola's sword from between her teeth. "That's been bugging me something awful. Finally managed to work it loose." She handed it down to Vola. "Is this yours?"

"Er, yes. Thank you." It was a relief to take the hilt in her hand again, even if it was covered in slime and a little bit of dragon flesh.

Pebbles cascaded down the slope behind them, heralding the arrival of Shereille as she slid down to join them on the cavern floor.

"How many of you are there?" Listrell asked.

"That's it," Vola muttered.

"I'm not really with them," Shereille said, making Lillie sag yet again. "I hired them to bring me here. Greetings, Great Listrell. It is so wonderful to finally meet you in person."

Shereille made a big show of bobbing her head to the dragon.

Listrell glanced between her and Talon. "Customs change so much when you sleep for hundreds of years. Are the cults that worship dragons still around, then?"

"I don't think so," Talon said. "I think this is just Shereille being Shereille."

"Oh, good. High Holy Days were always so awkward. How many times do you have to say, 'no unwilling sacrifices?' A nice roasted ox does the trick without all that tying up and screaming part."

Shereille froze, hands raised in some exaggerated gesture before she dropped them to her sides. "I'm not a worshipper. I'm Dr. Moonhallowed. I'm the lead researcher on the *draconis maximus* team based out of Firewatch. I've been studying you for nearly ten years now."

"Studying?" Listrell said.

"While you slept," Shereille said.

Listrell's whirling green eyes narrowed. "That's...unsettling."

"I was just hoping to ask you some questions." Shereille pulled her notebook and pen from her pocket.

"And you thought now was a good time? When we have someone draining magic out of the land and waking dragons before their time? If you think I was bad, you should see old Bothard when he's startled."

Shereille blinked. "That just means this is the best time. I must get all my answers before the world ends."

"I'd rather keep the world from ending," Listrell said and turned her shoulder, effectively cutting Shereille off with her bulk. "Now," she addressed Talon and Vola. "I know where you should start."

"With Nargilla Pipwattle," Vola said. "She's the one doing the draining. Do you know how to find her?" Perhaps dragons could sense the draining before it got out of control, the way Talon almost had.

"Yes, Pipwattle," Listrell said. "What an awful name. I've captured someone who works for her."

"Really?" Lillie said.

"I've actually rounded up several people wandering around my mountain in the last day. There are certainly a lot more of you little almost-humans than there were the last time I was awake."

"Master Bao!" Sorrel exclaimed. "You found Master Bao."

"Oh, I have no idea. I can't actually tell you apart most of the time. You're too small. And every time I stick my head in their cave to get some answers, they do nothing but scream. That's where you come in."

"You want us to interrogate your prisoners?" Vola said.

"They're only prisoners because I didn't want them escaping to Firewatch and bringing an army back here. They'll be free to go as soon as we move to another lair, and Renvick and the others have been taking good care of them in the meantime. He at least can tell them apart."

She nodded to her lead guardian, the one with green and blue streaks through his red-brown scales.

"I will show you to them," Renvick said with a small bow.

Sorrel scrambled to keep up with him as the big draconic

figure strode off toward the other side of the cave. Talon followed, but Lillie hesitated.

"You coming?" Vola asked.

Lillie bit her lip and glanced at her mother who had wasted no time filling the sudden silence with questions. Listrell grumbled under her breath.

"I think I'd better keep an eye on Shereille," Lillie said. "You can fill me in when you're done."

Vola just raised an eyebrow and followed Renvick and the others.

Across the cavern, the lead guardian disappeared into one of the wider air holes dug into the rock of the mountain. Not too big by Listrell's standards, but wide enough to sleep their entire party if need be.

The back end opened onto a cave about the size of the all-pantheon temple in Firewatch where several figures lounged on crates and canvas sacks. One small figure puttered around a pot over a fire against the far wall.

Sorrel scanned the small crowd, and her shoulders drooped. "I don't see Master Bao."

The prisoners eyed them curiously over cups of fine porcelain.

"More captives, Renvick?" one asked. He was a tall, slim elf dressed in hunting leathers with his hair tied up in intricate knots.

"Not today," Renvick said in his deep rumble. "But they're here to help. Then we can get you home faster."

The hunter shrugged. "No hurry. I haven't eaten so well in a long time."

The others made agreeable noises.

Vola addressed the hunter. "You're doing okay, here? Do you need rescuing?"

The hunter snorted. "Renvick's guardians are keeping us in fine fashion. They're better hunters than me. And the last one they brought in was a merchant who'd lost the rest of his caravan in the mountains. He was so grateful not to die on some mountain peak that he donated his goods. It won't hurt any of us to hang out here for a few days. Just so long as the dragon stays on that side of the wall."

"She will not fit in here anyway," Renvick said.

"Probably the only reason they're all so calm," Talon muttered.

Vola cleared her throat. "Um, do you know if any of you worked for a gnome named Nargilla Pipwattle?" She wasn't even sure it was a good question. Would someone who'd worked with Pipwattle volunteer that information?

The hunter spun on his crate and pointed. "You want Doddleben. She left him out on the mountainside for no good reason. But lucky for him, he ended up here."

"Thanks," Vola said. She moved the way he'd indicated with Talon and Renvick close on her heels.

Behind her, Sorrel asked, "Hey, while you were out there, did you happen to see an old monk?"

Vola left her to her questioning. Towards the back wall, an older gnome bustled around a makeshift living area wearing an apron over his tattered robe. He hummed while he transferred a steaming pot from a camp stove to a big rock made up like a table. Complete with a checkered table cloth and some mismatched plates.

Vola cleared her throat, and the gnome looked up startled.

"Oh, hello Renvick," he said, looking at the guardian. "Visitors?"

"I heard you were with Nargilla Pipwattle," Vola said.

Doddleben sniffed. "Worked for. Briefly." The old gnome straightened his tablecloth with gentle hands.

"We're looking for her. Any information you have would be helpful." From the hunter and Doddleben's reaction, it didn't seem like the old gnome was particularly loyal.

"Of course, of course. Join me?"

Vola blinked as Doddleben flounced to the other side of the makeshift table and sat down with a flourish. He stared up at her, waiting.

She felt eyes on the back of her head and glanced over her shoulder. All the prisoners watched her now with varying expressions of wariness.

Vola clanked over to the rock and sat, pushing her sword so it didn't catch against the ground.

Talon hunkered down beside her, her arm around Gruff.

"Would you like some tea?" Doddleben asked.

"I would love some tea," Vola said.

Talon grunted.

The gnome poured tea into tiny floral cups and slid them over. Vola took the porcelain carefully in her hands.

All around them, the prisoners breathed sighs of relief as Doddleben beamed. Like she'd passed some sort of test.

"Even when one is a prisoner one can never be caught without a tea service," he said. He eyed them both. "What do you think?"

Vola surveyed the floral pattern and was strongly reminded of Becky's Tea and Tap Room in Water's Edge, where she'd met the others.

"It's lovely," she said. "It reminds me of happy memories."

The gnome blushed. "Thank you. Nargilla was always making fun of my teacups. She preferred something a little more rugged, I guess. It irks me to no end to think of her throwing them out after I was gone."

"What happened?" Vola took a sip. The tea tasted like wilted grass but she didn't dare spit it out.

"She left me out there," he said, waving a hand vaguely at the wall. "Hoping I would draw the dragon's attention. I think she expected me to die. Luckily, I've found some new friends who appreciate the finer things in life."

He raised his cup to the other prisoners, and they all raised theirs back to him in a silent salute.

"Nargilla just left you?" Talon growled.

Doddleben shrugged. "It happens with people like me."

"No." Talon's hand sliced through the air. "You were her pack. Even if she was paying you. She was responsible for you. She should never have just left you behind."

The old gnome's eyes grew misty, and he reached across to pat her hand. "Thank you."

"We want to stop her," Vola said. She placed her cup back on the tablecloth and leaned forward. "We need to know how she's draining magic out of the land so we can keep her from doing it again."

Doddleben shook his head. "I'm sorry. You'd want one of her magic team for that. I was just looking for new places for her to hole up. She prefers old dragon lairs. They're spacious and they already have a link to the land that she's looking for." He brightened. "That means she could be nearby. She'll be trying to find another abandoned lair in the nearby peaks."

Vola nodded. "At least that gives us a place to start. What's she even trying to do? Why does she need all the power?"

"Oh, she has plenty of power. It's money she's after now. She's sending it along to her boss. Anders," the gnome said sipping his tea. "He's paying her for it. He'll be here to collect it soon."

Vola shot a look at Talon.

"Well, we knew it had to be connected," Talon said under her breath. "He's been stealing magic this whole time. Of course he'd be involved with Nargilla."

"And now we know why Rilla's sources said he was coming here."

"I have no idea what this Anders fellow wants to do with it," Doddleben said. "Except try to rival the gods."

Vola's chin jerked up. "What was that?"

"Oh, just a joke." He laughed to himself. "It's the next logical step, isn't it? If you control the magic of the land just like the gods. But a man can't rival the entire pantheon. Even one god couldn't control all of them. They threw out the Broken just for being powerful enough to think about it."

Vola wasn't laughing.

"Thank you," Talon said, glancing at Vola and evidently noting her wooden expression. "I hope Listrell lets you stay as long as you like. You seem at home here."

The gnome gave them a cheery smile. "I am. Which is good. I can't imagine leaving would be good for my health. Nargilla will not hesitate to finish the job if she found out I talked to anyone."

FIFTEEN

IN THE MAIN CAVERN, Lillie had started making camp, unpacking the bedrolls and cooking supplies from the swamp beast's packs. It seemed like most of their gear had survived the experience of being ingested at least. Though they were missing one or two pots that had been tied directly to the saddle. Vola wondered if they'd make an appearance again in a week or so.

The dragon herself shuffled around the immense cavern followed by Shereille, who chattered non-stop. As far as Vola could see, Listrell wasn't actually answering any of Shereille's questions. In fact, it looked more like Listrell was trying to run away, but Shereille had her trapped in her own lair.

Finally, the dragon flopped down, making the floor shake, and pulled her tail over her eyes.

Renvick stepped up beside Vola with the dry hiss of scales against his armor. "Listrell told your friends to make themselves comfortable."

Sorrel trotted up to the campfire Lille had lit with a quiet word and plopped down with a sigh.

"Any luck finding Master Bao?" Lillie asked.

"None," Sorrel said. "Waste of time."

"Well, not entirely," Vola said. "We did figure out where to look for Nargilla. But it will have to wait for morning, I think."

Renvick cast Sorrel a sidelong look. "Would you like to prepare for sleeping, as well? I am told I make an excellent bed."

Sorrel craned her neck to look up at him. "Do you mean you make the bed or you are the bed?"

"For you? Either."

Vola choked and tried to turn it into a cough. Lillie's eyes went wide, and she bit her lip hard enough to turn it white.

Sorrel's brow creased. "I think you're confused. Usually, people flirt with her." She cocked her thumb at Lillie.

"I am not familiar with flirting," Renvick said. "I only wish to make another warrior comfortable."

Sorrel frowned. "Then talk to Vola. She has what you want. Probably. I don't know. I'm not really well versed in..." She waved a hand. "All that."

Vola decided she should save the halfling, even if watching her deal with Renvick's attention was as amusing as hell.

"Come on, Renvick," Vola said. "You can show me a place where I can see the sky. I have someone I want to talk to."

Renvick gave a slow blink. He had two sets of eyelids. The first, an almost transparent flap of skin that slid over his eyes just before the scaled set did. "Very well."

He led her around the edge of the cavern. There were more alcoves like the one that held the prisoners, and Vola was struck by the idea that the cavern could hold nearly an entire city and they wouldn't even be crowded.

"Did I say something wrong?" Renvick rumbled once they were out of earshot.

"Maybe not wrong, but...unexpected? She's right. We're used to people going for Lillie. I'm not sure Sorrel knows what to do if your interest is serious."

"I have fought wizards before. Magic—and those who wield it —are uninteresting to me. And while you are an excellent warrior, you fight with blade and shield. Also very traditional. But I have never met so much skill and vigor in someone so small. It is fascinating."

"Then I suggest you focus on that. Sorrel's not much for romance, but if you present her with a good challenge and some-thing she can fight, you'll go a lot farther."

Renvick made a noise somewhere between a laugh and a groan. "Thank you for the advice."

They passed a massive opening where fresh air gushed, tasting of dry desert night.

"That is where Listrell comes and goes," Renvick said. "But up here…" He led her up a set of crude steps carved into the wall to an archway that led immediately to a long, wide balcony open to the night sky. "This is where the guardians come to watch when she flies."

Vola stepped into the cool breeze and lifted her face to the sky, which had gone black and deep, sprinkled with pinpoints of faraway light. The mountain stood between them and the city, so no human-made light marred the night.

Renvick didn't say more. He just stepped back out of her way. She could feel him standing beside the archway, either guarding her or guarding Listrell. But she didn't mind. She'd stopped caring if there were witnesses to what she was about to do.

"My lady," she said softly, and immediately another presence joined her on the balcony. Warmth pressed against her skin, like the arm of a comrade.

"My knight," Cleavah said, and her voice reminded Vola of the rush of wind as she'd stood on Listrell's back. A shaft of moonlight appeared beside Vola, and the beam coalesced until a figure stood there clothed in white, face too bright to stare at for long. The glow faded to reveal a woman with gold skin and dark curling hair that fell to her waist.

"You heard what the gnome said," Vola said. "About Nargilla."

"I did. I am…concerned."

From the feel of alarm that crackled through the air between them, Vola guessed that was an understatement.

"You think Anders really wants to rival the gods?"

"Perhaps that is his goal, but Doddleben is right. One man cannot take on the entire pantheon."

"Even with the magic of the world in his possession?"

"The gods still have their power. Which we might have to use if Anders gets much farther in his plan."

Vola had thought that was a pretty big worry. But if Cleavah was concerned about something else, that meant there was something even worse Vola didn't know yet.

"What's concerning you, then?" she asked.

Cleavah's lips tightened. "I am more concerned about Nargilla's ability to cut the gods off from their followers. You and I have one of the strongest bonds the pantheon has ever seen."

Vola blinked.

"And Nargilla severed it with one dead spot. If she can do that to us, it means she can sever the gods from the land itself. We would lose our ability to influence the world."

"And the rest of your power."

Cleavah shook her head. "It's not about keeping our power. We are the stabilizing influence of the world. We created it. Stripping the gods of their power would mean stripping power out of the world. It would end it, Vola."

Vola sucked in a breath. "End the world."

Cleavah attempted a smile. "We are not there yet. But…"

"But we could get there fast if Nargilla goes unchecked."

"Yes. It should be a concern for the entire pantheon."

"Even greater gods?" Vola asked carefully.

The goddess Vola had known as Cleavah hesitated. "Yes. Even us greater gods." Cleavah turned her head. "You know what I am."

Vola bowed her head. "I do."

"And yet you've never asked for my name."

Vola raised her chin and tried to meet Cleavah's gaze. The moon's brightness had faded, but the goddess's eyes still held an intensity that made Vola shake. "No."

"Why not?"

"I spent a long time worried about what people called you. What people thought of you. But in the end, it doesn't matter what any of them say. I know who you are to me. Your name won't change that."

Cleavah held her gaze for a moment longer before rolling her eyes. "Finally. Do you know how long I've been trying to teach you that particular lesson?"

"I guess I have a thick head," Vola said with a grin.

"Not as thick as some mortals. You were right to be worried about Nargilla. I will have to warn the rest of the gods."

"Will they listen?" Vola said. "They don't really listen to us, but if you're the one who's worried…"

"They do have a history of not heeding me, but I'm worried because I'm the prudent one. If I worry about everything, then nothing can surprise me. Personally, I think it's a better stance than some of my fellows who wallow in their presumed power and safety." She huffed a laugh. "I'd love to see Helleron actually heave himself off that sofa for once."

Her chuckle faded as the moonlight dimmed, and her presence retreated to that constant hovering just over Vola's shoulder.

"Your goal has not changed," Cleavah whispered in her ear. "Find Nargilla. And protect your people while you do it."

A nudge pushed Vola toward the right, along the railing. Vola followed, trusting Cleavah even in her confusion, and she found a small ledge wrapped around the side of the mountain. Two shadows sat hunched at the end, where another air hole opened to the sky.

Vola rubbed her hands over her face and leaned against the railing as close to Talon and Gruff as she could get.

Talon's hood was gone, torn to bits under Listrell's claws, and the ranger sat now with her face to the sky, her left hand buried in Gruff's fur. The wolf pressed the top of his skull into her side, leaning like he did when he was reassuring her. Without the cloak, her pink tunic was a lot starker against her dark cuirass.

"Hey," Vola said quietly. It was amazing how wonderful it was to see someone doing something as boring as sitting when the day before you'd thought they were dead.

Talon leaned her head back against the rock wall of the mountain, her overlong hair flopping away from her eyes.

"The others are bedding down in the cavern," Vola said.

"I'll come in a minute," Talon said. Her voice was still growly, the way it was when she wasn't paying attention and had something on her mind.

Vola waited. Cleavah wanted her to take care of her people, and taking care of Talon often meant giving her space to speak in her own time.

Finally, Talon spoke. "I wanted to thank you."

Vola tipped her head.

"For coming to save me. Even if I didn't end up needing it. I thought…when she dropped me I figured you'd think I was dead and…I didn't know what you'd do. I followed you through the mountains, trying to catch up."

"You made really good time."

"Well, I know what it's like to think someone's dead, but never know for sure. I didn't want you to live that way for too long."

"It was two of the hardest days of my life." Vola scratched at the rough stone of the railing. "And thank you. For coming to save us. You rescued me from a dragon."

Talon folded the edge of her ragged tunic over and over again, making the seams fray.

They were all alive, and they had a lead. So why was Talon still so agitated?

"What's wrong?" Vola said.

Talon surged to her feet and edged along the pathway back to the balcony. Gruff followed her, moving fluidly.

She vaulted the railing and paced from one end to the other. "I don't know."

Vola watched, silent, waiting for Talon to explain more.

Finally, she stopped beside the railing and gripped it with both hands. "I'm...I'm angry," she said.

Vola leaned back on her elbows. "Yeah, you look angry."

"And sad and frightened and-and guilty."

"Guilty about what?"

"The dragon that killed my pack. It was a victim, just like Listrell. It was forced awake, and it retaliated. And then we killed it. For nothing."

"Not for nothing," Vola said softly. "It was on a mindless rampage. You had to do something. The same way we had to do something about Listrell. You saved lives."

Talon sagged. "I still feel guilty about it. But it wasn't just the dragon. Nargilla is the one causing these dead spots. She was the one who woke it up. She has to have known what it did, but still, she came here and did the same thing. Who knows how many times she's done it since then?"

She pushed away from the balcony, her fists opening and closing like she wished Nargilla was standing right there, her neck ready to be wrung.

Vola wasn't sure she'd ever seen Talon truly angry. Even when

Vola had screwed up so royally in Lord Arthorel's cellar, Talon had been more disappointed than angry.

"You're allowed to be angry, you know?" Vola said. "She killed your pack."

"Yes, but what do I do about it? It's been years. I put it behind me. I recovered and moved on. It wasn't affecting me anymore." She gestured to Gruff, who lay at her feet, tongue lolling to take advantage of the cool air. "Like a wolf. Wolves don't dwell."

Vola wanted to put her hand on the ranger's shoulder, but she knew it wouldn't be appreciated. "But you're not a wolf. Not really. You're human. And you're allowed to have feelings and to remember."

Talon collapsed against the railing and clasped her hands. "But I don't want to remember if it makes me angry. I don't like being angry." She glanced up at Vola, who had plenty of experience with anger, both wanted and unwanted. "What do you do with it? How do you keep it from swamping everything else?"

"It's...hard. I try to make sure I'm using it for something. It's easy enough to stomp around and break things. But I want to make sure my anger changes the things that are wrong. When Inga kidnapped you all and turned you against me, I used my rage to get you back. I used it to beat Inga and make sure she never did it again."

"So I should use it," Talon said, staring at her hands. "That's the only way to get rid of it?"

"You could ignore it, I guess. But orcs believe that's not healthy." Of course, that didn't mean that Vola hadn't spent years trying to do just that.

Talon was silent for a long moment. "I'm not out for revenge. I don't want to be like Fedor Gerrickson, on a quest to kill every dragon just because one made a huge mistake."

Vola snorted. "I think you can seek justice without being like Fedor. Justice is different from revenge."

Talon took a deep, sweeping breath. "Wolves protect, they defend, and when they fail, they forget. I think I'd rather be a wolf." She rubbed her hands over her face. "But you're right, I'm not. I won't forget. I'll learn. And I'll use my anger to protect better the next time."

She put her hand on Vola's forearm and Vola just kept herself from jumping. "I won't let Nargilla Pipwattle take my new pack from me."

SIXTEEN

Vola slept like the dead that night, despite the fact that a dragon rumbled just a few feet away. The night before at the inn had been awful, and then there'd been all that traipsing around the mountains, fighting said dragon, and bouncing off a wall. After all that, Vola was one long ache.

For the first time since she could remember, she slept in. She woke to the sizzle of bacon and the metallic shing of a fork scraping the bottom of a pan.

"Breakfast, Vola?" Lillie said, tilting the pan toward her, revealing a wealth of grease and protein.

Vola didn't need to be asked twice. She threw her blankets back and reached for her pants. It was always nice when they found a spot safe enough that she could sleep without her armor on, and Listrell had assured them that the guardians would keep anyone from bothering them. Or at least give them enough warning that she would have time to armor up.

"I don't remember packing bacon," Sorrel said, skipping to the fire while Vola pulled on her boots.

"It was the guardians," Lillie said. "Apparently taking care of Listrell also means taking care of her guests. And Listrell said they don't need sleep."

"Wish I didn't need sleep," Talon said, rubbing her face as she settled down on her heels beside the fire.

Vola snagged up some bacon before it disappeared entirely and then stood back to survey the cavern.

Talon reached as if to pull up her head only to find it gone.

"We can get you another one if you miss it," Vola said.

Talon hesitated, then shook her head. "No. I'm sorry it's gone because it was a gift from someone who's gone now. But I don't need it anymore. And she would have been the first to understand that."

Listrell tromped up, shaking the ground with her footsteps while Shereille trotted along, trying to keep up.

"But I just wanted to know—"

"It is rude to ask," Listrell boomed. "Any decent person should know that."

"Yes, but I'm not a person. I'm a researcher."

Vola's mouth pulled, caught between a grin and a grimace. Shereille was certainly inhumanly persistent.

Lillie's glance flitted between her mother and the dragon. "Mo —Shereille, would you like some breakfast?"

Shereille eyed the pan full of grease and bacon. "Oh, no, my dear. My body just doesn't need that much fat in the morning."

Lillie flushed bright red and dropped her gaze.

Talon took a vicious bite of her bacon. Without her hood, she couldn't hide the glare she sent Shereille.

"We need to plan our attack," Vola said, deliberately drawing attention away from Shereille. "Listrell, do you think you could lead us to the old lairs in this area to look for Nargilla?"

"No."

Vola's mouth fell open.

"What?" Sorrel said. "I thought you were on our side now."

"I am. My priority is to keep any more dragons from waking early."

"Can't you do that by tracking down Nargilla and keeping her from draining any more spots?" Vola asked.

"Finding one gnome is too small for me to see clearly. But it is the perfect sized problem for you."

Sorrel narrowed her eyes up at the dragon. "Are you sure you're not just using that as an excuse to not even try?"

Lillie choked.

"Listrell's right," Talon said. "We don't want to repeat the dragon attack."

Listrell inclined her head to the ranger. "Your wisdom shines once again."

It was hard to argue with that, but Vola had really been hoping to have a dragon on their side. "Finding Nargilla would be a lot more helpful with you."

"I will go with you," came another rumble, not nearly as deep as Listrell's. Renvick stepped up to their fire and bowed his head. The firelight glinted across the green and blue streaks in his scales.

"I thought the guardians protected you," Lillie said, looking at Listrell.

"They do," Listrell said. "But they are many, and Renvick can make up his own mind. He will be able to lead you to any empty dragon lairs nearby," Listrell said. "Then at least you will be able to search out your enemy without wandering in circles."

"Thank you," Vola said, making sure she included both Listrell and Renvick in that.

"I'll go with Listrell," Shereille said, notebook clutched in her hands. "My research is barely begun and—"

"No, you will not," Listrell said.

Shereille gaped. "What?"

"I am not babysitting you anymore. I go into danger, and I will not protect you the way these four chose to. Your incessant questions will likely wake any dragons we come near anyway and defeat the entire purpose of my mission."

"But...but you're my life's work. You can't leave until I've learned enough to publish at least one paper."

"I'd like to know how you plan to stop me." The dragon snorted, a flicker of flame shooting between her lips, long enough to lick at Shereille's boots.

Shereille stumbled back a step and tripped over a bedroll. She landed on her butt amid the blanket.

She cast a glare at Vola. "This wouldn't be happening if you'd just killed her when you had the chance. I could be dissecting her right now."

Listrell ducked her head, smoke flowing between her teeth. "You planned to cut me apart?"

A low growl rose from the guardians arrayed around the edges of the cavern.

"Er, no," Shereille said, scrambling to her feet. "At least not originally. I just wanted to talk to you, so I tried to get closer. But then the swamp monster got loose and there was going to be a fight, anyway. I figured if there was a body left over, then I could examine it."

Vola rolled her eyes to the ceiling. This woman could not read a room to save her life.

"You should probably shut up now, Shereille," she said.

"Why is that so surprising?" Shereille glanced between the seething dragon and the guardians. "She wouldn't have been using her body anymore. Why not dedicate it to science?"

"I prefer not to share my space with people who only see me as a thing to be studied," Listrell rumbled.

"Give it up, Shereille," Vola said. "Your test subject has decided not to be a test subject, oddly enough."

"I'm an observer," Shereille told Listrell. "I see and learn and then I write about it. You can't just decide not to participate."

"Watch me," Listrell said. "You may take her with you, or I will take her out to the desert and drop her," the dragon told Vola. "Your choice."

Lillie's head shot up, and she cast a beseeching glance at Vola. Vola pretended not to notice.

The wizard scrambled to her feet and took Vola's arm so she could speak in her ear. "We can't let Listrell drop her," Lillie said. "Please, Vola."

"Her carelessness nearly got us killed, Lillie. I don't know if we can trust her if all she cares about are her results."

Lillie bit her lip. "It's actually a compliment, don't you see? She knows we can take care of ourselves."

Vola made a face. Lillie was being unusually dumb when it came to her mother, but she wasn't about to say that out loud. Vola's parents might have been super supportive, but that just made it more obvious how awful Shereille was and how Lillie deserved better.

Vola blew out her breath. There was a grain of truth in Lillie's argument. They could handle themselves, for the most part. They'd even gotten out of a fight with a dragon, albeit unconventionally.

But Vola was responsible for Lillie and Talon and Sorrel, and if Shereille was going to put them in harm's way, then Shereille was a threat.

Lillie stared up at her, big blue-green eyes wide. Vola sighed.

She also wanted to protect Lillie's feelings and convincing her that her mother deserved to get dropped from a dragon wasn't exactly on her list of things to do today. Maybe Shereille would take this one last chance and actually impress Vola and give Lillie the validation she was looking for.

Or maybe Vola was going to regret this. A lot.

"Fine. She can come with us. But only until we can figure out how to get her back to the city unharmed."

Lillie squeezed her arm and beamed. "Thank you, Vola," she said quietly, as if she knew the only way Vola would have agreed was for her sake.

Shereille moped and moaned the entire morning as they left Listrell's lair and followed Renvick through the hidden paths of the mountains. She was a lot less likable when she was complaining all the time. And Vola hadn't liked her much to begin with.

Lillie tried to distract her, asking about her research, but Shereille always managed to circle back to how they'd destroyed her one chance to study a *draconis maximus*.

Sorrel scrambled to the top of a jagged rock and then hopped from one rock to the next as they threaded their way through the rough terrain. "She's annoying the crap out of me," she told Vola. "But I'm a little disappointed, too. It would have been nice to just point and have a dragon swoop in to burn our enemies."

"She's preventing our enemies from doing more damage," Talon said. "That's our goal in the long run, isn't it?"

"Yeah, but it still seems like she's running away from the danger, not toward it. Hey, Renvick," Sorrel called to the guardian making his way through the boulders. They weren't even on a path, but he moved as light-footed as a goat, despite his size. "You're pretty handy with your weapon."

He paused a few paces ahead of them and glanced back, the

ridge above one eye raised. "I am very skilled with my weapon. Yes."

Vola choked on the euphemism. Talon covered her eyes and shook her head.

Sorrel just ran right on by without even noticing. "Great. Would you rather stand at the castle door to guard it against intruders? Or track down the threat and root it out at the source?"

"I am here with you, searching for the enemy. So what do you think?"

"Ah, good point. Good point." She turned to call over her shoulder. "He's a charger, guys."

"I am glad you noticed."

Vola snorted, and Sorrel paused on top of another rock.

"Oh," she said, her mouth screwing up with distaste. "There was another whole conversation happening there that I didn't even notice, wasn't there?"

Before Vola could think of an explanation, Renvick blinked his first set of eyelids and gave her a toothy grin. "I was speaking of battle. It has been many centuries since I've gotten to travel with worthy warriors."

Sorrel examined him out of the corner of her eye, but he just gave her a mild look and stepped up the path to a spot marked by a massive standing stone, carved with ribbed wings and claws.

The draconic warrior hunkered down beside it and put his shoulder to the rock. He heaved the stone and it shifted almost like it was on wheels, revealing a dark tunnel, similar to the one they'd crept through to invade Listrell's lair. Only this one was vertical and ran straight down into the mountain.

"Ooh, what's down there?" Sorrel said, sticking her head in the entrance.

"Another lair," Renvick said. "Possibly our enemy. Hopefully no rock wyrms."

Vola glanced back at their party. Lillie and Shereille still spoke, Lillie looking more red than usual and Shereille looking bored. Behind them trailed the swamp monster, which made grumbling noises and ground its teeth.

"I don't think lowering us down one by one is a great idea. Sorrel, do you want to do some scouting? Just don't alert anything to our presence."

"Sneaky, sneaky. Got it." She gave Vola a mock salute and disappeared down the tunnel, clinging to the walls like a spider with Maxim's Warhammer across her back.

Vola stepped back to see if she could rescue Lillie.

"I thought you were going to take me back to the city," Shereille said as soon as Vola came within earshot. "If I can't continue my studies in the field, I at least need to get back so I can lead my team. Maybe we can find another dragon who's still sleeping."

"I said you would come with us until we could find time to take you back to the city. Besides, I thought this trip was supposed to be an opportunity for other things, too," Vola said, nodding significantly to Lillie.

Shereille's pinched expression didn't change. "I'm not saying it wasn't. But now that's done, I really must get back to what's important."

"I'm beginning to see why you left Glenhaven in the first place," Lillie snapped.

"Oh, good," Shereille said. "I was worried you would never understand."

Lillie opened her mouth, but the only thing she could come up with was a wordless cry. Sorrel returned in that moment, interrupting them.

"Nothing's down there," she said, climbing from the hole and dusting her hands off on her pants. "But it looks like some kind of big operation might have been there a few nights ago. Probably Nargilla if that old gnome is to be believed."

"He seemed pretty pissed at her," Talon said. "I doubt he was lying to protect her."

She knelt and touched the ground.

Lillie's mouth went round. "Oh, can you feel if there are dead spots nearby?"

Talon grunted.

"Wait," Vola said. "Wouldn't Listrell be able to feel one if it was so close? We've only been walking a few hours."

Renvick shook his head. "We passed out of her territory. This is unclaimed since there's no one living in the lair right now."

"So, Nargilla can wreak whatever sort of havoc she wants," Vola said with a growl.

Talon's breath hissed through her teeth, and they all focused on her.

"Where?" Vola said.

"That way." Talon pointed. "I don't know how long ago. It doesn't feel like the last one felt, but it's there now."

She stood, then clambered up the slope. The rest of them hurried to follow. Even Shereille had shut up for once.

Talon was the first to make it to the ridge, with Renvick not far behind. Vola could tell something was wrong as soon as Talon froze, silhouetted against the sky. The moment Renvick joined her, he stiffened, the colors in his hide shifting into more vibrant hues.

"Another dead spot?" Lillie called.

"Yes," Renvick said at the same time Talon said, "Worse."

She turned back to them. "You'd better get up here quick."

Vola vaulted boulders to get to the ridge. At the top, she sucked in a breath.

It *was* another dead spot. A spreading, flat black, just like the one in the desert and the one outside Listrell's first lair.

But this one had a shape inside it. A body sprawled across the darkened stone, pale and limp in the harsh sunlight.

"Geez," Vola said and started skidding down the slope.

She lurched to a stop and fell to her knees beside the man, who lay face down against the rock. Her gaze raked him up and down, cataloging his hurts. But the thing was, he didn't seem to have any. His back moved with his breath but barely. She reached for his shoulder and tried to draw up enough healing power to tell what was wrong with him.

But it was like reaching blindly for a railing and finding it missing.

Damn, she had no connection to Cleavah in the dead spot, and therefore no way to heal.

The others skidded down the slope, sending gravel flying past Vola as she turned the man over gently.

She gasped. She hadn't paid any attention to his clothes while he lay there, but now she could see his face, she recognized him.

"Master Bao!" Sorrel said her breath escaping on a gasp.

The old monk didn't stir.

"Vola?" Sorrel said.

"Help me get him out of this spot," Vola said. She didn't need any help. She could just hoist the thin figure into her arms, but Sorrel needed something to focus on.

The halfling scrambled to lift his feet as Vola supported the old monk's shoulders. They dragged him out of the blackened area and laid him down in a clear spot.

"What's wrong with him?" Sorrel asked. "Is he hurt? Sunstroke? Did Nargilla do something to him?"

"I don't know yet," Vola said. "He doesn't seem wounded. And he hasn't been out long enough to have suffered from dehydration and starvation like he was planning."

Vola reached for Cleavah's power again, searching out the damage in Master Bao's wiry frame, but all she could see was an overwhelming grayness. The place where a person's bright spark of life usually resided was shriveled and colorless.

"It's like…his life is being drained."

Lillie sucked in a breath. "He must have been in the spot when Nargilla drained the magic out of it."

"But we don't have any magic," Sorrel said. She touched the staff over her shoulder. "I mean besides what little Maxim gives us."

"All creatures have magic," Lillie said. "It's attached to our life force. Those of us with more of it get a special connection to the land or it's gifted by a god." She gestured to Talon and then Vola. "The rest of us learn to use what's already in the world." She touched her chest. "Or we fight with more mundane means." She gestured to Sorrel. "But everyone has at least a little."

"So…she drained his life force?" Sorrel said, face going slack with horror as she surveyed Master Bao.

"Not all of it," Vola said. "Just the magical part."

"That still looks pretty bad," Talon said.

"Quiet, I'm going to see what I can do." Vola closed her eyes while the others held their breath.

Vola reached again for her healing power and poured it into the old monk, trying to sop up the gray like a dishtowel. When that didn't work, she tried infusing him with the power, repainting him from the inside to get rid of the frightening blankness.

He seemed to soak up the power like dry ground soaking up the rain, more and more and more, but none of it seemed to make a difference. Vola was left panting and shaky and suddenly she realized she was at the end of what she could provide.

She pulled back and her shoulders drooped.

Talon supported her before she fell over. "Are you all right?"

"No," Vola said, voice hoarse. "I can't fix it. I can't fix whatever is wrong with him. He's alive, but only barely. And whatever it is about being drained can't be fixed by healing."

"You are nothing if not predictable, Mishap's Heroes," a cheerful voice said.

Vola tried to stand too quickly and ended up on one knee as black rushed to crowd her vision.

At the opposite edge of the dead spot stood a cheeky gnome in a tattered robe.

"Nargilla," Vola growled.

SEVENTEEN

"I WILL ADMIT, I'm impressed you didn't get eaten by a dragon," Nargilla said, tilting her head to survey them. "Or burnt to ash in the burning city. But here you are after only a slight delay. Maybe this will be fun after all."

"You knew we would be here," Vola said.

"Like I said, predictable." Nargilla shrugged. "I knew you would be coming after me. Your honor would demand it. So I made myself easy to find."

"What did you do to him?" Sorrel asked, still supporting Master Bao.

"Pff, hardly anything. He tried to stop me from taking the magic out of this spot. And that's what happens when you get caught in the spell. It harvests you, too."

"Is he going to die?" Lillie said.

Nargilla looked affronted. "It takes your magic, not your life."

"Would you want to live without magic?"

Nargilla tapped her chin. "Huh. Hadn't thought of that."

Vola drew her sword.

Nargilla shook her head. "See. Predictable."

"I know how to deal with being predictable," Vola growled stepping closer.

Nargilla snorted. "What? Because you dealt with Inga? That stupid orc. She was a special case. She was obsessed with you."

Vola jerked. "You knew Inga?"

"Is there some sort of evil villains club?" Sorrel said. She was swinging her staff behind Vola ready for a fight.

"There's no such thing. We worked for the same boss, dummy."

"Anders," Lillie said.

"What does he want?" Vola said. "And what are you getting out of it?"

"Money, power, sex," Nargilla said with a shrug. "What else is there? He pays me, I get to keep the excess power from what I siphon off for him, and he's got the best butt I've ever seen. And believe me, at my height, I've seen a lot."

Renvick crept closer to the gnome from the other side and met Vola's eyes. Vola gave him a minuscule nod. And as Nargilla drew her next breath, Vola lunged.

Before Vola could touch her, Nargilla collapsed, as if she'd melted directly into the very stone. Vola stumbled, her momentum carrying her forward over the spot where Nargilla had disappeared.

Renvick glanced around, his weapon in his hand. "Where did she go?"

"Yoohoo," Nargilla waved from the top of a rock pile.

Vola ground her teeth.

"Talon, Lillie—"

"Already on it," Talon said, bringing her bow up. Lillie was whispering over her hands.

Vola turned to the most troublesome member of their little group. "Shereille, stay with Master Bao. And keep the swamp monster out of the way this time."

"I don't have to take orders. I was the one who hired you."

Vola ignored her and turned back to the fight.

Talon and Gruff had moved to flank Nargilla on her distant rock. Together, they drove the gnome back down to flat ground where Sorrel, Vola, and Renvick could engage.

Vola charged, swinging her sword around to cut the gnome's feet out from under her. Nargilla spun away, the tattered ends of her robe flying. Vola planted her leading foot and pivoted, bringing her shield around in a bash that should have taken Nargilla's head off.

But the gnome ducked and bounced back. "Ew, I don't want to touch that," she said, gesturing to Vola's black shield. "The evil might rub off on me."

"You're literally stealing the world's magic for money and sex," Lillie cried. "How is that not already evil?"

"Details," Nargilla said.

Renvick took advantage of her momentary distraction and swiped his warhammer through the air. Nargilla stepped back, tripped on her tattered robe, and fell, narrowly missing getting her head bashed in.

"Ooh, that one was close. I guess you guys aren't as bad as I thought."

Sorrel yelled a battle cry and leaped for the prone gnome.

She flew through the air, but halfway through her jump, the stone at her feet erupted, and Sorrel struck the unforgiving hide of a rock wyrm. It loomed over the halfling, who shook her head and tried to push up from the ground where she'd fallen.

Rock wyrms sprang from the stone all around in showers of dirt and gravel, making Vola and the others stumble back.

Nargilla climbed to her feet and brushed herself off. "There, see. I have friends, too."

"Lovely to meet you all," Lillie said, sourly.

The rock wyrms pulsed, their purplish veins throbbing under translucent skin. One leaned and lunged at Lillie.

Vola darted between them, sliding the last few feet on her knees, and caught the attack on her shield. She heaved upwards and threw the wyrm backward so that Lillie could throw lightning at it.

Sorrel flew by, her staff alight with crackles and sparks. She landed on the back...front? —it was impossible to tell —of one of the wyrms and clung there, beating the thing over the head.

A squeal rang out behind them, and Vola spun to see a rock wyrm lunging for the swamp monster. Shereille dropped its lead rope and cowered, covering her head.

The rock wyrm's mouth gaped wide enough to swallow the swamp beast whole. But somewhere between descending on it and eating it, the swamp beast twisted, and suddenly the rock wyrm was writhing on the ground as the swamp beast shook it from its neck.

Well, at least their rear was guarded. Vola remained beside Lillie, guarding the wizard as she rained lightning down. Renvick followed Sorrel, trying to guard the halfling's back, but getting left behind half the time.

In the center of the chaos, Nargilla stood, grinning at her rock wyrms.

Silent as a wolf on the hunt, Talon sprinted for her.

Nargilla pulled a hand up as if dragging something from the ground and spiky thorns sprang out of the rock, wrapping around Talon's boots and tangling in her cloak.

Talon's step hitched, but she spat out an angry word and the thorns let go as if they'd been burned, retreating underground.

Nargilla's eyes widened a split second before Talon tackled her.

"Ow. Hey, you're not actually supposed to get near me."

"No one told me that part," Talon said and drew back her fist.

Nargilla gasped and melted into the rock just as Talon's blow connected.

Talon cried out and cradled her hand against her chest, alone on the ground between all the rock wyrms.

"Talon," Vola called. She glanced back at Lillie.

"Go," Lillie said, face set.

Sorrel was atop yet another rock wyrm, her staff limned with lightning as she bashed the creature over the head. It moaned and threw itself on the ground, trapping Sorrel with its weight. She cried out.

Renvick rushed to her aid, hacking at the thick hide of the creature until it parted with a spurt of blood.

Vola skidded to a stop, halfway between Sorrel and Lillie with Talon on the ground at her feet. She couldn't reach everyone at once.

Lillie threw her arms up and pulled one last bolt from the sky, sending it arcing through the last rock wyrm. The wyrm moaned, but with its dying gasp, it lashed out, catching Lillie and throwing her into the rock pile where Nargilla had stood.

"Lillie!" Vola wavered. They all needed her help, but Nargilla was still lurking in the ground, waiting for her chance to strike.

Vola spun, surveying the battlefield, but the rock wyrms lay quiet, leaking dark purple blood into the dirt and rock, and no deranged gnomes leaped out of hiding.

"I think she's gone," Talon said with a grimace. She tried to uncurl her fist but hissed in pain and cradled the hand to her chest.

"Sorrel?" Vola asked Renvick.

The guardian heaved aside the rock wyrm's carcass and pulled Sorrel out from underneath its thick hide. He met Vola's gaze and nodded. "She will live."

Vola helped Talon climb to her feet, and together they stumbled to Lillie where she lay crumpled against the rock.

Vola fell to her knees as Talon propped herself up against the rock.

"Lillie?"

The wizard was breathing, and she had her eyes open, blinking at the sky. "I used...I used to think I would like flying," she said.

"What?" Vola laid her rough palm on Lillie's face, trying to get her to focus. One pupil was sluggish to respond. And the wizard wasn't making sense.

"It's not as much fun as it looks," she said, her words slurred. "Flying through the air."

Vola huffed a laugh. "It was only the landing that gave you a problem, little bird."

Lille tried to laugh, and her face went green. Vola rolled her onto her side in time for the wizard to barf up all her breakfast.

"How bad is it?" Talon asked.

Concussions had been common among the paladin candidates at the academy. Put a bunch of half-grown warriors in a ring with blunt weapons and grudges to work out and heads were bound to crack.

"She hit her head really good," Vola said. "She's gonna be loopy and dizzy for a while."

Lillie groaned. "No loops. No more flying, please."

"No more flying," Vola promised. She reached for the well of healing power in her soul but found it still empty. Just pulling a little thread out to examine Lillie's injuries made Vola break out in a cold sweat, and her hands started to shake. She cut off the thread of power before she could heave up her own breakfast.

Renvick stepped up to them, Sorrel in his arms. He'd crossed his forearms, gripping his elbows, and Sorrel sat in the seat they made, feet dangling.

"You all right?" Talon asked.

"The rock wyrm broke her leg," Renvick said as Sorrel winced.

Talon glanced at Vola. "What can you do?"

It was Vola's turn to wince. "Nothing. I'm out. I spent everything trying to heal Master Bao." She held up her hands so the others could see how they shook. Lillie went cross-eyed trying to focus on them.

"We can't stay here," Talon said. "We have to get back to the city. These two need healing, and Nargilla could still come back and decide to finish us off."

Lillie and Sorrel weren't the only ones who needed healing. Talon tried to hide it, but she still cradled her hand against her chest. And Master Bao remained motionless beyond the dead spot while Shereille dithered beside him, trying to yank the swamp monster away from the carcass of the rock wyrm it had killed. It was trying to eat it.

"Right. Renvick, can you handle Sorrel?"

The guardian's mouth twitched, flashing the end of a fang. "I am very capable of handling the halfling, yes."

Sorrel gave him a suspicious look. "There's a double meaning in there, I just know it."

Renvick, wisely, did not respond.

Talon sidled up next to Vola. "Why did Nargilla leave?" she said quietly. "If she was waiting here for us?"

Vola shook her head. "Maybe we were too much for her and she decided to cut her losses and retreat."

They exchanged a look, neither of them believing that explanation.

Vola gathered Lillie in her arms, trying not to jostle her too much. Vola would prefer to carry her the whole way to the city if only to keep an eye on her, but the draining and the fight had left her knees shaky as well. She'd never make it all the way back without some help. Lillie's head fell back, and she stared blearily at the sky.

Talon stalked up to Shereille and took the swamp beast's halter. She held it still while Vola placed Lillie on its back.

"No, anything but the monster," Lillie slurred.

"Shh," Vola said. "This is half the reason we have the dam — darn thing."

EIGHTEEN

THEY MADE it back to the city as night fell. Talon sent Gruff to the hotel to find Rilla while Rand circled above them, guiding them through the darkened streets that still smelled like smoke and wet, charred wood.

Vola had specifically asked the familiar to find a House of the Broken. The Broken might have been the Greater Virtue of Righteousness, but she had hospitals all over the world along with courts and homes for the homeless.

As they passed the first bridge in the city, Shereille stretched her arms out with a yawn. "Well, I appreciate your escort, but it's time I returned—"

Vola slung her arm around the elf's neck. "It's time you stayed with your daughter to be sure she's all right? Yes, I agree," she said, glancing back at Lillie. The wizard swayed on the back of the swamp beast. Talon wouldn't let her fall asleep, poking her when it looked like she was about to nod off. But she definitely wasn't completely aware of her surroundings, either.

Shereille opened her mouth as if to protest and stopped when she saw Vola's big, tusky grin. "Yes, of course," she said meekly.

The House of the Broken was clearly lit with lanterns and some wizard's fire lamps. This wasn't anything like the elegant marble facade of the hospital in Brisbene, but it was still bustling despite the charred roof and late hour.

Vola loved competent people. Less than half an hour later, they were all ensconced in a large treatment room that had been white-washed to cover the eclectic patchwork walls. Nurses and healers in calming blue uniforms floated in and out, putting together cots and bringing extra blankets, while others gently straightened out Sorrel's leg and laid Lillie's head down on a fresh pillow.

Beyond the open door, a couple of traveling judges dressed in red passed, whispering worriedly. And warriors hired to maintain the peace tiptoed by, doing their best not to clank.

No paladins, though. Paladins were chosen by their gods directly. And everyone knew the Broken had never chosen a mortal to act for her. The other gods had ranks and ranks of paladins called to serve their divine master on earth. But the Broken had always stood apart. In deed as well as appearance.

"There. You're all knitted up," one of the healers told Sorrel. "Be sure to keep the leg immobile through the night, though. The break is still weak and could be re-fractured." The healer brushed bushy black hair over her shoulders as she rose gracefully from the edge of the halfling's cot.

She moved down the row. Someone was already tending to Lillie who stared blearily at the ceiling from the next cot over, but the healer stopped at Talon and gestured for the ranger's curled hand.

More healers murmured from the far corner where Master Bao lay, all by himself, limp and unresponsive. His herd of care-takers shook their heads, as baffled as Vola had been up in the mountains.

Renvick stood in the corner, as still as a statue once again. His scales gradually faded from vivid streaks of blue and green to the red-brown color of rock.

"Do you need to sleep?" Sorrel asked him.

"This is my sleep," he rumbled, words coming slow and slurred. "Do not worry about me, fierce one. I will wake when I am needed."

Both sets of eyelids drifted shut even as his scaly lips pulled back in a draconic grin.

Sorrel stared at him, lips pursed and eyebrows drawn down.

"There is no lasting damage," the healer beside Lillie said. "And I have taken away the pain of the headache. I want you to try sitting up now."

Lillie cautiously pushed herself upright. She didn't immediately turn green and barf, so that was an improvement.

Lillie's healer moved on to check on Vola.

"I'm fine," Vola said. She'd taken off most of her armor, and now she was just stiff.

"Physically, yes," the healer said. "But I believe you are depleted in here." The healer touched her collarbone. "Allow me to bolster you, and you will replenish yourself faster."

Vola blinked. She hadn't even known that was possible, but then she was more of a field medic than a full doctor.

The healer lay a hand on her shoulder and closed her eyes. Vola felt something like a poke deep inside where her well of power normally resided.

The healer hissed and drew back, shaking her hand.

"What?" Vola asked.

"You…stung me." The healer tilted her head. "Your magic feels like the sun on a hot day. I don't think I can help you."

"I get my power from my goddess," Vola said with an apologetic smile. "So maybe it doesn't work that way. It's already coming back; I just have to be patient."

The healer's eyes narrowed. "I've worked with paladins before," she muttered as she moved away.

But Vola was more concerned about watching her party, making sure they were really okay, now. Talon was flexing her hand, and Lillie was cautiously craning her neck around, checking her range of motion.

Sorrel heaved a huge sigh.

"What's wrong?" Vola asked.

Sorrel's lips twisted, and she glanced at the motionless guardian out of the corner of her eye.

"Do you think he can hear us?"

"He did say he'd wake if he was needed."

Lillie's attention focused on him. "I think it's more of a passive awareness, though. Why?"

Sorrel plunked her head back on her pillow. "What am I supposed to do with him?"

"Whatever you want?" Talon said with a sly grin. "He seemed to make that very clear."

Sorrel glared at her. "That's just what I mean. He's persistent, and I don't know how to deal with that."

"If you aren't interested, you just have to tell him," Vola said. "There's nothing wrong with that."

Sorrel stared at the ceiling, her thumbs twisting over and over. "It's not that I'm not interested..."

Vola sat up as Talon spun around.

"Oh?" Lillie said, carefully.

"I'm just worried that I'm not interested in the same way other people seem to be. I like him. He's fun to talk to and fight with, but I'm still not into all that love and sex stuff. That's just not who I am."

Vola exchanged an amused glance with Lillie and Talon. That wasn't news to them.

"You know, you can like and spend time with someone

without the expectation of sex," Vola said. "It's a hard concept for some people, but there are other kinds of relationships. You like us, don't you?"

"Of course."

"But you're not ready to jump into bed with Lillie or Talon or me."

Sorrel screwed up her nose. "No, thank you."

"And that doesn't make how you feel about us any less important."

"Romance is only one type of relationship," Lillie said quietly. "It's up to you to decide if it's a necessary one for you. And if it's not...then it's not." Lillie shrugged.

"Yes, but how do I know if he'd be okay with that?" Sorrel asked.

Vola snorted. "You ask him. You won't know anything if you don't talk to him and tell him exactly what you're feeling."

"Communication is key," Shereille said, startling them. She'd been lurking beside the door, looking uncomfortable. "I recommend a contract. It is the only way to be sure hearts won't be broken."

"I'm not so sure of that," Lillie said sourly.

Shereille pressed her lips together. "Yes, it seems even that is not foolproof." She heaved a sigh and edged toward the door. "Well, since I'm not needed anymore, I will bid you farewell."

Lillie swung her legs over the side of her cot. "That's it?" she said, voice higher than normal.

Rand hopped from the little nightstand to her shoulder.

"Is what it?" Shereille lifted her chin. "I'm not a healer, Lilliara."

"No, I imagine such practical magic is beneath you," Lillie spat.

"Er," one of the healers said.

"I mean, don't you care at all?" Lillie said.

Shereille's brows drew down. "Care about what?"

"Anything!" Lillie threw her hands in the air.

"What a silly question. Of course, I care about things. I care a great deal about my research, which you might have noticed if you were paying attention."

"I mean about things that matter. People. Lives. Family. I was hurt. And…and you're just trying to get back to your books."

Vola raised an eyebrow. She'd never thought she'd hear Lillie admit that there was something more important than books.

"Let's be honest, Lilliara," Shereille said. "I barely know you."

The blood drained from Lillie's face. Vola would have leaped between them to spare Lillie this pain, but Lillie hadn't been willing to hear about it from Vola. Maybe Shereille herself was the only one who'd be able to convince her.

"What about people you do know, then?" Lillie said. "My brothers. The boys you helped raise when they were little. Did you know two of them are banished now? They tried to start a coup."

"That wasn't very smart of them."

"I had to do the banishing."

Shereille looked at Lillie like she still didn't get it. "Good for you. That's a hard spell."

Completely missing the turmoil and the anguish Lillie still felt over that decision.

"You really don't care, do you?" Lillie's shoulders sagged, and she sank back against the wall at the head of her cot.

"I never promised to care," Shereille said, and that was the gentlest tone Vola had ever heard from her. "It wasn't in the contract."

"That's what I mean. It's not that you don't care as a mother. You don't care as a person." She raised her gaze to meet Shereille's eyes, lips set in a hard line. "You care more about your research than you do about the people around you."

Shereille blinked. "Yes. I thought you understood that when I hired you."

"We thought you hired us to spend more time with Lillie," Vola said pointedly.

"I hired you to do a job," Shereille said. "The expectations were in writing and everything. You were supposed to help me study a dragon and you couldn't get it right. Even when I forced the issue, you still couldn't provide me with a subject."

"Forced the issue?" Vola said as Talon said, "Subject?"

"You stood at the end of that tunnel dithering for so long, and then you were just going to turn around and leave without letting me talk to Listrell. I figured a fight to the death would give me what I needed for my research."

Vola's stomach clenched. "You let the swamp beast go on purpose, to instigate the fight. You drove it into the cavern so we'd have no choice but to kill Listrell."

"You were talking about leaving!" Shereille cried. "That is not what I hired you to do."

"So you alerted her to our presence, made her angry, and risked all of our lives." Vola stood, looming over Shereille.

The elf shrugged. "You're adventurers. You risk your lives every day. What's the difference?"

"The difference is that we decide what's worth it and what's not. Your research is not worth our deaths."

"Maybe not to you," Shereille said with a pout.

They stared at her. Lillie stared at the ground, a heavy crease between her eyebrows.

"You risked her life, too," Vola said quietly, pointing to Lillie. "Was that worth it?"

Shereille remained silent, and Vola wondered if she even saw her daughter or just a means to an end.

"I can understand that you used me," Lillie said, her hands clenched together. "After all, I am only the result of a contract.

But you manipulated me into endangering them. They could have been killed, and it would have been my fault." Her eyes snapped up to her mother's face. "Mine and yours."

"Lillie," Vola started, but Lillie held up a hand, her eyes implacable as she stared at Shereille.

"I'd like you to leave, please," she said. "I won't bother you again."

Shereille didn't even hesitate. She walked out the door without looking back or pausing. As if she was finally free of an annoying obligation.

Vola reached across to take Lillie's hand.

Lillie remained staring at the empty doorway, but her fingers gripped Vola's hard enough to hurt. Vola didn't wince or pull away.

Sorrel hopped off her cot and hobbled over to put her arms around Lillie from behind.

"Immobile," the healer yelled. "You're supposed to keep the leg immobile! That means not moving!"

Sorrel jumped and guiltily tried to clamber back into her cot. But there was a stirring from the bed in the corner, and the healers in the room froze.

"What's the yelling about?" Master Bao said, voice as dry as a desert wind.

NINETEEN

Sorrel ignored the cries of the healers and hopped across the room. Vola caught her halfway and scooped her up so the healers would stop yelling.

"Master Bao," Sorrel said. "Thank Maxim, you're awake."

The old monk blinked at her for a long moment, and Vola found herself holding her breath. "Sorrel?" he finally said.

The color seemed to be leeching from his skin now, and his hair, which was already white and wiry, was going limp as well. But his eyes were alert and trained on Sorrel's face.

"I guess I'm glad you didn't stop following me," he said.

"You must have met Nargilla, then," Sorrel said as Vola placed her on the edge of his bed. The healers glared at her, but Sorrel didn't even notice.

Master Bao put a hand to his head and wheezed. "The gnome from hell? Yes, we're acquainted now. She interrupted my meditation to create that dead spot. I figured one last fight before I died wouldn't hurt anything. Except I didn't die, did I?"

"She drained the magic out of you as well as the land," Vola said.

"I'm sorry to say it's still happening," the closest healer said. "It seems to be a continual leeching process. But I don't know how to fix it."

He shook his head. "Forget that. We have a bigger problem."

"The dragons?" Talon said. She'd joined them with her bandaged hand.

Lillie sat on the edge of her cot looking like she was trying to get up. One of the healers rushed to her side and pushed her back down.

"I said you could sit up. Not that you could go jumping around."

"No," Master Bao said. "The...the city. Nargilla is going to drain the city. One big dead spot with all the power sucked out of it."

Vola gasped, and Sorrel went completely rigid.

"The spots she's already drained, she's using them as anchors. That's how her magic works. It builds on itself. If she drains even one more..."

"The whole city will be gone," Sorrel said. "Worse than burnt."

"We have to evacuate," a voice said from the doorway. They turned to see Rilla with Gruff beside her. Soot still streaked her green leather jacket, and she smelled like the burning city. Clearly, she hadn't slowed down in the days they'd been gone.

Fedor Gerrickson lurked just behind her, looking even more bedraggled. His beard was snarled and his shoulders drooped under the weight of his dirty chainmail.

Rilla stepped into the room and did a double-take when she saw Renvick beside the door. She cocked a thumb at him. "Did you guys stop to rob a tomb along the way?"

"Does it count as robbing if the artifacts walk away with you?" Renvick's voice rumbled through the room.

Fedor jumped and pulled his double-headed ax from his back.

Rilla tilted her head as the color started to pour into Renvick once more, greens and blues suffusing the guardian's scales.

"Does it count as an artifact if it talks back to you?" Rilla asked.

Renvick grinned, showing off a row of sharp, gleaming teeth. "It does not." He cracked his neck. "You are evacuating the city?"

"You heard?" Vola said.

"I hear everything in my fugue state.

Sorrel gulped. "Everything?"

"How else do you think I would know when to wake?"

"I don't know. Instinct?"

"Instinct is just action without thought. Thought alongside action is decision. You and I will talk, fierce one. But not immediately, I think."

He stretched his limbs, and Vola thought she heard a creak. Then he turned to Rilla. "I would like to offer the sanctuary of my mistress's old lair. If the people of Firewatch are in danger, we will shelter them."

Rilla raised an eyebrow. "Okay, I've missed a couple of steps here." She glanced at Vola.

Vola gestured to Renvick. "Rilla, this is Renvick. Guardian of the dragon Listrell and her representative at this moment. Renvick this is Rilla. Our boss."

Renvick gave Rilla a respectful little bow.

"Listrell," Rilla said, eyes narrowed. "And we're all friends now?"

"More or less," Sorrel said. "It helps that she didn't eat Talon."

Rilla glanced at Talon, who'd been half-hidden behind Vola. Talon gave her a little wave.

Rilla shook her head and raised a hand to rub her forehead. "Okay…okay, we're going to have to move fast so I can't ask all the questions I really, really want to. I trust you. That's why I hired you."

Fedor snorted loud enough to draw the gaze of everyone in the room. "You really believe this creature? This agent of dragons?"

Rilla's eyes narrowed. "I believe my people."

"They've been duped. Dragons are monsters."

"No," Talon said, standing so Fedor was forced to look at her. "We were wrong."

"How can you say that? Dragons kill and destroy."

"So do humans. So do dwarves and elves and orcs and every sentient creature. That doesn't mean we should make war on each other."

Fedor gaped at her. "You were the victim of a dragon. But you stand here and defend them to me."

"I was wrong. And an innocent creature died for it. I don't want to be wrong again. Listrell is not our enemy. Nargilla is. We have to go after her."

"This enemy can't be bigger than the dragon that is looming over all of us!" Fedor threw his hands over his heads.

"Is your revenge really more important than the lives of everyone in this city?" Talon said.

Fedor's face went hard as granite. "My revenge is everything," he said. "My heart still bleeds for the people I've lost. Your heart must be shriveled in your chest if you can forget what you've lost and feel regret for the death of even one of those creatures."

Talon reared back as if he'd struck her.

Vola stepped forward. "That's enough. How dare you judge what's inside someone else's head and heart?"

Fedor spat on the floor, making the healers cry out in disgust. "There's nothing wrong with *me*, paladin. But I'd seriously question the commitment of anyone in my party who backed out of their duty so easily."

"Good thing you're not in charge of my party, then," Vola said, dark and dangerous.

Fedor shook his head. "Don't expect any help from me. I have one priority. And it's to hunt this dragon down and kill it so that at least my honor will be satisfied."

He spun on his heel and slammed out the door. Renvick jerked as if to stop him before thinking better of it.

Talon stood frozen in the middle of the room, eyes wide and blank.

Sorrel caught Renvick's gaze across the room. "You want to go protect Listrell from that maniac?"

"I do. But I will first lead your people to a safe lair." He nodded to Rilla again.

She jerked her chin up. "I appreciate it. But I hope you don't mind if I vet this Listrell and her lair first."

"That sounds wise to me," Renvick said.

"While I do that..." She pointed to Vola and Talon. "I want you tracking down Nargilla. Your instincts are right, whatever that nutter says. Track her down and get rid of her. If there's no spellcaster, then there's no spell."

Talon remained quiet. So Vola answered. "We'll start, but we don't even know where—"

"I need a map of the city and the surrounding area." Lillie brushed aside the healer, who was trying to get her to lie back down, and snapped her fingers. "Now, please."

"You can find her?" Vola asked.

"The dead spots outside the city. She's using them as anchor points, which means I can predict where she'll need to cast her final spell."

"I can tell you how she forms her spells," Master Bao said from his bed. "So you will have a better chance to stay out of it. Unlike me." He cracked a weak grin.

"Then I leave you in good hands," Renvick said. He met Sorrel's eyes and gave her a solemn nod before leaving with Rilla.

One of the healers rushed into the room with a map for Lillie.

Vola stepped up to Talon and put her hand on her shoulder. The ranger didn't like to be touched, but Vola got the impression Talon needed something anchor her just then.

"Maybe he's right," Talon said.

"He's not," Vola said without even bothering to ask about what.

"Am I just running from a fight, though? Maybe it's human to want revenge and I'm more animal than I thought I was."

"Maybe you can be both," Vola said as Lillie did something arcane with rulers and a stick of charcoal across the map. "Take the best parts of both worlds. Animals run to protect themselves. But at some point, you have to stop running, Talon. At some point the best way to protect yourself is to turn and fight. Defense has to turn to offense. Or you'll be running forever."

Talon's shoulders straightened under Vola's grip. "It's not cowardly to want to protect what's important to you. To want to keep it as far away from the fighting as possible."

"No," Vola said. "Definitely not. But you don't have to do it alone. Your pack is with you."

Talon huffed a grim laugh. "Yes. That's what I'm afraid of."

TWENTY

LILLIE'S MAP had all sorts of lines slashing across it by the time she was done, but she assured Vola that the one they wanted was a dark angry x-mark near the top, a few miles north of the city.

"What do we do when we get there?" Sorrel said. "If Nargilla's there, too?"

"We disrupt her spell," Lillie said.

"Just like we've done the last two times, huh?" Sorrel said.

Lillie looked hurt. "We know so much more now than we did then. Master Bao can give us the details we need." She gestured to the old monk who lay on the cot, his head turned toward them. "If her magic works with anchors, on a large level as well as on a smaller level, then there have to be anchor points for the spell, anchoring on Nargilla herself when she draws power."

"Let me guess, we just have to find those and break her connection to them," Vola said. Sometimes magic could be so predictable.

"Exactly," Lillie said.

Master Bao cleared his throat. "They look like crystals."

"How do we keep from dying while we find them?" Sorrel

said. "She's thrown us around before and your head has to hurt as much as my leg."

"We couldn't get to her before because she was in the middle of the spell. And if we're caught in there, we'll end up just like Master Bao. But she couldn't move either…"

"If she's trapped there until she's done, then we can use that," Vola said, catching on.

"I also remember her being pretty good at dodging, whether she was trapped or not," Sorrel said.

"So we concentrate our fire. Sorell, that staff does lightning too, right?"

"Yeah." Sorrel touched Maxim's Warhammer and static crackled across its surface. "And I have a couple of bolts I've been saving especially for her."

"What about the rock wyrms?" Talon said.

Lillie raised her chin. "Leave those to me. I think I can take them out of the equation entirely."

"Then, you, Talon, and Sorrel concentrate on Nargilla," Vola said. "I'll have to go for the anchors. But be ready. Once we disrupt the spell, she can move again and I can't imagine she'll be happy."

"We have your back," Talon said. "Don't worry."

"Mountains look so much flatter on paper," Sorrel said the next morning as they made their way from the city.

This terrain was much harder than the meager trails they'd been following through the rest of the Firewall so far. Here there was no trail. There was no pass. It was just one ragged peak after another and finding ways to scramble up them.

Higher and higher they climbed. Vola tried to go slowly for the others. Talon's hand was fine, but Sorrel still limped and Vola didn't want her rebreaking anything. Lillie never complained, but every now and then she held her hand to her forehead as if the world still spun a little.

Vola tried to go slow, but she could still look over her shoulder and see glimpses of Firewatch through the peaks. It buzzed with the frantic movements of thousands of people trying to evacuate. They didn't have time to go slow.

"Lillie, how far?" Vola asked.

Lillie squinted at the map in her hands and then gazed around them. "We should be getting close. I don't know whether we should hope she got there first or not."

"Why would we hope that?" Sorrel said, puffing as she climbed up onto the next ridge.

"Because then we'd know for sure we got the right place," Talon said.

Lillie gave her a lopsided smile. "The map is not wonderfully detailed. I'm mostly just aiming us in the right direction."

"Great," Vola muttered under her breath. "Talon? Can you find her the way you did last time, now that we know where to look?"

Talon shook her head. "I don't feel anything. She must not have started yet."

It took them a few hours canvassing the area Lillie had marked on her map, but finally, they found a flat-topped cliff in the distance. A lone figure stood silhouetted against the early afternoon sky, and magic tingled against Vola's skin.

"There." That was all she had to say. They were as ready as they could make themselves even if Vola still felt shaky.

They converged on the peak.

At the top, it seemed like a god had taken a greatsword and sliced off the top, leaving a broad flat area with little peaks off to the side, serving as short edges to the bowl.

Nargilla stood in the center, staff planted in the rock. Black gathered at the tip in little tendrils, as if she'd just started.

The gnome sighed as the party climbed to her plateau.

"You know, you guys were fun at first. But your tenacity is beginning to irk me. Do you know what it's like when an annoyance just won't die?"

"Actually, we're familiar with the feeling," Vola said. They'd left the swamp monster with Rilla, who'd promised to put it to work evacuating the city. But if it managed to slip its leash and escape in the chaos…well, none of them would shed a tear over it.

"So, we're doing this again?" Nargilla said, leaning heavily on her staff.

"Unless you stop your spell," Vola said, drawing her sword.

Nargilla snorted. "Well, that's not going to happen. I've already explained this. If I stop the spell, then it doesn't get done. Does it?"

"That's the plan."

And Lillie hit her with a fireball.

When the smoke cleared, Nargilla coughed and brushed soot from her robe. "Good one, but—"

Lightning came from the other side as Sorrel let loose with Maxim's staff and Talon let loose an arrow.

Nargilla could only dodge one at a time and came out the other side, looking a bit singed. "Hey. Stop that. Do you know how hard it is to set this up? I'll have to start all over if you knock me out of sync."

Lillie sent another gout of fire at her, and when she tried to twist out of the way, Talon struck her with an arrow.

Nargilla cried out, Talon's arrow sprouting from her shoulder. "Fine." She panted. "I can work with this."

She reached down as if grasping a piece of earth and yanked upward. Just like she had when summoning the rock wyrms.

They all stared at the ground.

Nothing happened.

"Were you looking for your friends?" Lillie pointed over Nargilla's shoulder at a peak they'd passed on their way there.

A thumper like the ones the researchers used was positioned on top, just visible through the swarming bodies of half a dozen rock wyrms. Every rock wyrm in the area would be drawn to the thumper instead of them.

Nargilla's mouth thinned and her brows drew down. Sweat stood out on her brow as she clutched the end of the arrow with her free hand.

"You can end this now, Nargilla," Vola said. "By choice. Or it can be by force. Which will it be?"

Nargilla snapped the feathered end off the arrow, making the rest of them wince. "Guess," Nargilla said, eyes going to narrow slits.

She raised her blood-covered hand and dark clouds rushed to swirl over their heads.

Vola didn't wait to see what other spells she could call while working to drain the land. Nargilla was distracted, and that was all that mattered.

"Now," she shouted and rolled away to the edges of the plateau.

Behind her, her teammates pummeled Nargilla. They couldn't get close enough to hit, but they could send a variety of unpleasant things her way.

Vola sheathed her sword to give herself a free hand and leaped to the raised rock surrounding the plateau. The spell anchors would look like crystals, Master Bar had said. Vola scoured the ground, looking for anything out of the ordinary glinting among the rocks.

Thunder rumbled above and suddenly the heavens opened up. Except it wasn't rain that threatened to soak them.

Hail pounded the top of the mountains. Huge pieces of ice as big as her fist whistled past Vola's ear. She flung her shield up to cover her head and ran crouched over, hoping the others would be able to hold up under the onslaught.

She slipped and slid over the treacherous ice. Finding a crystal in this would be ten times harder. Vola kicked pieces of ice out of her way and noticed the others backing up a step out of the corner of her eye. The black was spreading from Nargilla's staff.

There, a glint of blue among the blanketing white.

Ice continued to pour out of the sky, hammering her shield and making it ring as she cleared the crystal of ice.

Perfect. She pulled her hand ax from her belt. Then slammed the blade into the crystal. It shattered, the sound of tinkling glass getting lost in the pounding of hail.

One down. Five more to go.

From the center of the circle, Nargilla screamed. She whipped around to fix Vola with a glare.

Vola stopped for long enough to meet her look. *See*, she said to silently. *We're going to make you stop.*

Nargilla lowered her chin. The ice storm ceased, a few last hailstones falling to the ground with a clatter. Then she lifted her staff, pulling it free from the spell.

Vola took a startled step back. She hadn't actually expected Nargilla to stop. They were supposed to force her.

The gnome disappeared into the earth, traveling through the rock itself, presumably. Vola skidded across the hail stones, trying to guess where she would come up.

"Where'd she go?" Sorrel asked. The three of them backed up, meeting Vola halfway as they scoured the mountaintop.

"Shit, we can't pummel her if we can't see," Talon said.

Lillie faltered, putting a hand to her head. "Does anyone else feel…woozy?"

"Is it your head?" Vola said. "Maybe we shouldn't have climbed so fast."

"I feel it, too," Sorrel said. She stared at her feet.

Vola reached for them both, pulling at her healing energy while she did.

Except she couldn't reach it.

It felt like a half-empty well, the surface of the water too far away to touch.

"What?" She gasped, and on a hunch, she knelt to clear away the hailstorms.

The ground was black, the last of the red-brown of the rock swirling away.

"Oh, gods," Vola said. "How did she—how did we—?"

"I had a second circle." Nargilla's voice came from the raised edge of the plateau, and they whipped around. She sounded weary, and she sagged against her staff as she glared at them.

From her knees, Vola swept armfuls of hailstones aside and found another line of crystals outside the first.

She looked back up at the gnome.

"I knew you'd turn up, so the first one was always supposed to be a decoy. Thanks for making it work."

"Oh, no," Vola whispered. "No, no, no." She tried to spring to her feet, to lunge at Nargilla, but a wave of weakness washed over her.

Around her, Lillie, Sorrel, and Talon fell to their knees and slumped over.

Vola growled, welcoming the wash of red across her vision. Rage would give her strength. She levered herself to her feet, using her knees to brace herself.

The breath left her lungs and suddenly she found herself too weak to draw another. Black crowded her vision, and she fell.

Laying on her side, the last thing she saw was the tattered ends of Nargilla's robe as the gnome stepped across the blackened rock to stand between her and her party.

She had no idea how long it took her to wake, but her dry mouth tasted like she'd licked the swamp monster when she finally cracked her eyelids open.

Short figures bustled around a large sprawling skeleton hung from a ribbed ceiling. The scene seemed familiar, but when would she have seen a floating skeleton like that?

Vola blinked, trying to clear the fog from her mind, trying to make sense of what she saw.

Light streamed from high windows, dawn from what she could tell. It had been early afternoon when they'd found Nargilla.

The windows stuck out over open space, like the back end of a ship but from the inside. And the skeleton was...?

A *dragon*, a piece of her mind answered its own question.

The field museum. She was in the field museum in the middle of Firewatch. How the hell had she gotten there?

Vola tried to sit up but a wave of weakness and disorientation kept her pinned to the ground as if she'd been tied there. Instead, she stuck out her elbow and heaved so she could roll.

Talon lay beside her. And beyond, she glimpsed Lillie's gold hair and Sorrel's brown arm.

At least they'd stayed together, whatever else had happened.

But what *had* happened?

The black. The crystals. Nargilla had trapped them in a second spell. She'd drained them along with the land. Just like Master Bao.

Vola's heart pounded, and she reached, trying to find Cleavah. But there was nothing there. No connection. She was empty inside, no healing and no calming presence.

Oh, gods. She groaned.

One of the small figures bustling around the skeleton heard

and came toward them. Vola recognized the tattered hem of Nargilla's robe from her spot on the floor.

"Ooh, one of you is still in the land of the living. So exciting. I always work better with an audience." Her misplaced cheer was back, and she leaned over so her face hung in Vola's sight, grinning ear to ear.

"Fffuck. You."

No lightning bolt. That was scarier than anything.

Nargilla clicked her tongue. Behind her, the skeleton dropped from the ceiling, bones shattering against the tile floor. Vola winced.

Talon stirred and tried to push herself up on her elbows. She didn't succeed any more than Vola had. "What...?"

"I'm clearing space," Nargilla said. "We're gonna need more room."

As she spoke, the gnomes behind her, dressed in shapeless gray shifts, made short work of sweeping the bones into a messy pile across the room. There was a low rumbling and another group of gnomes appeared in the doorway, rolling several tanks fitted with copper wiring into the center of the room.

Vola's eyes narrowed.

"You recognize them," Nargilla said, eyes on Vola. "Myron Vidal's work, you know. The man was an idiot if he thought he could get away from Anders, but he did have his moments of genius. These tanks can store the power I siphon from the land as easily as they stored the power he siphoned from the dead."

One of the tanks clanged as the gnomes stood it up in the center of the room.

"Careful with that," Nargilla said.

Lillie groaned and Sorrel thrashed about, trying to right herself.

"Well, I'd better get back to it, if I want to get those tanks filled. Anders will be here to oversee the draining of the city and to take the tanks back with him. I only get my bonus if I can prove it works." Nargilla straightened up again.

Vola tried to get her elbows under her to push herself up, but ended up panting, too spent to do anything besides stare at the floor. "Why haven't you killed us?"

"I thought about it. But I thought maybe Anders would prefer to do it. I'll also admit, I'm curious what the draining will do to you eventually. It'll be so much fun to watch. Thanks for clearing out the city, by the way. Much shorter commute now."

"They'll never let you live," Vola grated out.

"Who?" Nargilla paused. "The city counselors? They're not brave enough to come back. The dragons? They don't care enough to do more than defend themselves."

"The gods," Vola said, thinking of Cleavah and the burning anger she'd spoken with outside Listrell's lair. "They know what you can do. They won't let you threaten them or their people."

Nargilla's eyebrows went up. "Ha. Yes, that was a problem. Yesterday. Today, however, I've discovered a workaround. A happy little coincidence."

She flicked her fingers behind Vola, then trotted away, humming.

Vola fought the heaviness of her body and rolled to her other side. She sucked in a gasp and her vision went fuzzy.

One of the exhibits stood behind her, empty of everything except some fake rocks and lichen. And a figure bound to a stake.

Golden skin had gone dull in the dawn light and dark curling hair fell limp to her waist. Cleavah stood tied to the stake, her eyes closed and face wreathed with pain as gold light flowed out of her, spilled onto the floor, and flowed to one of the empty tanks.

TWENTY-ONE

VOLA FOUND A SURGE OF STRENGTH — OR at least, a surge of not weakness — and pushed herself to her hands and knees while her friends gaped at the captured goddess.

Vola shuffled to the display and fell over the railing into the diorama of the surrounding mountains made of foam and dry lichen. A fake rock disintegrated under her weight with a puff of dust.

"Lady," she whispered. A clear pane of spell glass separated her from her goddess. She pressed her fists against the smooth surface. She wanted to pound on it, but all she could manage was a dull thump.

Vola reached for her connection with Cleavah. It had always been there. Even when the paladin council had stripped her of her rank and stolen her emblem, Cleavah had still been there, just wrapped in fog, separated by the thinnest veil that Vola had spent too long shying away from.

Buried deeper than she'd ever looked before, Vola found her connection to Cleavah. At the very bottom of her well, power pulsed through a thin thread. It was pulled taut and stretched to the goddess. Was this how Cleavah normally fed her power? Except now, power sucked through that string, into Vola, and then immediately out and away, toward the closest of Nargilla's tanks.

A side effect of Nargilla's spell. Vola was connected to her goddess, therefore draining Vola meant draining Cleavah. The goddess had been right. Nargilla did have the power to rival the gods themselves. It was just way, way worse than they'd thought.

As if the end of the world wasn't bad enough.

Cleavah's eyelids cracked open, and she stared blearily at Vola. Even a greater goddess had been brought low by the maniacal gnome.

Vola thumped the glass again. It was just a simple ward spell to keep something valuable in and potential thieves out. Lillie could have broken it in a heartbeat. Vola could have smashed through it with no problem. Yesterday.

"Lillie?" Vola whispered. She knew the answer, but they might as well make sure.

"I'm out," the wizard said. She couldn't even muster the energy to sound grim. She just stared at the ceiling. "She's taken the magic out of our very selves. Even here where the world's not drained, I'm cut off." She raised her hand and a single sad little spark spluttered against her fingertips before dying out.

Vola definitely couldn't use Cleavah's power to heal. She was already the reason the goddess was hanging there, being bled like a butchered animal. How did Nargilla even get her physical form? Had Cleavah manifested while Vola and the others were knocked out? Or had her spell sucked Cleavah here like a summoning spell?

"I can't feel the land," Talon said. "I can't call on it anymore."

"Can't feel the land?" Sorrel said. "I can barely feel my legs." She rolled to her elbows and tried pulling her knees under her.

"Where's Gruff?" Vola asked. Maybe they had a friend on the outside, a lone wolf waiting to slink in and save them.

"I can't feel him either," Talon said. "He could be out there looking for me, but if he can't hear me..." She shook her head. "How can Nargilla cut me off from him? He's family."

"It's just like Master Bao," Lillie said. "She's tapped into our life force and is draining it away."

"Still?" Vola said. "She isn't done yet?"

"No, or we wouldn't be able to talk or move."

Vola swallowed. "So how long do we have?"

"I'm not sure I have all the tools I would need to calculate—"

"Then guess."

"A few hours."

Vola couldn't help the gasp that escaped her lungs.

"This appears to be much faster and progressing at a rate exponential to that of Master Bao's experience," Lillie said, discussing numbers like what she wanted for tea that afternoon. "Nargilla has stepped up her timetable, apparently."

The gnomes in the rest of the hall had finished setting up the rolling tanks and fiddled with the copper wiring between them. They'd seen the same kind of tank in Myron's laboratory so many months ago. He'd used them to collect magical energy from the dead and ship the result to Anders. This was no different, except it posed a threat to a much broader area.

Not to mention their own magic was swirling around in those tanks somewhere.

If they could just smash one...

Vola tried lifting her arm experimentally. Her fingers twitched.

The others didn't look like they were in any better shape. They'd all stopped trying for a minute, taking a breather to just lay there.

Vola squeezed her eyes shut. What could they possibly do

against Nargilla now? She'd been toying with them all along, if this was an example of the kind of work she could do normally.

The city was empty. There was no one left to help them, and really, there was no one left for them to save.

"We shouldn't have gone after Nargilla," Vola said, slumping to the rough floor of the exhibit.

"What?" Sorrel said.

She could hear Talon shift, but Vola kept her head down. It was easier than trying to wrestle it up.

"Why?" Talon said.

"We should have run with the others. We should have helped evacuate the city and stayed out of Nargilla's path. Then we'd be out there planning a siege that might work, rather than in here with no hope."

Vola could barely keep her lungs working, and she wasn't exactly sure why she was still trying so hard. She had nothing left to fight with. All she wanted was to lie down among these fake rocks and admit she'd been beaten.

It was a new feeling for her.

There was a long moment before Talon's voice finally came from outside the exhibit. "You've never lost everything before, have you?"

Vola opened her mouth and had to stop. She'd lost lots of things in her life. Given up a lot of things, too. But had she ever lost everything? Even when the paladin council had taken her emblem and burned her shield, she'd still had her team. She'd tried to give them up, but they'd followed her, anyway. She'd had her team; she'd had her family. She had so much that she'd never even thought of before.

"No," she said. "This would be a first for me."

"It's definitely not my first time," Talon said quietly. "I know what it's like to hit the very bottom of yourself and still be alive.

When you still have to go on despite everything that's happened because the world didn't have the decency to kill you."

Talon pushed herself to her feet, looking haler and healthier than she had any right to. "Maybe we should have run."

Vola stared.

"But you were right, when you said there's a point where you can't run anymore. Because you've hit a cliff or a pit or a wall. Or because you've run so far and so long that you're stronger now than the thing chasing you."

Talon stumbled to the railing of the exhibit and held out a hand to Vola. How did she have the strength to stand upright?

"There's a point when you have to turn and fight because you're human, and the only other option is to get slaughtered like an animal."

Vola felt like a slaughtered animal already. She had nothing left to give, nothing left to try. But neither did Talon, and she still stood there, waiting for Vola to take her hand. Waiting for Vola to find the last bit of hope or strength or sheer stubbornness that would propel her until she had the momentum to move on her own again.

Vola glanced back at the trapped goddess, around at the green tanks, and over at her team trying to pick themselves up.

Then she reached up and clasped Talon's hand.

Talon hauled her to her feet. Or at least halfway, and Vola ended up draped over the railing of the exhibit.

"Very motivational," Sorrel said from the floor. "But what the hell are we going to do against Nargilla if none of us can even move?"

"We'll figure it out," Vola said, huffing against the railing.

"Rilla called us Mishap's Heroes for a reason. We take misfortune and spit out gold."

"If that were true, we'd be a lot wealthier," Sorrel said. "And what if the misfortune kills us before we have a chance to get to the second part?" But she sighed and heaved herself to her feet, using the railing beside Vola as leverage. She and Vola reached down to give Lillie a hand up.

"It helps if you just concentrate on breathing," Talon said, once she was upright. "Keep the air going in and out and let muscle memory do the real work."

"You make it sound so easy," Sorrel grumbled.

"We haven't lost everything," Vola said. "Like Talon said, we're still alive. And we have a lot more than just magic. Nargilla didn't take Lillie's mind. And she didn't take the rest of our skills."

"So, ideas?" Lillie asked.

Talon's chin jerked up. "Can you distract her?"

They all stopped and looked at Talon. She was the only one who managed to stand there without support so far.

"Distract?" Sorrel said. "We can still talk, so yeah, we can be distracting as hell."

"Why?" Vola said, eyes narrow.

"I'm going for help."

Vola straightened and nearly blacked out. "What?"

"How can you go for help?" Lillie said. "She took your magic."

"I don't need magic to talk people into something they should already be doing. That's language, not spells."

"Talon, being a pack works both ways. You don't want us to put ourselves in danger. But we don't want you haring off by yourself either," Vola said.

"That time has passed," Talon said. "We're out of options." She met each of their eyes in turn. "Trust me."

"We do," Vola said without hesitating.

"Then distract her. Slow her down. Anything to kill time. And don't die."

"Only if you promise the same," Vola said.

Talon's lip twitched with a smile. "Promise."

"Then go. We're counting on you to get us out of this."

TWENTY-TWO

NARGILLA'S GNOMES eyed them as they wobbled on their feet and Vola hung her head trying to appear non-threatening. The gnomes left them alone. Like they didn't consider the party a threat in their current state.

They probably had the right of it.

Vola glanced around, taking quick stock of their equipment. All their weapons were missing, but Vola still wore her plate armor. Which seemed a bit silly right about now.

She yanked at the leather straps as she surveyed the room. Everything the gnomes did seemed to center around those tanks. She fumbled with the clasps of her pauldrons, and Lillie reached to help her. Vola pulled the armor from her shoulders and limbs. There, that felt a lot better. A piece of her was screaming that she needed that protection. It did no good on the ground. The rest of her was sighing in relief.

"All right. Distractions it is. Sorrel, I want those tanks to blow up or leak or something."

"I'll make it happen," Sorrel said. Instead of trying to walk, she flopped to the floor again and just rolled. Like a loose sausage rolling off an inn table.

"I'm hungry," Lillie said, absently.

Sorrel paused to let one of the gnomes pass, laying there like a dead thing. The gnome sniffed and stepped over her. As soon as she was unobserved again, Sorrel rolled between the legs of the tanks and disappeared from view.

A gnome stopped to peer underneath, and Vola's breath hissed through her teeth. She exchanged a look with Lillie.

The wizard wobbled a couple of steps to the center of the room and touched her head. "Oh, I feel so faint," she said and toppled over.

Vola lurched to her and fell to her knees. "Oh no, she's fainted. She's too delicate for this. Someone help, please!"

Lillie snorted, her arm over her face.

At least her cry had drawn the attention of the gnomes and while she couldn't hear it, she knew that somewhere behind her, Talon was slinking into the shadows.

There was a small clank from under the tanks, and someone swore.

Smoke poured out from under the glass containers and the mess of copper wiring and tubes.

The gnomes yelled and spun back to the tanks, racing to find the problem.

Vola didn't immediately feel an influx of power, so it probably wasn't their magic leaking into the air. That might take more work. But they'd obviously caused a problem, and that was the best she could hope for right now.

The smoke rolled over them as Sorrel crawled back to them.

"This will only work for so long," she whispered. "And we're too visible."

"Scatter," Vola whispered back. "Under cover of the smoke. If Nargilla's looking for us, she won't be looking for Talon. Stay out of sight. Sabotage what you can. And whatever you do, don't get—"

"Killed?" Sorrel said.

"I was going to say caught, but yeah, that, too."

Sorrel flopped onto her back and rolled away like a frenetic sausage. Lillie army-crawled her way toward a back hallway, and Vola heaved herself to her hands and knees and shuffled in the opposite direction. She found a table and ducked under it as the gnomes yelled frantically from the center of the room.

She peeked out long enough to check the high windows. Sure enough, someone yanked the edge of a pink sleeve free from the casement, and the window slapped shut, unnoticed by anyone below.

Good. Talon was away. Now they just had to keep her disappearance a secret from Nargilla for as long as possible.

Vola spotted a door that presumably led deeper into the museum and crawled towards it before the smoke could clear from the room. It wouldn't do Talon any good if she was caught here in the first chamber.

The hallway stretched long and skinny back into the mountain the museum perched on. Bare and utilitarian, this one was obviously not meant for the public. But Nargilla's people had been here already to lay down lines of copper tubing. They'd never experimented with smashing Myron's tanks to see if that released the stolen magic, but now Vola wished that they had. Not that she was strong enough to smash anything right now. But it would have been a nice goal to work toward.

As it was, she stopped several times to concentrate on breathing and yank copper tubing apart. She left a little trail of destruction along behind her.

It was not the most rewarding of battles, crawling along the hall breaking things. It didn't feel heroic at all.

But that was Talon's point. This was what they could do at the moment. This was how they could go on after Nargilla had taken everything away from them.

Maybe she could find the anchor points to Nargilla's spell. No, those would be somewhere beyond the city. Probably near those dead spots. Maybe they were the dead spots themselves. She would have to ask Lillie. Either way, she wouldn't find them here.

But she could follow this tubing to wherever it led. And screw up whatever she found there.

Voices from down the hall made Vola jump, and she scanned the corridor for an escape. Doors lined the hallway, most with windows at the top, but they were too high to see through when she was on her hands and knees.

It was a unique experience for Vola to be too short.

She picked a door at random and ducked inside, trying to close it quietly behind her.

She came face to face with a familiar elf, red-gold hair falling out of her bun, her blue-green eyes wide with surprise.

Vola slapped her hand over Shereille's mouth before she could scream or do anything to give them away.

They froze, locked together as the voices outside came closer.

"This had better not be like Myron or Inga," someone said. A low male voice Vola had never heard before.

"Those jokers?" Nargilla's voice scoffed. "I'm ten times better."

"Mishap's Heroes has managed to thwart me at every turn. Don't underestimate them."

"I've declawed those four. They won't be a problem anymore. Maybe we can take care of them for good together. And can I just say how fabulous your butt is looking today?"

"Please don't."

The tread of a sturdy pair of boots moved down the hall, accompanied by the patter of Nargilla trotting to keep up.

Vola slumped against the door and released the breath she'd

been holding. "Anders is here," she whispered, heart pounding against her ribcage. "Gods, we've been chasing him for so long, and now he's right on the other side of the door, and I can't do anything about it."

Her gaze fell on Shereille, and she scowled. "What are you doing here?" She was glad to find that curiosity and outrage fueled her muscles better than anything else right now.

"What do you think I'm doing?" Shereille pushed her hair out of her eyes with both hands. "Trying to stop that little shit, of course."

Vola raised her eyebrows at Lillie's mother's language. "I'm sorry, but you? You're trying to stop the bad guy?"

"You don't have to say it like that."

"Yes, I do. Not only have you had no interest in stopping Nargilla, you've actively gotten in our way when it's served your own purpose." Vola's mouth pulled down. "Unless...did Lillie's words actually get to you? Is that why you didn't evacuate with everyone else? You felt bad?"

"Felt bad about what?" Shereille said, shattering that idea. "This master plan of Nargilla's is completely interfering with my research. First, they tried to get me to evacuate with the others. As if I would leave my work unfinished. Then that gnome came in and started draining the magic out of everything. If anything is going to affect my results, it's that."

Of course. She wasn't doing this because it was the right thing to do. She was doing it because she was just as self-centered and determined as ever.

Really, it was a shame. Shereille and Lillie were so much alike in so many little ways. It was just the big ones that had sent them careening away from each other. Shereille was just Lillie, without any of the feelings attached.

"Why are you crawling around on the floor?" Shereille finally said, looking askance at Vola. "And don't you think you'd be more useful with armor and a weapon?"

"We were captured," Vola said shortly. "And Nargilla drained all the magic out of us. I'm crawling because it's easier than walking."

Shereille sat there gaping, without anything useful to say.

"What about you?" Vola said. "Have you made any progress? How can we beat her?"

"There might be a way to reverse what's happened. At least, to release all the magic back into the world that Nargilla has stolen. But it will require magic."

"You can't just smash the tanks?"

Shereille looked horrified. "Who knows what that would do? You could completely destroy us and yourself in the process. Or worse, Nargilla would absorb that power into herself."

Vola's stomach dropped. "No, no, no, she can't do that. She has the power of a goddess trapped in there. Cleavah herself is being drained. Through me."

"Oh my gods," Shereille said, eyes wide.

"Exactly."

Shereille bit her lip, and her eyes went unfocused and distant. Vola knew what that look meant when it was Lillie.

"What are you thinking?" she asked. "Do you have an idea?"

Shereille blew out her breath through her nose. "Only that if Nargilla has the power of a god, you will need a god's power to counter her. I wonder if any of the priests stayed in the city or if they were all sensible and evacuated."

Vola froze, hand raised to her head. "Not a priest," she said. "A weapon. We need to find wherever Nargilla stashed our weapons."

She scrambled to her knees and leaned up to check the hallway through the window.

"What good will that do if you can't even carry one?" Shereille said.

"Sorrel's staff," Vola said. "The staff she carries and fights with. It's part of Maxim's Warhammer. I've seen it shear through just about everything before. She can usually call it to her, but it must be locked away behind a door or a spell right now. If we can find it…"

Shereille pushed Vola aside—it didn't take much strength—and opened the door.

Vola hauled herself to her feet using the door frame, and surprisingly, Shereille slipped her slim shoulder under Vola's arm.

"Where would she have stashed our weapons?" Vola asked her. "We were unconscious when she brought us in."

"There's a back door by the delivery bay. Besides the visitors' entrance, that's the most likely. It seems to be where most of the equipment is being brought in."

They shuffled down the hall. Vola kept checking over her shoulder to make sure they weren't spotted. No one used the hallway right now, but they could hear shouting coming from the main room where she and the others had woken up.

Nargilla must have learned of their absence by now.

"I think they'll be coming after us shortly," Vola told Shereille. "Let's pick up the pace."

"Easy for you to say," Shereille said. "You're not the one hauling around a half-dead half-orc."

Vola glared at Shereille as she puffed, but for once she was pretty sure that had been a joke on Shereille's part. Huh. Maybe the woman did have a sense of humor.

The long hall ended in a doorway and light spilled through the cracks around the door.

"There are storerooms here," Shereille said. "If she brought you in this way, which seems likely, then she probably stashed your weapons here somewhere."

They checked the first room. Nothing but brooms and mops. The second held crates of antiquities.

"Oh, the Longbarrow collection came in," Shereille said. "I was looking forward to that exhibit."

"Focus," Vola said.

The third door they checked was locked.

"Bingo," Vola said. "Can you get it open?"

Shereille's mouth dropped open. "What do you think I am? Some common adventurer?"

"Mostly I was just hoping for helpful."

Shereille made a high-pitched squeak. "I am plenty helpful in my own field, thank you."

"Your daughter is much better at this." Vola twiddled her fingers. "A little bit of fire. A little bit of wind and ta-da. Magic is useful."

"Just because I refuse to debase myself for something so common —"

"You mean common like survival? You're right, you're too good for that."

Shereille let out a little scream and laid her hands against the door. Flames flashed out and licked at the dry wood.

By the time Shereille stepped back, the door was black and charred.

"See, that wasn't so hard," Vola said.

Shereille stared at her. "How did you know how to make me do that?"

"I've been traveling with another stubborn elf for a while now. Her block is self-confidence. I just have to goad her enough that she forgets to be worried. Your block is pride. Prick that and you'll bleed a river."

Shereille's mouth worked.

There was a yell from the end of the hall, and several figures appeared.

"We're out of time," Shereille said.

Vola let all of her dead weight fall against the door and it crunched open. They tumbled inside, and Shereille pushed it closed behind them.

She examined the rough surface. "I can hold it for maybe thirty seconds."

"It'll have to be enough," Vola said. She climbed heavily to her feet again as Shereille set her back to the door.

There, flung carelessly across a table in the middle of the storeroom, was their equipment. Vola pushed aside Lillie's spell book and Talon's daggers to grab Sorrel's staff. In her hands, the staff changed into a longsword.

"I appreciate the sentiment," Vola said. "But I can't do anything with you right now."

Her hands lingered on her own sword and shield, but there was no way she'd be able to carry them, let alone hide them from Nargilla and her people.

There was a thump against the charred door, and Shereille was knocked back a few inches. "Thirty seconds," she said, resettling herself against the barrier.

Vola glanced at their weapons again. She had to choose and choose fast. But with her arms feeling like noodles, there was no way she was going to get away with any of these.

"We can only take what we can hide," Vola said. Then she held out Maxim's Warhammer, disguised as a sword, and addressed it directly. "Work with me, please, and I'll get you back to your rightful owner. I need something small. Something I can hide."

The sword shuddered for a second, as if choosing, and then its surface rippled until she held a butter knife.

"That'll work," she said and stuffed it in her shirt.

The next thump on the door flung it open, and Shereille stumbled back into the table of weapons. She fell to the ground with a clang as Vola's sword and Talon's daggers cascaded around her.

Vola just slumped against the other end of it and refused to flinch as a couple of Nargilla's gnomes poured through the door into the little storeroom.

They were caught. No use fighting it. Her entire purpose had been to stall the inevitable. Well, that and get the Warhammer back. Hopefully they'd taken up enough time that Talon was well on her way to finding help.

The gnomes had no trouble manhandling Vola. They patted her down roughly, to see if she'd hidden any of the weapons from the room, but they didn't find the butter knife tucked between her breasts.

They hauled Shereille to her feet and gave her exasperated looks when she flinched and screamed with every sharp movement and word. Even Vola couldn't help rolling her eyes. They might have been caught, but there was such a thing as dignity.

The gnomes herded them back down the hallway Vola had so painfully traversed just a few minutes ago. Vola had to use the wall to stay upright, but Shereille walked with a stiff little hitch in her step despite the fact that she'd been perfectly fine before. Vola tried to catch her eye, but she stared straight ahead, her lips thin and her eyes pinched and worried.

Back in the massive foyer, one of the gnomes nudged Vola, and she lost what little balance she'd regained. She sprawled across the tile floor.

Shereille avoided the same fate by skipping forward to kneel beside her.

Lillie lay nearby. Not moving.

"Where are the others?" Nargilla snapped from somewhere over Vola's head.

"We haven't found them yet," one of the gnomes replied.

Nargilla's nostrils flared, and she glanced at a man who stood examining the tanks with a clipboard. His short brown hair was combed precisely away from his face, and he wore a pair of fitted trousers and a leather vest.

"I'll find them myself," Nargilla muttered. "Make sure these don't escape. Again," she told her gnomes.

The man didn't bother glancing up when Nargilla trotted off. He just turned another page on his clipboard and ran his finger down a list.

Vola narrowed her eyes. Was this Anders? The sinister presence they'd been chasing for years? The man who'd orchestrated the coup on the Thrones and hired Myron and Inga and Nargilla to steal all the magic out of the different pieces of the world?

Her fingers itched for her blade. He might be unassuming and unarmed, but she wouldn't fall into the trap of underestimating him.

His eyes met hers, almost as if he could tell what she was thinking.

But he didn't react. He just stepped around the tanks to examine the other side.

Vola's fingers flexed against the tile, but she was still weak as tepid water. And Lillie still wasn't moving.

"Lillie?" Vola croaked. She rolled onto her side.

"I'm all right," Lillie said without opening her eyes. "When one of them grabbed me, I tried to blast him. Fun fact: trying to draw magic you can't reach has unpleasant side effects."

"Good to know. I won't reach for Cleavah again if I can help it." She glanced over to the exhibit where the goddess stood trapped. Her head had slumped forward, so it was hard to tell, but Vola thought she looked paler than before. The stream of golden power flowing from her to the tanks had steadied, and no longer pulsed.

"On the bright side, I did fall down and manage to trip him at the top of the stairs." Lillie's expression hardened. "He won't be getting back up again."

"One down," Shereille said. "That's useful."

Lillie's eyes shot open, and she turned her head to stare at them. "Shereille? What are you doing here?"

"Long story short, Shereille is learning how to be an adventurer," Vola said.

Shereille made a face and opened her mouth.

Cries and the sound of fists on flesh interrupted them, and Nargilla returned with two gnomes dragging Sorrel behind her. The monk was nowhere near as fast as she usually was, but she did manage to get in several hits before the gnomes tossed her on the ground beside them.

Sorrel struggled to her feet while Nargilla stalked toward them.

"Where's the last one?" she said.

Vola glanced around and used her finger to count. "One, two, three, four." She shrugged at Nargilla. "Last one who?"

Nargilla growled. "The other one. Used to wear a hood. The one with the wolf. That one..." She pointed to Shereille. "Is new. I don't know where you picked her up, but where is the other fighter?"

"No idea," Vola said. The butter knife poked her in a rib but she didn't dare try to slip it to Sorrel now. Even if she did hand it over, there was little chance they'd be able to fight back. All that would accomplish was letting Nargilla know how special the Warhammer was. And who knew if Sorrel would be able to use the Warhammer's power without her innate magic?

Vola glanced at the others. "What about you guys?"

Sorrel shrugged expressively while Lillie shook her head on the floor.

"Sorry," Vola said. "Can't help you —"

Nargilla's fist struck her across the face, and Vola sprawled against the floor.

"Try again," the gnome said, cocking her head.

Vola rubbed her jaw.

Nargilla knelt and grinned at her, but the mirth didn't reach her eyes. "I can do anything I want to you in this state," she said, voice low. "You have no magic to protect you. No goddess. And your strength is draining out of you like water. Now, where is the last one?"

"I already gave you my answer once before. Fuck you."

Nargilla cocked her head. "I thought you didn't swear."

"My goddess doesn't like it. But you took her away, so..."

Nargilla smirked like she conceded the point.

"I told you not to underestimate them," Anders said, voice bland. He folded the papers smooth on his clipboard and hung it on the nearest tank. "This all seems to be in order. Do you need any help with them?" His brown eyes narrowed on the party laying on the tile floor.

"No," Nargilla said. Then she muttered, "Having a great ass doesn't make you better than me."

She struck Vola again.

Vola, who prided herself on her reflexes, couldn't even dodge.

"Stop that," Lillie said. She tried to push herself up on her elbows.

"Would you like a turn next?" Nargilla asked.

Vola glared Lillie down. She couldn't fight back, but Vola could still take a punch better than the rest of them. And she just had to hold out until Talon fetched help.

Nargilla struck her again.

Good gods, she was going to be beaten to death by a gnome with a god complex.

"You just have to tell me where she is," Nargilla said calmly, squinting at her knuckles. "If not, I'll see if any of them want to tell me." She gestured to Sorrel and Lillie.

Vola spit on her. It seemed like the only response. Her jaw burned when she pursed her lips.

Nargilla raised her fist again. "Where?"

A rumble rattled the tanks and made the floor vibrate under Vola's back, and the screeching sound of tortured metal stopped Nargilla.

They all turned their faces toward the ceiling.

A crack of light appeared between the top of the walls and the roof. It grew wider as the screeching sound grew louder.

And suddenly the entire roof lifted off, flung open like the top of a treasure chest, and standing over the opening like the scaliest treasure hunter in the world was Listrell.

She peered inside the museum, one arm holding up the roof and one braced against the far wall as her wings spread far enough to blot out the sun behind her.

Talon rode just behind her horns.

"Looking for me?" she said.

TWENTY-THREE

A FIERCE WILD light burned in Vola's chest as five of the smaller *draconis minimus* climbed up over the walls and hung there above them all. Vola recognized the red and gold scales of Hurren.

The front doors burst in, and Rilla and Renvick led a troop of guardians into the foyer, each one bristling with their choice of weapons. Behind them crowded the old gnome, Doddleben and his squad of former prisoners, now freed from Listrell's lair. They brandished broken teacups in the direction of Nargilla and her gnomes.

Beside the tanks swirling with magic, Anders shook his head. "Sorry, Pipwattle. You're on your own for this one."

He put his left hand on the tank that held Cleavah's power. The golden glow had filled it nearly halfway by now. Anders raised his right hand and a blue crystal glinted in his palm.

"Vola." Lillie struggled to her hands and knees. "He's getting away."

"No!" Vola lurched to her feet and lunged for Anders, but he was most of the way across the foyer.

The blue stone flashed and crackling light washed over

Anders and the tank. They disappeared just as Vola hit the ground a foot away, her hands closing on empty air.

She whipped around to check Cleavah. But the goddess still hung from her bonds. Her power drained into one of the other tanks now, along with the power pouring in from the city.

"What?" Nargilla screamed. "You're just going to leave me with all this? Fine," she muttered, lunging for the rest of the tanks. "Anders can live with that little bit of power. I'll take the rest."

"Stop her," Rilla shouted, gesturing to the guardians to spread out around the room as Nargilla yanked a copper tube from the tank where Cleavah's power was being siphoned to. She attached it to something else Vola couldn't see.

"Uh oh." Vola rolled onto her elbows.

"Vola—" Sorrel called.

"I know."

Myron had done the same thing once. And had become nearly invincible in the process. It had taken a god's weapon to stop him. And Nargilla had access to a goddess's power herself. That changed things.

Vola plunged her hand into her shirt for the butter knife.

"Sorrel," she called. "Here."

"What the—" But the monk's reflexes were better than Vola's right now, and she caught the knife. The moment her hand touched the handle, the Warhammer pulsed and flexed and became the quarterstaff Sorrel always favored. The Warhammer's magic didn't seem to mind Sorrel's state.

"Oh, yes," Sorrel said and surged to her feet.

Nargilla bent and attached the copper tube to a different tank.

A boom rocked the room and pressed Vola flat on her back again.

"What a rush," Nargilla said from the middle of a cloud of

smoke. Slowly it cleared, revealing the gnome, who was flexing her fingers.

Listrell lowered her head enough that Talon could slide down to the floor with them. "Hit her now," the dragon said.

Sorrel stumbled forward, then her gait evened out as if she drew strength from the Warhammer. Finally, she sprinted flat out and raised her staff.

"Hah!" She brought it down on Nargilla's head.

There was a flash, and Sorrel flew back. Listrell caught the halfling before she could slam into a wall.

Nargilla chuckled. "Oh, good try. But you're just a smidge too late." She held up her thumb and forefinger half an inch apart.

Nargilla raised her hands and a howling wind whipped around the foyer. Vola clutched the smooth tiles to keep from being blown away.

Rilla reached Vola's side with Renvick a split second behind her. The guardian gave Vola a hand to her feet and handed her a hand ax.

"Thanks," she said.

The guardian bent to lift Sorrel to his shoulder, and she clung there with one hand, her other holding her staff. "Watch my back," he said.

The wind tore at their clothes as Shereille hauled herself to her feet and produced Talon's daggers from the folds of her shirt. She tossed them to Talon. The ranger leaned out from Listrell's head to snatch them before the wind could fling them aside.

Vola stared. "When did you get those?"

"When the gnomes were busy trying to grab you. It's funny how if you scream and whimper, no one suspects you of conniving."

Vola laughed. "Connive away. Will you be Lillie's feet?"

Shereille nodded and stepped to help Lillie stand against the maelstrom.

Rilla hauled on Vola's arm. "I can't guarantee I'll keep you upright," she said. "But I can keep the worst from knocking you over."

"Sounds good to me," Vola said, ducking her head to keep Rilla between herself and the worst of the wind.

"All right. Spread out," Rilla said. "Maybe if we hit her all at once."

"Gods, you're taking forever," Nargilla said, rolling her eyes so hard her whole head moved. "Are we doing this or not?"

Listrell snapped at the gnome. Anyone else would have disappeared into the giant teeth-lined maw. But Nargilla's whole form flashed, and Listrell yanked her snout away with a snort.

"Ouch," the dragon said.

"She's basically a god right now," Vola said.

Rilla raised her daggers and stalked forward. "Not for long."

Vola followed, for the sake of staying upright. Rilla blocked at least some of the wind.

Those that could wield their weapons without falling over attacked. The five smaller dragons swarmed across the tile floor, trying to get close while Doddleben and his band of tea-toting prisoners darted in from the other side.

Nargilla swung her staff around, and Cleavah's gold light spilled out in a wave, knocking them all over before they reached her or the tanks.

"Again," Rilla called. "All at once."

Vola just tried to keep her fingers clenched around the haft of the ax. It wouldn't do her any good on the floor. Not that it was doing her a lot of good with the blade tipped toward the floor, but at least she felt better holding it.

Nargilla swept the ground again. Her staff scraped the tile and sparks sprayed out.

Rilla stumbled back into Vola, and they went down in a tangle of limbs. Vola managed to keep from stabbing the princess but only just.

"This isn't working." Vola's gaze focused on the golden light flowing from Cleavah to the gnome. Every move Nargilla made kept her between the goddess and her rescuers.

"We have to disconnect them," Vola said, pushing at Rilla with weak hands. "She's drawing away Cleavah's power. But if we can separate them—"

"Maybe it'll pull the power away. Got it." Rilla rolled off Vola's legs and helped haul her to her feet. She gave orders for the right ranks to close in and the left to give way, driving Nargilla away from Cleavah.

But the gnome narrowed her eyes and struck the ground with her staff. A rumble beneath Vola's feet told her what was coming a split second before the head of a rock wyrm broke through the tile.

"Shit," Rilla said, as rock wyrms erupted all over the floor.

Listrell snapped the head off of one, but three more rose to take its place.

It was no use. Nargilla would never let them get close to the source of her power. They just needed to do it from here.

"Sorrel," Vola called across the battle.

Sorrel still clung to Renvick's back, but she twisted around to make eye contact.

"We have to break the shield on Cleavah."

Sorrel looked down at the staff in her hand and squinted across the battle at the trapped goddess. "This is the first time in my life I think I've ever said this, but...I can't make that jump."

Vola opened her mouth, but Sorrel shifted her grip on Renvick and called across to Talon. "Talon, catch!"

She threw the staff like a javelin, and it whistled as it parted the air.

Nargilla's eyes widened when she saw it. It wasn't affected by her winds at all.

Vola's heart dropped as Nargilla reached out, close enough to intercept it.

But Listrell snatched the staff out of the air and twisted her head to offer it to Talon.

Vola let out her breath, but before Talon could take the staff, a cry echoed above them.

"Death to dragons!" A short squat shape leaped from the top of the museum wall, plummeting toward Listrell's head.

Fedor Gerrickson struck her snout and caught her eye ridges. Listrell grunted in surprise and dropped the staff which clattered and rolled between her feet.

Vola started for the staff, cursing under her breath, but she'd never get there before Nargilla. That had been the whole point of throwing it.

Listrell shook her head with a roar, making Fedor's feet whip through the air. And finally, with a snap, the dragon hunter flew across the room to strike Nargilla.

Clearly, she hadn't expected an armed and armored dwarf to fly at her or thought to guard against it, and she went down under his weight.

Talon slid down Listrell's flank, reaching for the staff.

With a cry of rage, Nargilla slammed her fists into Fedor's chest, and he flew across the foyer. Vola glimpsed his wide eyes and gaping mouth just before he struck the wall and slid down to lay still.

In Talon's hands, the staff shifted into a longbow complete with its own quiver.

Nargilla growled under her breath and leveled her free hand at Talon who lifted the bow and set an arrow to the string.

Listrell lunged, pulling more of her bulk over the museum wall, and threw her head between Nargilla and Talon.

Nargilla's god power struck the dragon square in the jaw and the dragon roared as Talon released her arrow.

Her shot sped toward Cleavah, ripping through the power Nargilla threw to stop it.

It whistled and struck the shield around Cleavah with a crack that shook the entire foyer. The shield shattered and dissolved in bright flames.

Talon tossed the longbow to Vola, and Vola dropped her ax to catch it.

"Listrell!" Vola called.

The dragon swung her snout around, and Vola flung herself aboard. Listrell cocked her head and sent Vola flying at the goddess, who stood tied to the exhibit.

The longbow warmed in her hand, responding to her touch, and it morphed into a longsword. It's keen edge hummed and sliced through the power Nargilla threw at her as she landed. A surprised rock wyrm fell in two pieces, and she stumbled across its corpse into the fake lichen of the exhibit.

Nargilla screamed as Vola righted herself.

Cleavah's eyes fluttered, and she tilted her head enough to stare blearily at Vola.

Vola brought the sword edge down to slice through the goddess's bonds. They sizzled as flames licked across the ropes and burned away the remaining strands.

Cleavah slumped, and Vola reached to catch her without thinking. Her arms went around the goddess, but her knees buckled and they fell.

For a moment.

And then that moment froze. The sounds of battle faded, Nargilla's scream muted, and Vola stared up into Cleavah's serene face. The goddess's eyes fluttered closed, and she breathed deep.

The gold power flowing out of her across the floor to Nargilla stopped. Then it started flowing the other direction, pouring back into Cleavah, filling her skin with golden light. Light so bright, it burned Vola's eyes.

She scrunched them shut and suddenly sound returned. Nargilla's scream still echoed around the walls, and she could hear the moans of the rock wyrms and the clash of weapons.

Cleavah's arms closed around Vola and gently lifted her to her feet. Strength filled her limbs until she felt like she would split in two and pour herself out into the world. Her own feet held her again and her fingers closed around the hilt of her sword, lifting it without any trembling.

Vola could still feel the searing heat of Cleavah's light against her face, and she held a hand over her eyes as Cleavah finally let go of her.

Vola could feel the goddess through their bond once more but more clearly now than ever before.

Cleavah had always felt like that friend standing just over her shoulder, waiting to be called on. But this...this was the burning of rage. This was the feel of righteous anger held barely in check. Vola could feel Cleavah as a white-hot torch shot through with her cool concern for the mortals in the room. If she released her true power, if she allowed herself to act on her rage, she would incinerate everyone and everything. Friend and foe alike.

A touch left a mark of heat on the back of Vola's hand. And then the burning presence moved away. Cooler air stung Vola's sensitive cheeks, and she gasped still hiding her eyes.

This was ridiculous. She was a paladin. Her goddess had returned to her strength, and Vola was too afraid to open her eyes to see it?

Finally, she pulled her hand away. One glimpse. One little peek was all she needed.

A figure stood at the edge of the exhibit, but that was all the detail Vola could discern. The blinding radiance of the goddess's true form burned across her vision, blotting out everything else in a figure of white light.

The burning goddess stepped down from the exhibit. Listrell's guardians and Doddleben's squad cowered back, ducking their heads and hiding their eyes from the searing light.

Vola couldn't look away.

Neither could Nargilla. She stood frozen in the center of the room, her eyes fixed on the dazzling figure. Tears streamed down her cheeks and the skin around her eyes went tight and red, but still, she didn't break away.

The goddess's expression remained implacable as she brought her hands together, and Nargilla's tanks exploded in a shower of light and glass. Someone screamed. Several someones. But it wasn't Nargilla or Vola.

Glass rained down, tinkling against tile, claws, and scales. But the power remained in the air, floating over Nargilla's head, flashes and sheets of color that looked like streamers in a carnival sky.

The goddess tipped her head back to gaze at the power hanging in midair. She held up one searing glowing arm and seemed to gather it to her. Her other arm hung limp at her side, blending in with the brilliance of the rest of her.

The power roiled and eddied and flowed toward the goddess and then she flung her hand out.

The power exploded. Like the tanks, but this time it was like a cloud of light fractured into a million tiny motes of dust that sped out back into the world.

Three streams of it gathered and speared toward Talon, Lillie, and Sorrel. The three of them clutched their chests and fell to their knees as their strength and magic returned.

The goddess shifted, and her burning aspect turned until she looked directly at Vola. Coal-black eyes rested in that light, the only break in the expanse of burning divinity.

Nargilla squeaked and finally broke her frozen terror. She darted away only to be grabbed by a glowing golden spear that could have been a hand.

She struggled in the goddess's grip but couldn't rip away.

The goddess's eyes never left Vola's face and as they stared at each other, the burning aspect dimmed and subsided, drawing in as if her skin absorbed the light and fire of her true self until she was something fit for mortals once again. Her figure didn't shrink or hunch. It just drew the light together into a more compact space.

She subsided until she had the same golden skin which Vola could now tell held all the light of the world underneath. The same dark curling hair, but now it was cropped short, curling around an ear. She was missing an arm and one leg was gone from the knee down. Half of her face was that serene beauty Vola had met in a defaced temple in Brisbene. The other half was covered in a mess of scars. Burns that had left the shining skin puckered and marred.

The same black eyes stared back at Vola, and the figure of light had been burned into Vola's gaze so that it hung like a halo around the self-contained outline of the Broken.

"Lady," Vola croaked. Her eyes burned from the memory of light, and she rubbed the moisture from her stinging face.

"Volagra," the Broken said, her voice the same sound of rushing wind that it always had been.

Nargilla tried to struggle again, and the Broken raised wings of flame to steady herself against the unbalance.

The Broken glared at the gnome in her hand, and Nargilla shrank away from the wrath of a goddess.

"Righteousness demands I don't kill you," she said. "But you should know, it's going to be very, very hard for me."

Glass tinkled as those present picked themselves up off the floor where they'd been thrown after the tanks exploded.

Rilla was the first to her feet, brushing the bits of broken glass from her clothes and hair. A cut across her forehead was bleeding down the side of her face.

The princess raised a bloody finger. "Er, hi. Yes. That's our prisoner." She pointed to Nargilla.

Vola climbed carefully out of the exhibit and made her way to her team. Talon stood, shaking her head as if trying to clear it. Renvick set Sorrel on her feet, and the monk winced as she cracked her back. Vola started to reach to help Lillie up, but Shereille was there already with her hand under her daughter's elbow.

The Broken's eyebrow raised as she looked at Rilla. "Yes. And your point?"

Rilla's head jerked. "My point is, I want to take her in for trial and judgment. She nearly leveled this city. She's stolen power out of the land—"

"And from the gods themselves," the Broken said. Her eyebrow remained raised without even a twitch.

"Yes," Rilla said. She wasn't easily cowed, though Vola could see her thumb shaking. "But you can't just walk off with her."

"You think your authority supersedes mine?"

A stupid question if ever there was one. Rilla was not stupid, and her mouth snapped shut on any sort of answer she could give. But she still fumed a little as the Broken took Nargilla more firmly in hand.

The Broken paused for a second. "Would it make you feel better if I told you there is no reprieve where she is going? I have friends in high places. The Greater Virtue of Justice for instance. She'll be more than happy to see this one serve for eternity."

Nargilla gulped.

"I suppose that makes it slightly better," Rilla said. She glanced at Vola and added. "My lady."

The Broken also glanced at Vola and the twitch in the unburned corner of her mouth was so reminiscent of Cleavah's grin that the last of Vola's uncertainty fell away. Vola gave her a little shrug.

The Broken gave her an almost imperceptible nod. "I like you. And Vola says you'll do, so we'll be speaking again."

Rilla flashed Vola a wide-eyed look as the Broken spread wings of flame. Instead of leaping into the sky, the goddess wrapped the fire around herself and Nargilla before they disappeared in a swirl of sparks.

TWENTY-FOUR

LISTRELL SWOOPED low over the blackened earth, and Vola hung out over her shoulder to get a good look.

"Looks the same to me," the dragon rumbled.

"Talon?" Vola called across the dragon's scales to the ranger, who clung to the dragon's other shoulder.

"The magic has returned, but the land…it's still dead," she said over the rushing of the wind.

"All right, put us down at the city gate, Listrell."

The massive dragon took another lazy turn and had them back to Firewatch in less than five minutes. Vola and the others covered their eyes to guard against the sand and grit kicked up by the dragon's landing.

"Thanks for providing transport," Lillie said as she crept carefully down the dragon's side to the ground. Vola jumped down and stepped to offer her a hand.

Sorrel leaped without looking and landed on her feet. "Very handy having a dragon in your back pocket."

"It was no trouble," Listrell said. "I was curious as well. I could feel the spot still, but the others are outside my territory."

"Firewatch isn't in your territory either, is it?" Sorrel said.

The dragon tilted her head. "Firewatch doesn't belong to any one dragon," she said. "But to all."

"So if the magic is back but the land is still dead, what does that mean?" Vola said.

"It means that whatever Nargilla did caused permanent damage," Lillie said.

Listrell's massive shoulders rolled. "And we don't know what that will do in the long run. At least the culprit is gone for good."

Vola winced. Nargilla might have been gone, but Anders had escaped and she didn't want to think about everything that could mean.

Still, Listrell was right. They'd succeeded yesterday. Won the battle if not the war.

"Thank you for coming to help," she said, walking around to the front of the dragon so Listrell didn't have to crane her neck to hear.

"You saved our butts," Sorrel said.

"Talon just said she was going for help. She didn't say she was going to come back with you." Lillie beamed up at Listrell.

"I didn't want to promise something I didn't know if I could deliver," Talon said, coming around the dragon's massive forearm.

"I'm sorry it took me as long as it did. I...did not want to believe that such small things could affect me or the other dragons. But Talon convinced me small bodies can contain big enemies." Listrell shook her head like a dog. "But this is the time for all of us to focus on one threat. Are you headed for the meeting? I can give you a lift."

Vola shook her head. "We wanted to check in on Sorrel's master first. We'll meet you there."

"Suit yourself," Listrell said. "And cover your eyes."

The dragon launched herself into the air, sending up another cloud of dust and dirt. When they could finally look up to track her flight, she had already alighted on the cliff above the field museum.

Lillie chewed her lip as they turned to start their trek up into the city. "I don't like that those dead spots are still dead."

"I definitely thought it would all go back to normal when Cleavah...I mean...the Broken did her thing," Sorrel said.

"Have you spoken to her yet?" Lillie asked quietly.

"Not since she left with Nargilla," Vola said. And she wasn't sure what she would say when she finally did. There was so much roiling around underneath Vola's skin that she wasn't sure what would rise to the top when she finally stood face to face with her goddess again.

She could feel her there, deep inside, still connected. If she needed to heal someone or if she really needed to talk, she could just call and the goddess would be there as always. But the Broken hadn't reached out to her yet, and Vola wondered if the goddess needed her space as much as Vola did now that the truth was known. She had to have been hiding herself, making Vola think she was a lesser goddess for a reason.

Outside the House of the Broken, where they'd brought Master Bao, a scaled creature with a filmy green crest and a menacing expression stood tethered to the railing by a thick chain.

"Oh, dear," Lillie said.

"I'll admit I kind of hoped it would disappear during the evacuation," Sorrel said.

Talon grabbed a note that had been tucked under the swamp beast's halter, deftly dodging its teeth. "It says it tried to eat one of the patients, so they left it behind. Too bad it's still here. They also said please, please don't bring it back."

"I'll second that, since I was the patient it tried to eat," a voice as dry and cracked as the desert said behind them.

They turned to see a slim, straight figure in a monk's tunic leaning against the doorframe.

"Master Bao," Sorrel said.

She trotted up to him, and he smiled in greeting. Then she took his hand in hers and flipped him over her shoulder.

The rest of them cried out as the martial arts master hit the ground rolling and sprang back to his feet.

"What are you doing?" Lillie cried.

"Making sure he feels better," Sorrel said.

Vola forced her shoulders to relax as Master Bao grinned.

"Much better," he said. "I never thought of myself as magical before, but it's amazing how not having any takes it out of you."

"It's a matter of balances, sir," Lillie said with a brilliant smile. "All life carries some magic and without it, a body has a much harder time just existing."

"I don't know, I felt like I was getting used to it, by the end," Sorrel said.

The rest of them stared at her, and she raised her hands.

"I'm not saying I wanted to stay like that. I just had an easier time convincing my body to fight after I had a chance to get used to it."

"I'll take your word for it," Master Bao said. "All I know is I felt like a long-dead weasel beaten against the rocks until it's nothing but a bag of skin holding some bones and some mush."

Vola made a face.

"That's exactly how I'd describe it, too," Talon said.

"But I'm back to normal now," he said, raising his chin.

Sorrel crossed her arms. "Great, so you can go back to trying to kill yourself."

Vola rolled her eyes. She didn't disagree, but there was such a thing as tact. She'd have to introduce it to Sorrel sometime.

The old monk examined his nails. "Actually, I'm heading back to the monastery."

Sorrel eyed him sidelong. "You are?"

"There was a point there while I was watching a psychotic gnome drain the life out of me when I realized I wasn't done fighting. If I was, I wouldn't have minded someone else taking the choice away from me. But it turns out, I do mind. And I don't want someone like that taking the choice away from the rest of the world either."

"We think that's what Anders is trying to do," Vola said.

He met her eyes, his glinting with something much stronger than steel. "Yes. I'm returning to the monastery to rally Hazel and the others against this threat. This is much bigger than even Maxim."

"It's a threat to the world," Sorrel said. "Maxim is only part of it."

Now that he was recovered, Master Bao was the last person in the world who needed an escort to the edge of the city, so they collected the swamp monster reluctantly, and continued up to the field museum.

The roof still hadn't been replaced after Listrell hinged it open like a huge treasure chest, and considering that she was still coming and going over the edge, it didn't seem likely that she would replace it any time soon.

The dragon herself was overseeing the transformation of the foyer under the bright desert sun. One of the museum's employees shuffled by with a broom, sweeping up the last of the broken glass from Nargilla's tanks while others righted the fake lichen and the mossy rocks in the exhibit where the Broken had been tied. Still more followed Listrell's directions, hauling square tables together in the center of the room.

Rilla stood arguing with the councilman of Firewatch and the curator of the museum while Renvick looked on with his arms folded over his chest.

A glowing portal of dark green stood open behind the princess, and as they watched, the Princess of the War Throne and the Princess of the Defense Throne stepped through. And behind them came the Princess of the Magic Throne. Four rulers of Southglen in one room together. Rilla must be worried.

No one had seen them yet where they stood beside the door, and Vola took a deep breath before starting forward. She nearly ran over a young woman with short, curling brown hair.

"Aster?" Vola said, recognizing Shereille's assistant.

"Oh. Hello," she said with a bright if harried smile. "Sorry, I didn't see you. We're in a hurry."

Vola caught sight of Shereille directing the rest of her crew to collect the crates just inside the door. Vola's lips thinned. "I can imagine."

She stalked over to the elf woman. "Heading out again?"

"Oh, you know how it is," Shereille said. Her bright hair was perfectly contained in its bun again, and she didn't seem any worse for wear from her adventure the day before. "There are still undergrads to harangue and research assistants who absolutely need to finish by a certain time or they won't receive their certification."

"What can you possibly be studying?" Lillie asked. "Listrell said they're going to be waking all the dragons to warn them of the threat and enlist their help."

The lines around Shereille's mouth deepened for a moment. "All the more reason to hurry then, isn't it? If we want to talk to any of the *draconis maximus* before they leave dragon lands, we must go now."

Especially since Listrell still wouldn't talk to her.

"You don't care that Anders is going to try what he did here again?" Talon said.

Shereille blinked. "Why would I? Nargilla is no longer a threat to my research. Tell your goddess thanks for that, by the way. Aside from that, my life is going back to normal."

Vola glanced at Lillie, but the wizard just watched her mother calmly.

"Good luck, then," Lillie said.

"Thank you." Shereille bent to pick up a crate and then thought better of it. "I'm sorry," she said abruptly, meeting Lillie's eyes. "I'm sorry I'm not the person you wanted me to be. I actually feel rather guilty about that."

"Don't worry," Lillie said with a thin smile. "I'm sure you'll get over it soon enough."

"You know, I'm sure I shall," Shereille said, completely missing the veiled insult in Lillie's words.

"Goodbye," Lillie said, voice steady and firm. And Vola noticed she didn't say anything like "see you later" or "be sure to visit for the holidays."

Shereille lifted the crate in her capable hands and didn't even look back as she followed her team out the door of the museum.

"Are you all right?" Vola asked Lillie, who stared after her.

"I am not going to fall apart if that's what you're asking," Lillie said quietly. "But that's as good as it's going to get right now."

"I'm sorry," Talon said. "We all are."

Lillie shook her head and squeezed her eyes shut. "You shouldn't be. She is who she is. I cannot force her to be someone else just because I had silly dreams as a child. She cares about her research and only her research. A fact I should have picked up on long ago. Even before I met her."

"We're still sorry," Sorrel said.

"I know. But not every story has a happy ending." Lillie's mouth firmed, and she lifted her head. "My father more than made up for her. And I prefer the family that I have now." She glanced at them from under her lashes. "The one that I chose."

Rilla spotted them, finally, and waved impatiently for them to join the others at the makeshift council.

Vola and the others took their places along one side of the pushed-together tables beside Fedor Gerrickson, who still served as the captain of the city militia even on the injured list. He sat with his arm in a sling and his bandaged leg propped on a stool. The stout dwarf was missing his ax and his chainmail, but he glared at Listrell as if he wished he still had both.

Vola cleared her throat. "I hope your recovery is going well," she said as politely as she could manage. A growl still managed to rumble through the good intentions. This man had interrupted at exactly the wrong time and could have ended the world with his misplaced fanaticism.

Fedor glanced at her, breaking his stare at Listrell. "A few broken bones." He winced. "And some ribs. Dwarf bones are sturdier, but that makes them harder to heal, too."

"What will you do now that the dragons are all on our side?" Lillie asked. "Surely you're not here to ambush Listrell." She chuckled, but her eyes flickered between the dragon and the dragon hunter.

Fedor grunted. "I guess I'll have to find something else to hunt."

Talon settled herself on the chair directly beside him. "What about your revenge?"

He met her eyes, and his mouth screwed up in a grimace. "My revenge completely misses the point if it hurts other people," he said. "I can't claim to be protecting others if I'm just trying to get them killed. Besides, I have another personal target now." He raised the arm that was still in a sling. "Nargilla threw me against a wall while she was under orders from this Anders fellow. I'm ready for a little payback." He cracked his knuckles.

"So...more revenge," Sorrel said as Renvick stepped up beside her and pulled out a chair.

"Is this seat taken?" he asked.

Sorrel glanced at him. "No. Be my guest."

He settled himself so his tail draped comfortably to the side.

Lillie leaned over to whisper in Sorrel's ear. "Have you had your conversation yet?"

Sorrel batted her away with a mild glare. "No, and this isn't really the time for it." She cast a look at Renvick full of chagrin and a little bit of longing. "I think we're both okay with leaving it at that for now. Maybe when this is all over, we can figure out what our relationship will look like."

Vola raised her eyebrows but did her best to hide her expression. Sorrel might have wanted to stay non-committal, but it sounded like there was a relationship there already, whether they'd figured it all out or not, yet.

The leaders of Firewatch arrayed themselves along one side of the tables, and Listrell had her own side opposite them. Rilla sat with the three other princesses directly across from Vola and the others.

Rilla stood. "We know now the threat Anders presents." She braced her hands on the tabletop in front of her. "He is trying to drain the magic from the world."

There was a sudden hush in the museum's foyer. The councilman of Firewatch shifted in his chair. "I hate to say it like this, but Firewatch is one city outside of any country's jurisdiction. An attack on us hardly indicates an attack on the world. How do you come to this conclusion?"

Rilla's eyes narrowed, but she jerked her chin at Vola's group without speaking.

Vola stood and ticked points off on her fingers. "He was using a necromancer to suck magic out of dead people. He tried to steal the magic from the Thrones of Southglen. And we know now he's been using Nargilla to suck the magic out of different lands for years."

"And when we first met, he was buying living people from desperate nobles," Lillie said. "We thought it was for slavery, but now I'm sure he was going to steal their magic out of them, the same way Nargilla did to us just a couple of days ago."

Rilla nodded. "And these are only the incidents we know about. We've thwarted him so far, but we know he has these capabilities. He has Myron's tanks and Nargilla's spell. He can set up shop whenever he likes."

"If this is true," Listrell said, her voice making the tile under their feet rumble. "It means war. We cannot allow him to take what does not belong to him. But more than that, we cannot allow him to destroy so much of the world to do it."

"Yes," Rilla said. "This means war. War with Southglen, war with the world."

"And war with the gods themselves," a voice like rushing wind said.

Vola felt her before she turned her head to see the Broken standing just behind her right shoulder.

The goddess's presence was muted somehow, as if she was holding some of herself back so as not to scare the mortals. She wore her Broken aspect, the scarred, unbalanced body with the hint of fiery wings raised behind her.

Vola's breath caught in her throat, and she forced herself to swallow. "My lady," she said quietly.

The Broken's eyes flicked to Vola, and the scarred corner of her mouth lifted.

Rilla gave the Broken a respectful nod. "We welcome all the help we can get, of course."

The Broken winced. "I don't know how much help it will be. Anders escaped with a piece of my power."

A gasp went through those assembled.

"With it, he can cut the rest of the gods off from the land and thereby end the world."

The councilman clutched his chest and swayed in his chair.

Rilla didn't flinch. The only reaction Vola could see was the twitch at the corner of her mouth that looked like a split-second grimace.

"Well," Rilla said. "Won't this be fun?"

The Broken actually smiled.

Vola felt torn. There was a big piece of her that felt like she stood beside a stranger. A benevolent leader who had taken a strange interest in her. She didn't know this woman, this entity that had chosen to stand beside her.

Except she did. There was an even greater piece of her that recognized Cleavah in the figure beside her. The aspect was different, but the feeling of comaraderie, benevolence, and humor was the same. The bond that pulsed in Vola's center was the same that had been there for five years as she'd trained and worked under Henri and Cleavah's leadership.

Everything she knew about the Broken came from legends and myths surrounding the mysterious Virtue. She was the Greater Virtue of Righteousness, but since righteousness could rule over all the Virtues and Obstacles, they'd tried to throw her out. They'd tried to burn her. They'd only let her return to the pantheon on sufferance with the understanding that she would remain an outcast, a recluse who wasn't allowed to seize power for herself.

But everything Vola knew about Cleavah was something she'd learned firsthand along the way. And if the two were one and the same...then Vola knew more about the Broken than any mortal alive. Maybe even more than the gods who'd harmed her.

"Then the gods are declaring war on Anders," Rilla said, her diplomatic princess face stretched thin across her features.

Vola wouldn't have noticed it if she hadn't been standing right beside her, but the Broken flinched.

"*I* am declaring war on Anders," she said firmly.

The Broken had once been powerful enough to rule the rest of the gods. Even apart from the pantheon, she would be a formidable ally.

Rilla gave her a formal nod. "I'll assign a liaison to serve as a go-between for you—"

"I like Vola just fine," the Broken said.

"I know that," Rilla snapped, then she cleared her throat and straightened her jacket. "She's obviously your chosen, my lady. Though she might have called you by a different name. I just meant I would make it official. That is if you don't mind making that information public."

The princesses stared at the Broken. Listrell and the Firewatch officials looked a little more confused. They might not be as well versed in Pantheon politics or realize that the Broken had never taken a mortal representative within written history. She'd never chosen a paladin or a prophet or even a heroic farm boy to carry out her will. Probably because the other gods would assume she was maneuvering to assert her dominance.

The Broken put her good hand on her hip and cocked her head. "Have you ever tried to shove a cat back into a sack once it's escaped?"

Rilla's mouth quirked as she saw the goddess's point.

The Broken pointed her thumb at her own chest. "Cat," she said. Then her face and form shifted to that of unblemished Cleavah for just one second. "Bag. Vola is my chosen. For good or ill, I'll not forsake her now."

The words meant more than just what she was saying to Rilla. Vola's hands tightened on the edge of the table, and she swallowed down the sudden knot in her throat.

"Unless Vola has a different opinion," the Broken said quietly.

This was her out. She hadn't signed up for this. She'd just wanted to be a normal paladin. Not the first and only paladin to serve an exiled Greater Virtue. She was rocking the boat enough just by being herself.

But she didn't have to imagine herself without Cleavah or the Broken or whatever she chose to call herself to know how miserable she would be. She'd lived that life already.

"My opinion has not changed, my lady," Vola said, voice steady and strong in the quiet foyer. "Although…" She glanced up and met the Broken's black bottomless eyes. "We are going to have a talk about this, you and I."

Her chest tightened as the words left her mouth. But she'd earned a little familiarity after all of this.

The Broken's throaty chuckle filled the empty spaces of the room, and it was Cleavah's laugh and everything was okay.

"I can't wait till someone explains this to the paladin council," Talon muttered. Vola caught the amused glance she shared with Sorrel and Lillie.

"I came to tell you where we will find Anders," the Broken said, ignoring them for the moment.

Rilla straightened. "Nargilla talked?"

A toothy grin spread across the Broken's face. "She didn't have to. I do have some friends in the pantheon. And once I'd convinced them of the threat, the Greater Virtue of Perception found him easily enough."

"And since you didn't just snap your fingers and disintegrate him just as easily, I'll assume he's going to be a tough nut to crack," Rilla said, raising an eyebrow.

"War was an understatement," the Broken said. "Muster your strength. This is going to be fun."

DID YOU ENJOY?

Keep reading for a preview of the next book, *Wastelands and War*!

ONE

"What are you supposed to pack for war?" Sorrel said, holding up a loose white shirt Vola had never seen her wear before. The monk always wore the same gray wrap-around tunic and loose pants that she'd tied close around her calves.

"I suppose the same kinds of things you've always packed," Lillie said. Her lilting voice which would have done well when paired with a lute was distracted as she stacked books in her own saddle bag. Vola was waiting for her to drop something on her foot because she wasn't paying attention.

"Knives, swords, daggers, bow, quiver, armor, two pairs of pants, boots, and new gauntlets from the vendor down the street." Talon ticked off the list on her fingers.

"That's oddly specific," Lillie said, pausing with her head cocked. "Especially for Sorrel who doesn't wear armor and fights with a glorified stick."

Talon looked up, blue eyes confused. "What's Sorrel got to do with anything? I was going through my bags."

Lillie rolled her eyes. "Sorrel was asking what to pack for war."

"I think Lillie's right," Vola said, folding her own shirts. "Just pack normal."

"Sexy underwear it is, then," Sorrel said and tossed a couple scraps of black fabric at her bags without folding them first. "Might come in useful."

Talon snorted under her breath. "If you like to wear it for yourself, that's fine. But I think you might have to actually have sex to call it useful."

"Bleh," Sorrel said, making a face. "Whatever for?"

"Maybe because you love someone," Talon said.

"And want to feel close to them." Lillie's gaze was distant and unfocused again. Vola scooted a stack of books closer to her reaching hand so she could grab them without having to look down.

Vola was already packed. She'd spent the night rearranging it all over and over again, mulling over what they were about to do. Too bad she couldn't repack her thoughts out of the way where she wouldn't trip over them every five minutes.

"Not sure I need to be that close to anyone," Sorrel said, shoving another shirt into her pack and sitting on it to make it close. "I mean, you guys are my best friends and we don't have to have sex to feel close, do we?"

Lillie's fair skin flushed bright red, clashing painfully with her strawberry blond hair. "That's not what I meant, Sorrel."

"Actually, she has a point." Talon swung her saddle bag over her shoulder and stood, the big black wolf, Gruff, flicking his ears at her feet. It was strange to see her without her cloak so the light from the window hit her sandy colored hair, now long enough to curl around her ears. Her chin gleamed the way it did when she'd shaved recently.

"It's alright, Lillie," Vola said. "We all know you're a romantic."

"Says the woman with a couple of cheap romance novels in her bag," Talon said.

Vola didn't flush the way she used to. She just shrugged. "It's research."

"For what?" Sorrel said, brow furrowed. She pulled her bag off the bed. It was nearly as tall as she was.

"I'm trying to figure out how to weaponize your underwear." Vola spun for the door while Sorrel spluttered in outrage.

"Come on, Lillie," Talon said. "If the books don't fit, you'll have to leave some behind."

Lillie's mouth fell open. "No!"

"How'd you even have time to acquire more? I swear your books procreate by themselves," Vola asked as Lillie tried to tighten the straps over the last couple of tomes. She winced when she heard a seam pop. "We've spent all of the last week running after dragons and putting out fires."

Sorrel sighed with a happy smile. "Good times. Hey remember that day and a half when we thought Talon was dead?"

"You thought that was fun?" Vola said.

"Well, not the thinking she was dead part, but the finding out she wasn't part was great."

"I'm not leaving any of my notes behind," Lillie said, ignoring the ominous popping and trying to hoist her bag over her shoulder. "We need everything we have to go up against Anders. He has Nargilla's plans. Between those and the piece of the Broken's power he stole, I want every advantage we can get."

The others went quiet and sober for once, and Vola took the pack from Lillie without saying anything.

They left the hotel room that had been their home since they'd arrived in Firewatch and headed down the narrow, creaky stairs.

"At least now we have a god on our side," Talon said. "That should give us an advantage, right?"

"Has Cleavah—I mean the Broken said anything to you, yet?"

Sorrel asked Vola. "She likes you a lot. And Maxim has never been the talk in your ear sort of god, so he's not saying much."

From everything Vola had heard since she'd met Sorrel, Maxim wasn't the sort of god to give his followers any sort of feedback. There'd been a time when Vola had envied Sorrel for her connection to the Greater Virtue of Strength and Courage. It had taken her a while to realize just how worthless a connection it was when the Virtue refused to use it.

"She hasn't said anything to me since we met with everyone at the museum the other day," Vola said quietly. The common room of the hotel was patched together with a variety of woods and pieces of wagons and it was empty this time of day. "She might have declared war on Anders, but I'm not sure how much help that's going to be in the end."

"Why?" Lillie said, tilting her head.

Vola ran a hand over her dark braid and tried to come up with a coherent argument for what she was thinking. It wasn't just about the knot in her chest and the way she felt a little woozy every time she thought about her goddess. Vola had served the minor goddess known as Cleavah for years now. She'd grown in so many ways, some very unexpected for a paladin, all with the goddess's help.

But now Vola knew that Cleavah wasn't just Cleavah, Goddess of Vengeful Housewives. She was actually the Broken. The Greater Virtue of Righteousness. One of the greater gods and quite possibly the greatest god in the pantheon. If the others would ever agree to such a hierarchy.

"The Broken isn't exactly popular with the rest of the gods," Vola said. "She has some friends, some of the Greater Virtues on her side, I think. But there's a reason they call her the Broken."

"She was cast out, wasn't she?" Talon said. "Kicked from on high when the other gods realized that righteousness could rule all the rest of the Virtues and Obstacles."

"Yes," Vola said quietly. "She fell in flames and was missing from the pantheon for millennia while she recovered. She's still marked by it." The figure who'd broken free from her bonds and blazed her image across Vola's vision while she'd shattered Nargilla's magic tanks had been that of a woman with one arm and one leg, burn scars masking the left side of her face.

"So you don't think she's going to ride into the pantheon on a cloud and tell the rest of the gods what to do," Sorrel said.

"Actually that sounds like the beginning of another Divine War," Lillie said. She tapped her lip. "Perhaps I should take notes the next time we see her."

"They didn't even trust her to hold Nargilla after she brought her to them," Vola said. The gnome was being held by the other gods.

"Yeah, but we don't have time for another Divine War," Talon said. "If the gods take it into their heads to beat their problems out of one another, Anders will have stolen all the magic of the world and we'll be better off dead."

"Maybe that's why the Broken chose a paladin for the first time ever," Sorrel said. "To convince the gods that this threat is bigger than their squabbles."

"They're gods," Talon said. "Do you think they'll recognize anything as bigger than them?"

Vola rubbed her brow, trying to smooth out the lines left by worry. Her friends weren't saying anything she hadn't already been over in her head a thousand times a night since the Broken had revealed herself. Why had she finally chosen a paladin? Why had she chosen an orc? Would Vola be strong enough to protect everyone from whatever came at them, whether that was a man who thought he could strip the whole world of magic, or a collection of gods too busy with their own troubles to notice the world they presumably ruled?

It would be nice if the Broken had explained anything to her when she'd decided she was done hiding. Anything at all.

Vola pushed through the door of the hotel. Outside, a walkway snaked up the mountains between the buildings made up of leftover wood lashed together with cords brought across the desert in caravans.

The harsh sun beat down on Vola's head, and she raised a hand to shade her face. Her green tinted skin didn't burn as easily as Lillie or Talon's fair complexions, but she seemed to soak up the heat faster than the locals. Even without her plate armor.

There was an angry hiss and Vola instinctively dodged as a squirt of greenish goo landed across the boards at her feet. The liquid sizzled and began to eat through the wood, throwing off a wisp of smoke.

Vola sighed. A creature waited across the walkway, tied to a railing, but it had already chewed most of the way through the rope. It looked like the unhappy love child of a crocodile and a donkey. Slimy, scaled, and ugly enough that both parents had probably dropped dead at the sight of it. It oozed a bit at both ends and gave Vola a toothy glare.

"One day we will find a way to be rid of you," Vola said under her breath as she ducked the swamp monster's teeth and yanked what remained of the lead rope from the railing. She knew better than to assign the creature to one of her teammates. It was her turn and she'd been the one who insisted they couldn't sell the thing to Lillie's mother at the field museum. "Don't make me regret saving you from dissection."

"I still think it would look ten times better inside out," another familiar voice said, and Vola turned to find a dark slim woman leaning against the wall of the hotel. Even in broad desert daylight she looked like she lounged in a shadow. The dark green jerkin she wore gleamed against her dark skin and her black hair rose in a fluffy halo around her head.

One day Vola wanted to see Rilla actually wear the crown she was entitled to as the princess of Southglen's Dagger Throne.

"Have you been lurking—I mean, waiting long, Your Highness?" Vola said as Sorrel and Talon slung their packs over the swamp monster's back. She yanked its head around as it tried to lung for one of them.

"Just getting some sun while I can," Rilla said, holding out a hand. Vola was surprised it didn't sizzle in this heat. "It's probably raining in Southglen. I hate soggy leather."

Vola waited till the others had strapped their bags to the swamp beast's back before slinging hers on and fastening the straps. "Oh, shut up," she murmured as it glared. "It's the only thing you're good for besides eating everything."

A huge shadow swooped over them and they all glanced up instinctively. But the red shape swinging by wasn't familiar to any of them. Listrell and her lead guardian Renvick had already said their goodbyes and were presumably off collecting the rest of their dragon allies for the war ahead.

"Right," Rilla said, pushing off from the wall. "If you're ready, I'd like to get going before Anders wins this war by default." She didn't bother ducking into an alley or finding a more private spot to do this. She took hold of an amulet around her neck and drew a burning shape in the air with the fingers of her opposite hand. The flames flickered, floating in midair for a second before spreading to form a large green doorway in the middle of the walkway. On the other side there were a couple intricately carved doors twice Vola's height, and you couldn't see the rest of the palace that stretched above them because the portal was too close.

"You know it's hard to take your complaining seriously, Rilla, when you can open a portal directly to the front door of your castle," Sorrel said, grinning up at the princess.

"Don't take this away from me," Rilla said, her lip twitching. "Griping is my thing. It's part of my persona."

"Not taking it away," Talon said. "We like your grumpy highness. Honest."

Rilla's eyes narrowed. "Just get through the portal. I can only hold it open for so long. And if we're going to war, then I have a lot of work to do to make sure Southglen stays safe before we leave."

As the princess of the Dagger Throne, Rilla was essentially Southglen's spymaster. She kept the country safe from invasions and sabotage by being faster and more clever than the threat. Or by throwing Vola and her team at the problem. Rilla might have first called them Mishap's Heroes as a joke, but they were really good at taking bad situations and making them turn out all right.

All right, if Vola was being really honest, they usually made it worse before they made it better, but that was splitting hairs.

Talon gave Rilla a cheeky salute before stepping through the fiery portal, hand on her dagger, Gruff on her heels. Knowing the ranger, she'd make sure their landing zone was clear before any of them stepped through into an ambush. The castle stood in the center of Glenhaven and if it was under attack, then they had a lot more immediate problems than a war between gods. But Talon's paranoia kept them all from making stupid mistakes, so Vola wasn't about to complain.

And there was that one time nobles had taken over the palace in a coup, so…

Sorrel trotted through next.

Lillie stopped on the threshold. "One day you really must show me how to make one of these."

"Later, Lillie," Vola said. "You literally don't have any more room for notes."

Lillie flushed and stepped through the portal.

And like a good leader, Vola brought up the rear, stepping from the hot desert afternoon into the muggy evening on the other side of the world.

ACKNOWLEDGMENTS

I started out thinking I was writing something fun and light and hopefully hilarious. But it turns out I can't just write fluff. Meaning creeps in from the sides and makes its home between the lines. And then someone likes it, and I have to write more, and more meaning forces its way in, and suddenly it's a whole "thing." I blame these people:

First, the Kickstarter backers, for making all this possible. And for believing in the series before I'd ever sold a copy.

Mom and Dad, for reading every book ever. And always asking where the next one is.

Arielle, Betsy, and Alison, for being the first inspiration for a group of inept heroes who have no idea what they're doing and manage to save the day anyway.

Miranda and Lacey, for sisterhood which looks a lot like party dynamics sometimes.

Kevin and Andrew, for inviting me to play this little game called Dungeons & Dragons.

Kyle, Mary, Amy, Clark, Tim, Greg, Lauren, and Dave, and a

host of other party members, for providing endless opportunities for inspiration. These books are all your fault.

Lucy Lin, for all the amazing cover art. I don't think anyone else could have brought Vola and the others to life the same way you did.

Fiona McLaren, for copy edits and flexibility. And for enjoying my humorous fantasy as much as my slightly more serious stuff.

And Josh and Abby, for endless support. Especially when I decided to launch a series the same month I was supposed to have a baby.

ABOUT THE AUTHOR

Books have been Kendra's escape for as long as she can remember. She used to hide fantasy novels behind her government textbook in high school, and she wrote most of her first novel during a semester of college algebra.

Kendra writes familiar stories from unfamiliar points of view, highlighting different types of heroes.

When she's not writing she's reading, and when she's not reading she's playing video games.

She lives in Denver with her very tall husband, their book loving progeny, and a lazy black monster masquerading as a service dog.

Visit Kendra at
www.kendramerritt.com

facebook.com/kendramerrittauthor
twitter.com/Kendra_Merritt
instagram.com/kendramerrittauthor
goodreads.com/kendramerritt

CPSIA information can be obtained
at www.ICGtesting.com
Printed in the USA
LVHW021428010821
694139LV00001B/65

9 781951 009236